T0378245

Praise for

BY INVITATION ONLY

"Brilliance, wit, and high style abound in *By Invitation Only*, as we get to know the extraordinary Piper and Chapin and how their contrasting personalities draw them into an unbreakable bond of magnetized opposites. With Paris as its runway, this story soars—dynamic, empowering, and unforgettable."
—PAUL TAZEWELL, 2025 Academy Award winner for Best Costume Design for *Wicked*

"This book is pure fashion fantasy: runway-worthy gowns, Parisian glamour, and the kind of high-stakes drama you'd expect backstage at a couture show. But what really stole my heart? A heroine who's smart, grounded, and unapologetic enough to outshine even the chandeliers at the Ritz. I devoured every stylish, swoony moment."
—JOE ZEE, Professor of Fashion, journalist, and celebrity stylist

"I loved spending a week in Paris with these badass debutantes. A modern and empowering spin on a century-old tradition."
—KAREN McCULLAH, screenwriter of *Legally Blonde, 10 Things I Hate About You,* and *She's the Man* and author of *The Bachelorette Party*

"Lights, camera, fashion! *By Invitation Only* is big screen ready, with its winning combination of irresistible heroines, glittering gems, and iconic style moments, all set against the shimmering backdrop of the City of Lights."
—REBECCA SELVA, Chief Creative Officer of Fred Leighton and Kwiat

"Dazzling and cinematic, *By Invitation Only* offers an exquisitely fun look into the worlds of high society and haute couture. A love letter to fashion, this novel is escapist, witty, and delightful!"
—CHRISTIAN SIRIANO, CFDA designer and *Project Runway* mentor

"A dazzling blend of humor, opulence, and heart, following brilliant and beautiful young women as they navigate ambition, romance, and family in a high-stakes world—exactly my kind of story."
—ABIGAIL HING WEN, *New York Times* bestselling author of the *Loveboat, Taipei* series

"RSVP immediately to *By Invitation Only*! Alexandra Brown Chang's debut novel is teeming with charm, glitz, romance, and humor. It is a true confection, but it also has much to say about class structure and privilege."
—HEATHER HACH HEARNE, screenwriter of *Freaky Friday* and book writer of *Legally Blonde: The Musical*

"A decadent dessert of a book: frothy and fun, with a heapful of heart. In this zingy, swoony affair, Chang offers a glimpse into the world of the mega-rich and famous with scintillating detail and lancing wit. An exciting new voice to watch in YA."
—ALEXA DONNE, author of *The Ivies*

"An instant classic! A fairy tale for our modern times, Chang's debut is a charming coming-of-age story about unexpected friendship, following your dreams, and finding your voice along the way. Escapist, emotive, and exceptionally easy-to-inhale, *By Invitation Only* is one of those books that's instantly impossible to put down! I want to read this again and again."
—BECKY CHALSEN, author of *Kismet*

"An electric blend of humor, heart, and glamour with Paris as the backdrop, *By Invitation Only* is the perfect fall book for readers craving romance, friendship, and an escape. RSVP now!"
—EMIKO JEAN, *New York Times* bestselling author of *Tokyo Ever After*

"Alexandra Brown Chang's *By Invitation Only* is a funny and fast-paced YA contemporary set against the backdrop of an elite competition focused on poise, fashion, and philanthropy. It is a charming, honest look at the mother-daughter dynamic that celebrates sisterhood without compromising swoon-worthy entanglements. Together, Chapin and Piper redefine what it means to be young ladies of consequence."
—KRYSTAL MARQUIS, *New York Times* bestselling author of *The Davenports*

BY INVITATION ONLY

BY
INVITATION
ONLY

ALEXANDRA
BROWN CHANG

Margaret K. McElderry Books

New York Amsterdam/Antwerp London
Toronto Sydney/Melbourne New Delhi

MARGARET K. McELDERRY BOOKS

An imprint of Simon & Schuster Children's Publishing Division

1230 Avenue of the Americas, New York, New York 10020

For more than 100 years, Simon & Schuster has championed authors and the stories they create. By respecting the copyright of an author's intellectual property, you enable Simon & Schuster and the author to continue publishing exceptional books for years to come. We thank you for supporting the author's copyright by purchasing an authorized edition of this book.

No amount of this book may be reproduced or stored in any format, nor may it be uploaded to any website, database, language-learning model, or other repository, retrieval, or artificial intelligence system without express permission. All rights reserved. Inquiries may be directed to Simon & Schuster, 1230 Avenue of the Americas, New York, NY 10020 or permissions@simonandschuster.com.

This book is a work of fiction. Any references to historical events, real people, or real places are used fictitiously. Other names, characters, places, and events are products of the author's imagination, and any resemblance to actual events or places or persons, living or dead, is entirely coincidental.

Text © 2025 by Alexandra Brown Chang

Jacket illustration © 2025 by Elena Masci

Jacket design by Sonia Chaghatzbanian

All rights reserved, including the right of reproduction in whole or in part in any form.

MARGARET K. McELDERRY BOOKS is a trademark of Simon & Schuster, LLC.

For information about special discounts for bulk purchases, please contact Simon & Schuster Special Sales at 1-866-506-1949 or business@simonandschuster.com.

Simon & Schuster strongly believes in freedom of expression and stands against censorship in all its forms. For more information, visit BooksBelong.com.

The Simon & Schuster Speakers Bureau can bring authors to your live event. For more information or to book an event, contact the Simon & Schuster Speakers Bureau at 1-866-248-3049 or visit our website at www.simonspeakers.com.

Interior design by Irene Metaxatos

The text for this book was set in Questa.

Manufactured in the United States of America

First Edition

2   4   6   8   10   9   7   5   3   1

CIP data for this book is available from the Library of Congress.

ISBN 9781665972437

ISBN 9781665972451 (ebook)

For Annabelle, Audrey, and Ames

Playlist

"Paris" by Taylor Swift

"Royals" by Lorde

"Uptown Girl" by Billy Joel

"Dreams" by The Cranberries

"Walking on Sunshine" by Katrina and the Waves

"Just a Girl" by No Doubt

"Butterflies" by Kacey Musgraves

"gold rush" by Taylor Swift

"Head Over Heels" by The Go-Go's

"Over My Head (Cable Car)" by The Fray

"Liability" by Lorde

"You Get What You Give" by The New Radicals

"The Way It Was" by The Killers

"White Flag" by Clairo

"BIRDS OF A FEATHER" by Billie Eilish

"Wannabe" by The Spice Girls

"get him back!" by Olivia Rodrigo

"You're So Vain" by Carly Simon

"Bad Reputation" by Joan Jett and the Blackhearts

"Just What I Needed" by The Cars

"You've Got the Love" by Florence + the Machine

"so american" by Olivia Rodrigo

"I Wanna Dance with Somebody (Who Loves Me)"
by Whitney Houston

"Welcome to New York" by Taylor Swift

Meet *Teen Vogue*'s College Women of the Year

These 22 exceptional students are scientists, entrepreneurs, athletes, content creators, and even elected politicians.

#1. Piper Woo Collins

COLUMBIA UNIVERSITY

As a rising college freshman, Piper Collins has already accomplished more than most people do in a lifetime. The eighteen-year-old from King of Prussia, Pennsylvania, recently won the grand prize at the annual International Science Fair, a prestigious science and engineering competition, beating more than ten thousand other applicants. Collins's star invention—an eco-friendly, low-cost polymer made of biodegradable orange peels—has the potential to save thousands of farming jobs across the United States while also increasing crop yields by up to 75 percent. Collins's scientific brilliance has powered more than just crops. The high school senior—with an IQ higher than Albert Einstein's—was recently accepted to every Ivy League school. She will attend Columbia University this fall, where she hopes to major in environmental science.

PROLOGUE

Paris, France

"*Merde!*" Amélie bellows, exhaustedly burying her face in her hands as she hangs up the phone. Behind her, the lights of the Champs-Élysées twinkle, the Arc de Triomphe visible through the office window.

Across from Amélie, her assistant, Bardot Sinclair, looks shocked by Amélie's uncharacteristic outburst. The Storey Ricci scandal has broken her.

"Dior is panicking," Amélie says. "I don't blame them: This publicity is terrible. Elizabeth Drake insists we find a debutante to replace Storey, and *she* will be dressed by Dior instead."

"Another girl . . . by this weekend?"

Amélie lets out a groan of frustration. "I spend nine months curating each year's list. Each girl invited to La Danse is hand-selected. The right family. The right look. The right profile. We are not an app. I cannot select 'intelligent, beautiful, special eighteen-year-old' and press order!" Amélie rises and begins pacing the room.

"These 'eat the rich' bores have been braying for my head for years. Where am I going to find somebody deserving, who will give us positive publicity, not some pampered brat who doesn't recognize how lucky she is, dragging us to hell like Storey Ricci? She doesn't exist!"

Bardot looks down at her laptop, where TeenVogue.com fills the screen. An Asian American brunette beams. She's adorable, with obsidian eyes, and creamy skin, yet dressed like a preppy school-girl. She's begging for a glow-up. Everybody loves a Cinderella story. . . .

Words float up:

Piper Woo Collins . . . rising star . . . IQ higher than Einstein . . . scientific brilliance . . . accepted by every Ivy League school . . . This is her.

Bardot swivels the computer toward Amélie. As Amélie's expression morphs from thunderous to intrigued, it's clear: *Piper Woo Collins, your life is about to change forever.*

CHAPTER ONE

Piper
King of Prussia, Pennsylvania

I scroll through the *Teen Vogue* article. Wow. I sound impressive. Too bad it's an exaggeration.

Plus: The fawning article fails to mention that I spent my entire afternoon piercing the ears of surly middle schoolers at Claire's. Sure, biodegradable orange-peel polymers are thrilling and all, but you haven't really lived until you've sliced and diced the lobes of fidgety, Snapchatting twelve-year-olds.

"Earth to Piper," Seb says, snapping me out of my daze. I put down my phone. We're in my living room, snacking on popcorn and watching *My Best Friend's Wedding* for the millionth time. "You look more miserable than Ben Affleck at an awards show." He points at my screen. "This is a huge deal. *Teen* freaking *Vogue!*"

I don't want to burst his bubble. Seb is looking at me with

such love and pride that even a stranger could probably tell we've been BFFs since middle school. So despite the fact I've been drowning in misery for the past day, I can't keep this secret any longer.

"I have to tell you something not great," I blurt out.

"You're having Timothée Chalamet's baby."

"I said *not* great."

He nods knowingly. "Ezra Miller's baby."

"I was awake till two a.m. last night tinkering with polymers while watching nineties rom-coms. Do I *seem* like I'm getting some celebrity strange?"

Seb laughs, and I briefly forget the pangs in my chest that have been plaguing me ever since I got the call yesterday.

"My scholarship has been revoked," I confess. It hurts to say the words out loud. "I'm not going to Columbia."

Seb slams his bag of Sour Patch Kids on the coffee table. Sugar flies everywhere.

"Unacceptable. You've been dreaming of Columbia forever. What the hell happened?"

I catch him up. "Remember how I won that huge grant that covered like sixty percent of my tuition because my research impressed somebody who owns half the planet?"

"Yeah, the microchip dude. Or, wait, was it the space-tourism guy?"

"Different billionaire. Hedge funder who funds scientific endeavors."

"Potato, potahto. All rich people are literally interchangeable. Except Oprah. And TSwift."

"Apparently, the university revoked his son's fraternity charter and kicked them out of their house on 114th Street."

"And Fratty McCanceled is your problem because . . . ?"

"Because he was so pissed that he's pulling *all* funding in protest until the current president steps down."

Seb looks scandalized. "That's outrageous! Like, be normal and write a strongly worded letter to the dean. Don't punish poor kids who can't afford it."

I shrug, feeling despondent all over again. "I got a call from the bursar's office yesterday. 'Circumstances change, we extend our sincerest regrets, blah blah blah.' The woman who called me was mortified."

"But *not* mortified enough to cough up the extra 50K they promised you."

"I guess not."

"Does your dad know yet?"

"No." I shake my head miserably. My dad is an EMT who pulls long shifts to give us a better life. He was so proud when I accepted Columbia's offer. "He's gonna be devastated."

"Deep breaths. We can figure this out." Seb stands up and starts pacing around the living room. As he does, I notice an alert on his phone: *SCANDAL: STOREY RICCI EXPOSED!* Storey's tearful face fills his phone screen in miniature—somehow, even while crying, the world's highest-paid teen model looks better than 99 percent of eighteen-year-olds on the planet. "There has to be some way for you to make up the difference."

I shake my head. "Short of selling an organ on the black market, it's not happening. First semester's tuition is almost due."

"So that's it? Presto chango, college bye-bye? You're national news for getting into every Ivy League school and now you're just . . . *giving up*? That is not the Piper Woo Collins I know."

I try not to feel sorry for myself. "I'm not giving up on college. I just don't have any scholarship options left—they all disappeared after I committed to Columbia. I should have taken the full ride to Cornell."

"But it's not Columbia."

"It's not Columbia," I affirm.

We both stare at Julia Roberts on the TV, depressed. Seb sits back down and wraps his arms around me. "I'm sorry, Pipes. You worked harder than anybody. You don't deserve this."

I hug him back but don't say anything. Instead I point to the Storey Ricci headline on his phone to distract myself. "Wait, what did she do?"

Seb grabs his phone and opens the article. There's a photo of her being led out of a Sephora in handcuffs. "Looks like . . . okay . . . wow. She stole eyeshadow? But she's got her own makeup line!"

He mutes Julia, then clicks onto a gossip page, and we huddle over the phone together. A glossy reporter in high heels addresses the camera soberly, as if reporting from a war zone. "Since we first broke news of Storey's arrest this morning, she's released an apology video on Instagram. The video has created quite the stir, with over ten million likes." Storey's glowing face takes over the screen.

"I would like to apologize first and foremost to the House of Dior," Storey says as a lone tear slides down her poreless cheek.

"Being the face of Dior is the honor of a lifetime, and this transgression does not reflect who I am. I didn't want to be seen buying products from a competitor, so I had a momentary lapse in judgment that I immediately regretted. I want everybody to know that I value nothing more than diversity, equity, inclusion, and a business's right to detain shoplifters." Storey takes a tremulous sigh, as if to center herself. "Finally, to my adoring fans, I adore you even more. Thank you for your support, and I look forward to seeing you outside the Ritz Paris for La Danse des Débutantes, where I will be happy to sign autographs. Love to you all."

"What a bunch of useless buzzwords," I say, tossing my phone. "Anybody who says they love DEI definitely doesn't have any of it in their own life. She just doesn't want to get canceled. And what's this Danse des Débutantes thing?"

Seb gasps as if I've scalded him. "How are we best friends? You cannot call La Danse des Débutantes a *thing*. It is the primo debutante ball. It is a debutante ball on steroids. It is the *ne plus ultra* of debutante balls."

"AP Latin for the win," I joke. "Okay, it's fancy. I get it."

Seb clutches me by the hands. "Piper, you so do not. La Danse is a once-in-a-lifetime event. People would die to be invited. Paris! Couture! Celebrities!"

"Archaic! Elitist! Horrifying!" I shoot back.

Seb drops my hands, looking grumpy. "There's nothing wrong with a little fashion diversion in this ongoing hellscape. Besides, La Danse is very into charity these days. They don't only select poor little rich girls." He pauses for dramatic effect. "They select poor little rich girls *who give back.*"

We share a giggle.

"Why are you so obsessed with La Danse?" I ask.

"Because of the insane opulence," Seb says. "La Danse is the last throwback to a golden era—"

"Where only straight cis white dudes had rights?"

· "Where glamour still meant something! The gowns these girls wear put the Oscars to shame. It makes the Met Gala look like a middle school Halloween party."

He shoves his phone into my face. I catch the hashtag he's searched: #LaDanse. It has scores of videos with millions of views.

"So it's not just you into this?"

"Oh please. Trying to cancel La Danse is so boring. When you find out about it, how could you *not* be obsessed?"

"Welcome to La Danse," a girl intones, before images quickly flash, displaying snippets of impossibly gorgeous teenagers in impossibly expensive gowns. They pose in front of luxury cars, try on diamond necklaces, sip from gold-leaf lattes in ornate sitting rooms. I spy some familiar faces: mostly a few recognizable nepo babies who followed in their parents' footsteps and are now actresses, singers, or models themselves.

"For the past seventy-two years, top French fashion houses, including Dior, Chanel, and Givenchy, have competed to dress young women making their societal debuts," the TikToker expertly narrates. "Widely known as the teenage Met Gala, and listed by *Forbes* as one of the ten hottest parties of the year, La Danse hosts sixteen debutantes from around the globe every year in Paris."

Despite my deep disdain for the very concept of a debutante

ball, the glamour is admittedly seductive. I stare as the images flash by, wondering what it must be like to have access to so much luxury . . . so much privilege . . . so much *money*.

I couldn't be prouder of my dad, but for a fleeting, disloyal moment, I think: *Oh, to care solely about which couture gown to be photographed in, not how to finance your entire future.*

"Okay, so if they're all exclusive and into *giving back*"—I stifle a snicker—"why is Storey Ricci still invited?"

"I mean. She's *Storey Ricci*. I doubt the La Danse people even care. They're Teflon."

Suddenly there's an aggressive *knock-knock-knock* at the door. Seb and I look at each other, frozen. The only thing worse than somebody calling instead of texting is somebody stopping by in person unannounced. I swing open the front door, confused by the sight greeting me in our apartment's hallway.

The delivery guy looks like he walked straight out of Halloween City, the discount costume store at the King of Prussia Mall. Upon closer inspection of this guy's attire—a classic footman's outfit that makes him resemble an extra from the live-action *Cinderella*—I feel severely underdressed in my black camo leggings and pink Champion hoodie. This man takes Oscar Wilde's quote "You can never be overdressed or overeducated" to a new extreme. He hoists an oversized card-stock envelope out of his bag.

"Mademoiselle Collins, your invitation has arrived," the courier dramatically intones, committing to the bit.

Yeah. This guy definitely does Revolutionary War reenactments on the weekends.

I take the heavy envelope, feeling its heft. My full name,

Piper Woo Collins, is inked on the front in perfect calligraphy.

I'm confused. I look back at Seb.

"Seb, was this you?"

He shakes his head no, wide-eyed.

Now the delivery guy is confused too. "You are Piper, right?"

"Unfortunately."

He breaks character. "Look. I gotta get a signature from you so I can justify what they're paying me. So can you just . . ." He thrusts a digital signing machine in my face, and, not sure what else to do, I add my signature. "Okay, cool. Thanks."

We make eye contact again, unsure what to do. He bows. Weirdly, so do I. I smile, preparing to thank him.

"You have a kernel stuck in your teeth," he deadpans as he walks away.

Okay, rude.

I fish out the kernel before inspecting my prize. What *is* this thing? There's no return address.

"The hell is that?" Seb asks.

I hold up the envelope. "I think I just got invited to the Hunger Games."

Seb laughs. "Do me a favor and choose Hemsworth." He stares at the envelope like it's a lottery ticket. "Piper, I have *a feeling* about this," he says dramatically.

"A feeling I'm part of a Rian Johnson murder mystery?"

"Open it! Stop leaving me in suspense."

I gingerly open the envelope as Seb bangs his fists against the table, mimicking a drumroll. I pull out the card-stock letter, staring dumbly.

La Danse des Débutantes

MADAME AMÉLIE BOUCHON

CORDIALLY REQUESTS

THE HONOUR OF YOUR PRESENCE

AT LA DANSE DES DÉBUTANTES.

THE FIRST OF MAY

HALF AFTER EIGHT O'CLOCK

HÔTEL RITZ PARIS

PARIS, FRANCE

I hold up the invitation, stunned. Seb snatches it out of my hands.

"Piper, is this a joke?"

I'm too dazed to reply.

"This is insane," Seb says, practically hyperventilating. "It's La Danse. You're going to *la fucking danse!*"

I examine the invitation once again. I notice a small, handwritten note stuck inside the envelope. I pull it out and read it to Seb:

Piper, we are beyond thrilled to invite you.

Congratulations on your scientific achievements.

You are an inspiration to girls everywhere.

Sincerely,

Bardot Sinclair

Amélie Bouchon Communications

A phone number is listed at the bottom.

"Bardot Sinclair. That sounds fancy."

"It does!" Seb replies gleefully. "It all does!"

"How is this possible?" I ask, still dazed. "Why would they pick me, out of all the high school seniors in the world? The farthest I've ever traveled is Toronto."

"The polymer! The International Science Fair prize! *Teen Vogue!* Who cares? I'm so excited for you!" Seb yells. "And for *me.* Imagine the clout I'm gonna get from this. Caleb is so gonna regret rejecting my promposal."

I pull out a second piece of card stock from the envelope. It lists the debutantes set to make their societal debuts at La Danse.

~~STOREY RICCI~~

CHAPIN BUCKINGHAM

LOTTIE STUART-JONES

VALERIA AGUILAR

LUCIA AGUILAR

CHLOE HUGHES

MARGARITA VASQUEZ

PEACH DAVIS

ZELLA DE PERIGNON

KARINA NEMEROV

MCRAE LAWRENCE

SEA REILLY

ANANYA SANWALKA

TREVI GRAHAM

NIHAT FAROU

IMOGEN WANG

Finally, at the bottom of the page, handwritten in calligraphed ink:

PIPER WOO COLLINS

This is overwhelming. "They already wrote my name in. See?" I point. "Right under Imogen Wang. That's me."

"Ooh, Imogen Wang," Seb said. "Her parents founded the biggest telecommunications firm in China."

"How do you *know* this stuff?"

"TikTok. Obviously."

I stare at the cards. "You don't think it's a little presumptuous? How do they know I'm free next week? What if I have plans?"

"To do what? Go to Costco?"

"I have school!"

"For La Danse, you skip it. Besides, Piper, you *have* to go. Making your debut at La Danse is literally once in a lifetime. It's once in a billion lifetimes. Nobody gets to experience this."

I push the cards away, suddenly feeling repulsed. "Why would any girl want to be paraded around like a piece of meat? Even the British royal family canceled debutante balls. It's weird!"

"You gotta get over that," Seb declares. "This isn't some Jane Austen marriage market, with rich bachelors plucking middle-class girls out of obscurity. These chicks wear Cartier like it's Claire's—no offense."

"None taken," I mutter.

"It's about fashion and fun and partying in Paris! And making new friends! And dancing!"

"I'm a terrible dancer."

He reverses course. "Or maybe it's not about dancing!" Seb looks increasingly desperate. "Do it for me? You know I live for this high society shit."

"I drive a Toyota. They *own* Toyota. People like these have yacht captains on speed dial. We don't mix. This is not my scene."

"How do you know something's not for you until you try it?"

"What if I have to curtsy? I'd fall flat on my face."

"Sure, sure. Counterpoint: You meet a prince from a country that no longer technically has a royal family, and you become a princess in exile. I'm just saying."

"I thought this wasn't a marriage market."

"Can I help it if a gorgeous prince falls head over heels for your wit and charm and Mensa-level genius?"

We explode into giggles. Seb grabs the cards, and we retreat for the couch again, collapsing onto the cushions.

"I wouldn't even know what to do at La Danse," I admit, letting my guard down. I pull a blanket around me, self-protective.

"You'll figure it out. You can take classes or whatever."

"Classes?" I quip. "Should I go on Yelp and search 'Debutante class for billionaires near me'?"

He laughs. "I meant in Paris. Just go and learn on the fly!"

I pause for a moment, thinking this through—I would have the opportunity to visit Paris and travel outside North America for the first time. That wouldn't be the worst thing. . . .

But what if I fail? What if everybody laughs at me? What if the girls all band together and reject me like an impermeable cellular membrane, keeping me out, unable to penetrate their circle of friendship?

He studies my face. "Oh. I get it."

"Get what?"

"You're scared."

"I'm not scared."

He nods, sympathetic. "You know what, you're right. Tell them you need to work a double shift at Claire's that weekend."

I narrow my eyes. "You're trying to reverse-psychology me."

"I'm not!" he says innocently. "I'm being mindful of my best friend's mental health. You should decline. Put it behind you and definitely don't wonder what magical experiences you missed or think about it ever again. Two roads diverged and all."

"Okay." I pick up the card. "There's a phone number at the bottom."

"Just do it. Rip off the Band-Aid. Tell them you decline."

"Maybe I will," I say, ready to call his bluff.

Seb's bravado wavers as I begin dialing France. "Or maybe you hear her out, you know?" he says in a rush.

I laugh, hanging up. "So you *were* trying to reverse-psychology me."

"Piper, you are the bravest, coolest girl I know. You've been working your ass off for years, and you've had a real shit run of luck. You deserve this. Go to Paris, party for a week, and *have fun*. Please."

Seb is as serious as a heart attack. Tears come to my eyes.

He's right: It's been an especially grim several years. My mom's breast cancer . . . our family's tight finances after her death . . . the college-application grind. I try to stay cheerful and press forward, but it's been a lot. Before Mom died, I felt as if I was in control of everything. Work hard, study hard, reap rewards.

But since losing her, I feel like I've been spinning plates, desperately trying to keep control of the uncontrollable.

"Hey," he whispers, wiping my tears away. "Don't cry. Crying will age you. And then you'll need to waste your minuscule college-scholarship money on preventative Botox in your twenties."

I start laughing through the tears. "Get out of here, you weirdo."

He stands up and gives me a big hug. "Promise me you won't call Brigitte Bardot back until *after* you spend all night maniacally googling how your life is about to explode into unicorn goodness, okay?"

After Seb leaves, I can't stop staring at the envelope.

I'm not a very dramatic person. I'm sensible ol' Piper. Dependable. Sturdy.

But I can't help feeling like this is about to change everything.

CHAPTER TWO

Chapin
Upper East Side, New York City

I stare at myself in the private dressing room at Bergdorf Goodman, horrified. I'm wearing a voluminous cocktail dress that my mother insisted I try on. I leave for Paris tomorrow and—true to form—Mom worried my already-bursting suitcase wasn't full enough.

Ugh. I look like a meringue cream puff.

I exit the dressing room to find my mother. Her eyes brim with excited tears. She carefully dots them away, not wanting to ruin her makeup. I'm reminded of the tremulous, wonder-filled look on her face when she was nominated for Best Actress for *Breaking News* (before she lost to Meryl Streep and had to hide her fury).

"Oh, Chapin. My darling. You look perfect!"

I turn away so she can't see my stupid, grateful smile. Compliments from Mom are rarer and more valuable than musgravite gemstones—which is really saying something.

She clasps her hands together, delighted. "You're so beautiful, darling."

But my mother's beatific countenance evaporates when she clocks my feet.

"Are you wearing . . . *sneakers*?"

I look down at my favorite pair of Nikes. They're limited-edition lime-green Dunks. Nowhere near as valuable as an elusive Australian gemstone beloved by collectors . . . but freaking awesome nonetheless.

"Yeah! These were a collab with—"

"I don't give a damn if they're from Manolo Blahnik—you cannot wear sneakers in Paris in front of Amélie Bouchon. God, Chapin. Common sense." I flush, humiliated.

She sighs at the stricken expression on my face. "Please don't be dramatic. I just want you to be thoughtful."

I wince, desperate to please her, as always. "Sorry."

"You're fine, honey." She stares at me, sizing me up. I see a flash of regret flit across her face. She suddenly steps forward to engulf me in a hug, a cloud of Le Labo perfume surrounding me. It's a familiar dance: hurt my feelings, apologize, hurt my feelings, apologize. I lean into her hug, taking the scraps.

Better than being ignored altogether, right? Half my friends barely *see* their parents, who are constantly schlepping between various vacation houses and leaving them to nannies they've long outgrown. At least my mom likes to spend time with me, even if it is 25 percent bonding, 75 percent me disappointing her no matter how hard I try.

The sales assistant hurries back into the dressing room, smiling eagerly. "She looks ah-mazing." She's barely even spoken to me all afternoon, instead gluing her eyes firmly to my mother. I'm used to it. When Ella Somerset is around, I'm invisible. "Which ones will she take?"

Some of the items were winners, bringing a smile to Mom's face. But otherwise, the dressing area is full of clothing that Mom has rejected: *too slutty, too common, too boring, too poor.* (Her words, obviously.) When I exited in one sleek black pantsuit she'd selected for consideration, she shuddered. "You look like a waiter."

"We're only taking a few things today," Mom says apologetically, waving her hand toward a rack by the door. Her notion of "a few things" is predictably twisted. The "yes" rack holds about fourteen different frilly dresses, jumpsuits, bouclé jackets, pussy-bow blouses, and trousers, most in pastel colors so vomitous I want to offset them with a face tattoo for some edge.

I smirk at the notion of permanently marking myself, fantasizing about a huge Old English neck tattoo saying "HARD-CORE." Ella would have a coronary.

Mom looks at me, suspicious. I smile back winningly.

"Now for the shoes!" Mom says, clapping her hands together. My glee fades. Time for more torture.

After another hour of shopping, we finally drive back to the apartment in the Escalade, where we sit side by side. Mom's weighed down with the bags of clothes she picked out for me.

I'm now the not-so-proud owner of several pairs of designer stilettos and pumps that look like they were stolen from Miss America's closet circa 1998.

"So are you excited?" she asks. "You're going to have the best time, lovebug."

I nod, even though I'm only half excited. But I know what she wants to hear. "Yeah, I figure—"

She interrupts me, poking me in the back,. "Please don't slouch in front of Amélie." I straighten my back.

"A little more." She thrusts her shoulders back, her elegant neck elongating. In profile, my mom looks like a Greek goddess. It's not hard to imagine her as Helen of Troy, the most beautiful woman in the world, men risking their lives and sanity for the merest hint of a glimpse of her. "See? Like this?"

I imitate her perfectly.

She sighs imperceptibly but manages a smile, patting my hand.

I stare out the window as we drive up Madison Avenue, nursing hurt feelings. The anonymity of New York City is a marvel. Here, nobody cares that you live in an Upper East Side penthouse filled with your parents' Grammys, Emmys, and Oscars. Money and power and fame are a given. Next. What do *you* bring to the table?

I know what it looks like from Instagram. It seems like I have it all. Movie-star mom, rock-star dad, a wardrobe that rivals the *Vogue* fashion closet. Last year *Vogue* actually interviewed me (*me!*) for *73 Questions*. They called my family "the closest thing America has to royalty beside the Kennedys" and said I'm "queen of my tony private school." Which: *Queen* is a bit dramatic, but yeah, the social part's easy.

So why do I feel like such a colossal failure all the time?

When I was younger, I thought my mom was the most beautiful, glamorous, wonderful person in the entire world. Of course, it wasn't just me who thought that: Mom has had the entire world in thrall for two decades. For somebody who made her bones as America's Sweetheart—carefree, hilarious, effortlessly charming—in private she's moody, mercurial, and intense as hell. Sometimes she's the best mom on the planet (especially, let's be real, to my brother Dalton, who basically walks on water in her eyes). But the rest of the time she's a bitch on wheels. She doesn't do anything by half, and that includes painstakingly curating my life to fit the perfect image she's determined to present to the world.

Believe me, you do not want to grow up as the daughter of Ella Somerset. Maybe if she'd given me her last name instead of Dad's, it would have conditioned me to live up to her expectations.

"Are you still pouting?" she asks, poking my leg as the Escalade turns onto East Seventy-Seventh Street. "C'mon. Cheer up, buttercup. You're going to have the best time!" I smile half-heartedly and she brightens, mollified.

"Now remember, we're aiming to win Debutante of the Year—"

"It's not *winning* Debutante of the Year. It's being *named* Debutante of the Year."

"Sure, but there can only be one. And that's you."

Normally I let this sort of thing go, but all week I've been in A Mood. Probably because of my Columbia rejection. *Not a rejection, a wait list,* in my brother Dalton's words, but it's hard to break free of Mom's binary thinking. If you don't win, you lose. Besides: He already goes to Columbia, so of course he's optimistic they'll eventually let me in too.

Mom doesn't know about Columbia—and what's worse is she'll probably celebrate it. I got into USC, which was her alma mater before she quit halfway through sophomore year after NBC picked up her pilot. She's always complaining that Dalton didn't follow in her footsteps, which gives me the tiniest hint of glee, because otherwise Dalton would get off completely scot-free. (It's okay, he deserves it; he's the best brother on the planet and was basically engineered in a lab of awesomeness.) But when it comes to college, it won't matter that Columbia was *my* dream—all that'll matter is it wasn't hers.

I'm not trying to be a brat. USC is a perfectly good school. A great school! But I spent years literally torturing myself with AP classes, SAT tutors, and Columbia application events. I sent handwritten thank-you cards to so many people, I was one note away from mailing the receptionist and janitor. Trying to get into Columbia has been killing me. If I'd known USC was endgame, I would have waltzed through Spence and not given myself a stress-induced ulcer.

I've been trying to stay even-keeled, as always, but I suddenly can't stop myself. "It's not like it matters who gets Deb of the Year. It's all pointless bullshit."

Mom swivels toward me, horrified. Her driver, Ephram,

eyes me from the front seat apprehensively. He's seen Ella Somerset make mincemeat of lesser targets. "Okay, you've been a complete jerk to me all week." I flinch. She's not wrong. But the insult still hurts.

"I'm not a jerk," I mutter.

"I had all sorts of invites for next week. I could be off the coast of Sardinia with Jeff and Lauren on their yacht!"

So go, then. Who's stopping you?

"Chapin, honey. This is our magical mommy-daughter time. But, frankly, I'm not looking forward to it very much if you're going to keep up this sullen attitude. This is *not* like you." She roots in her purse, pulling out a compact to check her reflection. She turns her head from side to side, admiring herself. "My sister always told me girls were harder in their teens, but I never believed it until now."

Don't fight back. Remember why you're doing this ball in the first place. It means the world to her.

"I'm sorry," I offer dutifully. "I know La Danse is very important to you."

They're not just empty words. La Danse *is* important to her. I really *do* desperately want to make her happy. Because when my mother is happy, it's like God herself is shining on you.

She turns to face me, gearing up for a patented "Ella Somerset speech," as Dalton and I call it: the kind where she acts like she's accepting an Academy Award even though she's just choosing between red or white wine at dinner.

"Lovebug, you don't know how lucky you are. Your father and I left behind everything—our families, our friends, our sanity—and we made it here. To the top." Our car comes to a stop in front of our building, right at the corner of Seventy-Fifth and Park. "My parents were carrot farmers. I grew up with nothing. We had to spend months saving up just to buy a new pair of shoes or a pretty dress. But you've never known anything but abundance. Look around. You have the world at your feet. *Our* world. This is where we belong." Two older female tourists stand in front of our building, no doubt hoping for a selfie with Ella. I wonder how many hours they've been waiting.

I start to exit the car, but Mom touches my arm. Her thin hand is cold against my skin. "I give you everything and I don't ask much. But this is a once-in-a-lifetime opportunity. The sort of thing I endlessly dreamed about when I was a girl. Please don't embarrass me. Take this seriously. You're so talented. You could win if you just *try*, for once."

I look into her piercing blue eyes, my heart aching for her approval, and I think: *If I ever have kids, I will be nothing like you.*

"Okay, Mom," I say. "I won't let you down."

She squeezes my arm gently. "That's my girl."

CHAPTER THREE

Piper

King of Prussia, Pennsylvania

As much as I find the whole concept of La Danse detestable, I can't stop thinking about how, for one magical night in Paris, I could be dancing in a gilded ballroom alongside movie stars and royalty.

After Seb leaves, I spend the next hour googling the other girls on the list. When I type in Imogen Wang's name, the first search result is a lengthy profile in *Tatler Hong Kong*, featuring Imogen, her mother, and their full-time clothes nanny, named Venetka. These are not my kind of people. Are these girls anyone's type of people? That's the real question.

I proceed to look up several more debutantes. Hundreds of millions of results pop up on my screen—countless photos of the girls at premieres, store openings, fashion shows, and music festivals, with some paparazzi pics and street-style shots sprinkled into the mix.

Chapin Buckingham has by far the most photos. She's effortlessly stylish in a way I could never be. Of course, Chapin exited the womb into a glamorous, friction-free life of parties, vacations, and backstage passes: movie-star mom, rock-star dad, everybody knows the Buckinghams. When Chapin was born, her parents' personal assistants placed an official baby announcement on a golden easel outside the hospital, as if they were British royals. To be fair, Chapin Buckingham is probably the closest anyone has ever come to being American royalty.

Then there's Lottie Stuart-Jones, who's just actual royalty.

I go further down the rabbit hole, stumbling across a blog post and reading about the history of the ball:

> La Danse des Débutantes has been around since the 1950s. After Queen Elizabeth stopped allowing debutantes to be presented at court, it provided an outlet for well-bred young women to make their societal debuts. For a while, La Danse coasted on its laurels, but it eventually fell off the social calendar, floundering until fashion publicist Amélie Bouchon decided to make it relevant again. Under Amélie's steely gaze, La Danse reimagined itself, making haute couture more relevant and increasing its now-inescapable social media presence. In recent years, as the world has become more attuned to elitism, Amélie has savvily fought back, inviting a more diverse class of debutantes in an attempt to keep La Danse relevant. But while the debs

now hail from around the globe, often with a charitable component, they're still gobstoppingly rich. Whether you're a celebrity, a CEO, or a political magnate, if you have a daughter, La Danse is the hot ticket.

In *theory*, however, as I learn, La Danse's vision isn't concerned with family lineage. Instead, it "celebrates modern womanhood" and honors accomplished (ahem, sample-sized) young women—and their proud parents—by introducing them to society via the *Daily Mail, Tatler*, and *Vanity Fair*. For one Parisian evening, in a gilded hotel ballroom, oligarchs and movie stars waltz with their daughters alongside European royalty and titans of industry as their imagined equals—and the press covers them as such. In addition to Chapin Buckingham—a *major* get for La Danse—this year's crop of debutantes includes the daughter of a UNICEF humanitarian, the daughter of a C-list game-show host, and twelve other young women selected from the most prominent dynasties of Chinese business, Indian aristocracy, and European royalty.

And then there's me.

I hear the front door open and jump to my feet. "Dad!"

His EMT instincts kick in. He runs over. "Is everything okay? Why do you sound like that?"

"Something . . . weird happened today."

He sits down, looking at me expectantly.

I hand Dad the La Danse invitation, sitting next to him. As he studies it, quizzical, I watch his face anxiously. "A debutante ball? In *Paris*?"

"I know, I know. Thing is . . . this is the biggest societal event of the year. Way bigger than prom. It's a huge honor to be invited. They only invite sixteen girls in the whole world."

The tiniest part of me fears Dad will say, *So why would they invite* you? but of course he doesn't. My dad is the most supportive human being on the planet.

I can't imagine becoming a parent at eighteen, like my parents did, but they always made the best of it. From the time I was a little kid, I always felt loved and cherished. Sure, we had less *stuff* than all my friends. And, yeah, my parents weren't able to take us on vacations (besides the time Dad chaperoned a school trip to Toronto). Mom was working double shifts; Dad was on-call. Financially, we were always on a razor's edge.

But I felt like my voice mattered. My parents respected me. Lifted me up.

That's worth more than all the money in the world.

"And is this something you want to do?"

I stop. Is it? Do I really want to spend a week tagging along with spoiled little rich girls whose biggest worry in life is whether to align themselves with Chanel or Dior?

"I'm not sure," I say truthfully. "It doesn't feel like *me*. I can't imagine what I'd have in common with the debutantes. Running around Paris with them playing dress-up?"

But Seb's words reverberate in my head: *Have fun.* It's not about the girls. It's about me. Dad doesn't know about Columbia yet, and when I think about how disappointed he's going to be for me, my chest seizes. Tears come to my eyes again. Dad notices.

"Your mom always wanted to go to Paris," he says quietly.

I nod. "I remember."

Mom didn't just want to go to Paris. She was not-so-secretly in love with it. She adored movies like *Amélie* and *Midnight in Paris*. One weekend when I was in elementary school, I caught her watching *Before Sunset* two days in a row. I assumed it was because of her enduring crush on Ethan Hawke, but it occurred to me years later that it may have been because the movie was the closest she came to truly walking the streets of Paris herself.

He looks between me and the invitation. I can practically see the wheels turning in his head.

"Okay, then," he says firmly. "Just say the word, and you're going." He pulls me into his arms for a massive bear hug. "Whatever you want to do, Piper. I'm in." I squeeze him back tightly. Best. Dad. Ever.

After an epic spaghetti dinner—seriously, Dad's homemade marinara could give Rao's a run for its money—I retreat to my room to dive into hours of homework. But instead of focusing on calculus, I ignore the books for once and somehow find myself down the rabbit hole of La Danse again.

These dresses are bonkers.

I find a photo of one of the debs from last year, a Brazilian girl whose father is some fancy film director. Setting aside the fact that she's basically royalty, it's the type of dress that indicates not just a better fashion sense but a better *life*. I don't even possess the language to describe what she's wearing: It's all tulle and lace and metallics, everything geometrically draped across her body in an epically perfect fit.

I wonder what kind of dress my mother would have chosen if she were invited. Mom had a kooky fashion sense: She'd throw inexpensive things together, seemingly without a care in the world, and yet everything would still look incredible on her. I bet she would have chosen a bohemian dress, something with fringe and feathers. Or maybe she would have gone for something soft and silk, but in an eye-catching shade like chartreuse. Whatever she wore, she'd have killed it. Honestly, she'd have looked great in a paper bag.

I picture myself in one of those gorgeous confections—something royal blue, to flatter my complexion?—gliding down a grand staircase on Dad's arm. And at the bottom of the stairs, instead of some hot young European prince waiting for me (sorry, Seb), my mom would be standing there, smiling proudly. The daydream brings tears to my eyes. I suddenly miss her so much I can't breathe. What I wouldn't give for just one hour with her in Paris.

If Mom had been there when the invitation arrived, she would have backed Seb up, grabbing me by the shoulders, shaking me (metaphorically speaking, obvs), and agreeing: *You can do this, Piper! You deserve to be there just as much as these girls do!*

But as I look through the jaw-dropping dresses—ooh, this one has white-and-gold appliqué flowers all over it—something occurs to me that's so painfully obvious I physically squirm. The gowns are unique, bespoke creations from the finest luxury fashion houses in the world . . . literally created for each individual girl . . . which means the debutante needs to *buy* the dress.

Right.

Duh.

Maybe I could get a lesser gown: something that's still gorgeous and sparkly but that doesn't give *I mortgaged my penthouse in Monaco to pay for this.*

I open a Google spreadsheet. *Let's run the numbers!*

Flights to Paris for me and Dad . . . quick Google search . . . $388 each on some Portuguese airline I've never heard of. Not that bad.

Hotel in Paris . . . over to Expedia . . . Fifteen minutes away from city center is close enough, right? . . . Okay, this one is kind of decent and it's only $151 per night. Doable.

I'd probably need new clothes . . . that's a Target run, obviously. . . . I bet if I browsed the sale racks I could keep it to a hundred bucks. How many new clothes would I really need?

And then the dress . . .

How much *is* an haute couture gown?

After a Google search, my eyes pop out of my head:

Gowns usually begin at $25,000, although depending on the brand can run from $40,000 to $100,000.

Wait, what?

Twenty-five thousand dollars for a *dress*? And that's on the *low end*?

Seeing the costs laid out in black and white, I feel like a moron. *Of course* I can't go to the Met Gala for baby billionaires. *Of course* this is out of my league. I allowed myself to get seduced by the glitz and the glamour and I completely lost my head. It's no loss, really—those girls and I have zero in common. It's fine. Just another silly daydream.

I shut my computer, feeling embarrassed to have ever entertained the notion.

Before I turn off the light, I look at the photo of Mom on my bedside table. She and my dad had a dream of backpacking through Europe after high school. Like Dad said, Mom especially always wanted to go to Paris. They didn't have the money, though, and suddenly they were two teenage parents with a baby, dreams dashed.

And then Mom died.

I allow myself one last tiny moment of fantasy.

We'd walk along the Champs-Élysées together. She loved chocolate ice cream—I once saw something on TikTok about this shop called Berthillon with scoops the size of your head, so we'd definitely go there. She liked Monet, so the Musée d'Orsay would be a must. . . .

I turn over, sighing. Back to reality: I'll call Bardot and Amélie in the morning to decline.

But as I stare up at the ceiling, unable to sleep, I can't help feeling like I'm letting Mom down.

CHAPTER FOUR

Chapin
Somewhere over the Atlantic

"And then she said, 'No, it's *twenty* thousand!'" Lottie says, laughing.

I'm on a private jet with Lottie and a few of the other debs: Margarita Vasquez, Peach Davis, and Imogen Wang. Lottie stopped in New York after Frieze, while Margarita, Peach, and Imogen keep apartments in the city. When we were younger, I remember going with Lottie on the royal jet once or twice. But recently, the king has started wallet busting—appearances and all—and it's forced Lottie's parents to ask friends for favors. I'm pretty sure this jet belongs to the Beckhams.

"Such a nightmare," Margarita says.

"Rude, honestly," Peach nods.

"What do you think, Chapin?" Lottie asks me.

I've barely been listening. I'm watching a documentary on YouTube about the crystal caves in Naica, Mexico. They're full of these gorgeous milky-white crystals called gypsum, as wide as tree trunks. Mom sometimes pokes fun at my other "weird" interests—I still maintain that magic tricks are cool—but the one preoccupation she can totally get on board with is geology. Mom loves jewelry even more than she loves fashion.

I remember the first time I fell in love with gems. I was six years old, and my mother was on her way to the Met Gala. Our apartment was bustling with makeup artists and personal dressers and hairstylists, everybody fluttering around with the singular goal of making my mother look as gorgeous as possible. I sat on the edge of her bed, watching my mom get dolled up. She was in the best mood, and she kept smiling at me through the mirror, giving me little winks and funny faces.

And then a man entered with a briefcase. He opened it, and it was like the room exploded with light: a necklace made of diamonds, plus another gemstone I'd never seen before. Obviously, the diamonds were beautiful, but it was this *other* gem that enthralled me. It changed colors, from emerald to red to turquoise, the light catching and dancing and shimmering through the stone. It was enchanting. Even my mother gasped, momentarily speechless. I asked the man what it was, and he said the whimsical jewel was called alexandrite. He then placed the necklace around my mother's neck. I thought I had never seen anybody more beautiful in my entire life.

Once my mother was fully ready, she insisted on taking a photo with the two of us together: me standing on the stairs, her at the base, our heads together. I still have that photo tacked up to my mirror, and I don't know what's more radiant: the jewels, or the smiles on both our faces.

As luck would have it, our nanny took Dalton and me to the Museum of Natural History the following day, where I spent an hour wandering around the Halls of Gems and Minerals, hungry for more radiance. It wasn't just alexandrite—which I now know offers up its trademark brilliance thanks to a unique crystal structure and trace elements. There was an entire world of gems to discover: garnet and tanzanite and larimar and red beryl.

Of course, Mom's always had a substantial jewelry collection of her own—some bought, some gifted, some occasionally loaned, like that gorgeous necklace. But even though my mother has the attention span of a gnat, as I got older, she'd actually *listen* when I explained to her why certain items in her collection were rarer and more valuable than others. (Don't even get me started on the artificial scarcity of diamonds.) I cherished those moments; it doesn't take a PhD in Freud to guess it's probably why I love gems now.

"Earth to Chapin," Lottie says, waving her hand in front of my face.

Oh right. She asked me a question.

I pause the documentary and turn my phone over on my lap. "I think . . . I agree with you?" I say, hoping that's the right answer.

They all exchange looks before bursting into laughter.

"You could at least *pretend* you want to be here," Lottie says.

She waves a finger and the flight attendant arrives, topping up everybody's glass of champagne. I've barely had two sips of mine. I don't understand why everybody loves champagne so much. It tastes like the bottom of an old shoe. And it's not like I'm *not* drinking the good stuff. I've had more Dom Perignon than a supermodel in Cannes.

I try to see us through the flight attendant's eyes—a bunch of pampered eighteen-year-olds drinking expensive (illegal) alcohol and glued to our phones, flying unchaperoned from New York to Paris. Cringe. I call "Thank you!" after the flight attendant as she retreats back to the galley. *We're not all bad!* I want to say.

I refocus my attention on Lottie. She's too far down the line of succession to be of any consequence (twenty-first, to be precise), yet as granddaughter of the king is too high up to get an actual job. If her mother hadn't refused a title for her at birth, she'd be Her Royal Highness Princess Charlotte of Cumberland. Instead she's just Lottie. Surprise, surprise, my mother adores her. (The fact that her mother is the Princess Royal and the king's eldest daughter is *entirely* irrelevant, I'm sure.) Mom's ridiculous theory is that people with money need to stick to other people with money: Mere fame isn't enough for entry past the velvet ropes.

Despite all of Lottie's advantages, she's a mostly good egg. But down-to-earth? Big no.

Lottie's been rocking couture since she was twelve.

By contrast, I'm wearing a The Row-esque thrift-store outfit with my favorite lime-green Dunks. (High heels are a torture device invented by men and you will never convince me otherwise.) I might be a walking fashion encyclopedia thanks to copious hours spent at the Costume Institute after school, but I think *true* style comes from making an outfit your own—societal expectations be damned.

Sure, I agreed to this whole debutante nonsense to make Mom happy. And I'm gonna curtsy and preen and promenade with the best of them . . . but in my dream world I'm wearing platform Celine sneakers underneath that gown.

"Chapin's way too cool to *try*," Peach says. "And that's why she's going to get Deb of the Year." Her smile doesn't quite meet her eyes.

"No, thanks."

"Oh, Chapin, get over it," Lottie says. "You want Deb of the Year just as much as the rest of us."

"So I can get an extra quarter of a page in *Vanity Fair* and even *more* pressure from Ella to conform? Pass."

"Well, I hope it's me, and I'm not sorry about it," Lottie declares. "The king pretends he doesn't give a toss, but he absolutely does."

"It's so weird you call your *abuelo* 'the king,'" Margarita Vasquez says. (Yes, *that* Vasquez family, the Colombian beer billionaires.)

"What should I call him? Harry Styles?" she quips.

"Okay, what about you, Margarita?" Peach asks. "Why do you want queen deb?"

"So I can smoke you fools," Margarita purrs.

Everybody laughs, and then they all start talking on top of

one another about why they're the one to deserve the honor. I'm not completely clueless—I understand that it's a big deal being named Deb of the Year. But truly, I don't give a damn; it's not like it's going to get me any credibility inside a science lab. I've spent my entire life in my mother's shadow, and I'm only doing this ridiculous ball to bond with her, and it's all a waste of time anyway. None of us are escaping our gilded cages. I could be writing my essay to get off the Columbia wait list instead.

My phone buzzes, startling me. I turn it back over to find a text from Bardot Sinclair.

Bardot: how's it going? just checking in on you! on the plane, right?

She's Amélie's assistant, and she's awesome. Way better than the last girl, who had zero personality and lips that were firmly glued to Amélie's backside.

I reply:

Chapin: yep. with lottie and the girls

Chapin: hope you're okay. seems like 24/7 drama with storey

Bardot: it's been a nightmareeee

Bardot: luckily the new girl taking her place seems great

My heart leaps. New girl taking Storey's place? What new girl?

"What did you say?" Lottie asks. Everybody's frozen, staring at me. Oops—I must have said that last part out loud.

I point at my phone.

"I was just texting with Bardot." Shit. Am I betraying Bardot's confidence? She didn't ask me to keep it secret. "Maybe I misunderstood. . . ." Lottie grabs my phone out of my hands and scrolls back up.

"You did not misunderstand. It says right here: 'New girl taking her place.'" She begins texting Bardot back, oblivious.

I gently pluck my phone from Lottie's hands.

"Well, come on, then," she demands imperiously. "Ask her!"

It's not a stretch to imagine Lottie's ancestors yelling *off with their heads!* and completely remaking the fabric of society because they were mildly displeased.

Chapin: sorry . . . what new girl?

Bardot: oh

Bardot: shit

Bardot: maybe it's still a secret?

Bardot: she hasn't actually accepted yet haha

Chapin: what's her name?

The phone goes silent for a while—the ellipses appearing and then disappearing.

Meanwhile, all the girls on the plane are staring at me, ravenous for the latest detail. Finally . . .

Bardot: Piper Woo Collins

"Piper Woo Collins," Peach announces to the cabin. I startle, realizing she's been reading my phone over my shoulder. "Does anybody know Piper Woo Collins?"

"Is she Lily Collins's sister?" Margarita asks.

"Her sister is *way* older," Lottie says authoritatively. "I know Phil."

"Maybe she's related to Joan and Jackie," Peach says.

"Do they go to Aiglon?" Margarita asks.

"Or she could be a member of the Woo family," Imogen Wang says. "You know. John Woo?"

"What about Cho Seung-woo?" Peach says.

"How do you know Cho Seung-woo?" Imogen is impressed.

"Oh, please. Like I'm not addicted to K-dramas."

Lottie is already searching for this Piper on social media.

"Nothing on TikTok . . . Insta's got like four photos of chemistry beakers . . . Wait, is *this* her?"

Lottie holds up her phone. It's a *Teen Vogue* article about some girl. Wow, she won the International Science Fair. That's prestigious.

I pull up the article on my own phone. Eighteen years old . . . she's pretty, in a boring sort of way . . . accepted at every Ivy League school . . .

My stomach tightens. I didn't get into Columbia but *this* girl did? And to make matters worse, *she's* a science geek too?

I study her more intently. She *is* pretty, even though she's clearly never set foot inside Sephora. She needs better eyebrows. Maybe some highlights? And that posture: disaster. But with a few fixes, she could be a brunette bombshell.

Wait. I sound like my mother. Gross.

"She's some rando," Lottie says. "They cannot be serious."

"This is unacceptable," Peach agrees. "There's a certain standard to La Danse. You can't just let anybody in."

"This drags us all down," Margarita agrees.

I secretly feel guilty for picking Piper apart. I foist my guilt onto the girls. "You sound like my mom, you snobs. She's very accomplished. The International Science Fair is a big deal."

Imogen throws her arm around my shoulder. "Chapin Buckingham, defender of strays everywhere. You know the Mother

Teresa routine doesn't help your chances of winning, right?"

I throw her arm off, laughing. "Well . . . we're supposed to be charitable, aren't we? Don't say anything about Piper yet. Bardot isn't sure if it's still a secret or not."

Lunch arrives and we all start eating, followed by a group watch of *The Office*. Lottie keeps cracking up, which I find deeply weird. As if she can relate to any of it? (Okay, I can't exactly relate to it either, but funny is funny.)

Two episodes in, however, Margarita gasps. "It's already on Insta."

She swivels her phone around to show us Deuxmoi. It takes me several seconds to understand what I'm looking at. It's the same photo of Piper from *Teen Vogue* we saw earlier.

The post is from an hour ago.

anon@ladanse.com
Anon pls! Rumor has it that Piper Woo Collins—a nobody from Pennsylvania— is set to take Storey Ricci's place at La Danse.

Everybody scrolls . . . except, I realize, for Peach. I look at her, suspicious.

"Peach?"

She looks back at me innocently. "Mmm?"

"You didn't text anybody about Piper, did you?"

Peach suddenly becomes very interested in her cuticles. "No . . ."

"I told you it was a secret!"

"I didn't tell anybody!" she protests. "Only McRae." Another deb. McRae Lawrence is an enormous gossip, which makes sense because her father is literally the most powerful newspaper magnate in the world.

"Great. It'll be on the *Daily Fail* in five seconds." I check. Sure enough, it's already an item in the sidebar column.

"Cat's out of the bag." Lottie shrugs. "Hope Piper's ready."

I look at Piper's Instagram account again. Her account has exploded: She already has over fifteen thousand new followers. I can't help it—my competitive juices stir.

Be nice, Chapin. Be nice.

Still, something about this Piper girl feels like trouble.

CHAPTER FIVE

Piper
King of Prussia, Pennsylvania

"You said *yes!*"

Seb's elated voice bellows through my phone. I haven't heard him this excited since he scored Chappell Roan tickets.

I look at the clock. It's 10:57 a.m.

"Why are you calling so early?" I ask. "I thought you never woke before noon on the weekends."

"What's more normal: a high school senior who hits the snooze button twenty times, or one who's voluntarily awake in time for the breakfast special at Denny's?"

"Early to bed, early to rise—"

"Makes a man want a stronger Ambien prescription," he jokes.

"I can't help my internal clock!"

"Yeah, but only nerds and sociopaths are early birds."

"So you're calling to insult me," I laugh. "Gotcha."

"No, I'm calling to praise you! I'm so proud! This is going to change everything."

Now I'm confused. "I literally have no idea what you're talking about."

"La Danse? Your acceptance? It's all over social media."

"Wait, what?" My heart stutters.

I put Seb on speaker while I search Instagram. My feed is mostly full of science accounts and chemistry memes. "Where do I look?"

"Deuxmoi, Diet Prada, Just Jared—pick your poison."

I pull up Diet Prada and am greeted by a photo of *me*. It's the *Teen Vogue* article, where I look approximately seventy-five billion times more glamorous than normal. On top of my photo, they've placed a headline:

Polymer Princess:
Science Winner Takes Storey Ricci's Place at La Danse

My jaw drops as I read the caption:

After Storey Ricci was disinvited from La Danse, organizers aren't sleeping on a new pick.

Enter Piper Woo Collins, an 18-year-old from King of Prussia, Pennsylvania. Piper won the International Science Fair and is a future Ivy League whiz kid, according to Teen Vogue, who recently featured her. Watch this space.

"I am loving this for you," Seb declares.

"It's not . . . I didn't . . ." I reread the post over and over, kicking myself for not calling Amélie sooner to send my regrets. It's late in Paris already.

Seb hears the anxiety in my voice and understands. "You haven't accepted yet?"

"I was going to say no."

"Piper! I thought we had a breakthrough!"

I click on my notifications to find a sea of red. Somehow I've accumulated thousands of followers. "It's too much money." I have to put a stop to this, before the news gets out even further.

"Call you later, love you, bye."

I hang up before Seb can say anything else. I find the invitation and dial Paris.

"*Allô?*"

"Um . . . Amélie Bouchon, please? This is Piper Woo Collins. I'm calling about—"

"Oh my God, Piper, hi!" A friendly American voice chirps back at me. "I'm Bardot, Amélie's assistant. One sec, let me get Amélie for you."

"Yes, but—"

"Piper! *Bonjour!*" An older woman takes the line. "We are so thrilled to have you at La Danse! As soon as we read about your incredible academic accomplishments, we thought, 'Now *she* is a debutante!'"

"Thank you. You're too kind. But, um—"

"What day will you arrive? Most of the girls will get here this weekend, although a few arrive today. Hotel availability is difficult, but of course I will pull some strings. Bardot will be able to—"

"I'm so sorry, but I can't accept," I say in a rush.

Silence.

A *long* silence.

"Um, sorry. Are you still there?" I ask.

"I'm afraid I don't understand. What do you mean, you cannot accept?" Amélie says icily.

A flush creeps up my chest. I hate confrontation. I don't know what else to say, so I fall back on the truth. "We don't have the money."

Amélie doesn't respond.

I hasten to fill the silence, embarrassment fueling verbal diarrhea. "Of course, I do appreciate the invitation, but I think it's probably for the best. I'm not your typical debutante. I work at Claire's. I've never been outside North America. I'm only going to college on scholarship. Or at least, I *was* going to college on scholarship."

"Pardon?"

"I was supposed to go to Columbia, but they rescinded my scholarship last minute, and now I can't afford it and it's a mess." I suddenly remember I'm talking to some fancy French lady, not a therapist. She doesn't care about my problems. "Sorry. Anyhow. Money's extra tight right now and . . . yeah. Can't afford it. Plus I have school. But thanks. It was fun to dream for a few hours."

Normally I'd feel awkward about unloading on a complete and total stranger, but (1) it's not like I'm ever going to speak to her again, and (2) I just want to get off the phone and back to real life so I can forget this ever happened.

I hear some muffled whispering on the other end. It sounds like Amélie has her hand over the phone, conferring with somebody.

"Piper."

"Yes . . . ?"

"If you could afford La Danse, would you come?"

"Well. I guess. But like I said, I'm not exactly who you have in mind—"

"You are, indeed, *exactly* who we have in mind," Amélie says, her voice firm and clear. "So that's settled. You're coming to La Danse, and we're paying for it. Perhaps Columbia University isn't smart enough to keep you on scholarship, but we are. La Danse des Débutantes is not some elitist, old-fashioned affair. We are a modern organization, devoted to hand-picking extraordinary young women who give back to society in a myriad of ways, and I can think of nobody more deserving than you, Piper Woo Collins." As she speaks, her voice gets louder and more triumphant, as if she's giving a stirring speech onstage. I half wonder if Bardot is filming an Instagram live.

"Um. Thank you?"

"*Superbe!* Bardot will arrange everything. You will—"

"I'm so sorry, *really*, but I just don't think it's a good idea."

The silence takes on a new tone. I think Amélie is going to reach through the phone and strangle me. "And what, pray tell, is it now?"

"Listen, La Danse sounds like a dream. But I have to focus

on making up the difference for my scholarship. I have to focus on my future. And it's not just my scholarship. It's the funding for my polymer, my inventions . . . it just wouldn't be smart for me to ditch a week of class and go gallivanting around Paris for some dance party with a bunch of rich people I'm never going to see again and who don't give a damn about me." The words fly out of my mouth before I even think about what I'm saying. I hope I didn't offend her.

"*Dance party?*"

Okay. Yeah. I offended her.

"I didn't mean—"

"Piper, *ma chère*. La Danse des Débutantes is not a *dance party*. Do you understand who comes to La Danse? The mothers and fathers of our debutantes and cavaliers could fund the next twenty years of your research."

"Yes, I'm sure but—"

"I've been selecting girls for nine months. Girls would kill for this. Nobody says no to La Danse."

"Of course, I didn't mean to—"

"The fact that you do not understand the opportunity that has been presented to you is concerning, but I cannot fault you. You do not know what you do not know. You do not need to spend your life hustling like a stripper for a hundred dollars here and a hundred dollars there, Piper."

"I mean, there's nothing wrong with exotic dancing for—"

"There are people in life who understand the difference between working hard and working smart. I read your *Teen Vogue* article, and I think: Here is a girl who works hard *and* who works smart. You seem like a very smart girl, Piper, so now it is my turn to speak plainly. This is rarefied air, and you have been given the once-in-a-lifetime opportunity to come breathe it. This is not about a *dance*. This is about connections that will set you up *for life*. Perform at La Danse, impress the right people, put your best foot forward, and you will never need to look for funding again."

Now it's my turn to be silent.

"Are you still there?" she asks.

"Yes." I'm considering her offer. The silence stretches, but for once I don't rush to fill it. I hadn't really considered the exposure La Danse might offer. And, despite what I said to Amélie, I don't really think missing a week of the final semester of senior year would be a big deal. I spend so long working through the tantalizing possibilities that Amélie jumps back in.

"Okay, fine," she says, sounding increasingly panicked. "I understand you are on the fence. How about this? If you agree to come to the ball, I will also pay for your first year of college."

"Wait, *what*?"

More conferring in the background.

"La Danse des Débutantes is all about charity, and it pains my heart to know that one of the most accomplished young high school graduates in the country cannot access a school that desperately wants her. I can think of no better use of our considerable discretionary funds." There she goes with that announcer voice again.

"Amélie. That's insanely generous. Thank you."

She switches back to a normal voice. "You understand, yes,

Piper? *No bad press.* You will be an exemplary debutante. You will rise to the challenge. You will be our Cinderella story. Benefits you, benefits me."

"I understand. Thank you."

"*Bon.* We have a deal. Bardot will call you back in a few minutes to arrange everything. Welcome to La Danse."

Amélie hangs up before I can change my mind. What on earth have I gotten myself into?

CHAPTER SIX

Chapin
Paris, France

My room at the Ritz is perfection.

I'm in the Coco Chanel Suite, on the top floor of one of the most opulent hotels in Paris. It has an enormous wraparound balcony with views of the Eiffel Tower, which even I find wildly impressive. Sure, I've stayed in the world's best, but show me a person who isn't moved by a picture-perfect view of the Eiffel Tower from a seven-star hotel suite and I'll show you a jaded robot sociopath I want nothing to do with.

Of course, the suite was pristine when I moved in a few days ago, but now every inch has been taken over by my clothes and sneakers. Here's the thing Mom doesn't get about me. Just because I'm not into the boring clothes *she* likes doesn't mean I don't adore fashion. I just don't go for that lacquered, cookie-cutter, *let's impress people* thing she's obsessed with. She buys an expensive label and mistakes it for style.

Speaking of Mom, she's staying in the hotel's coveted Suite Impériale, which was described as "the crown jewel of the Ritz" by *Condé Nast Traveler.* That iconic suite is only available for royalty, Hollywood royalty, heads of state, and high-profile guests.

"To think that she grew up in a town where the nicest 'hotel' was a Motel Six," I say, pouring two glasses of sparkling water. I hand one to Dalton, my brother, who's lounging on the couch as we catch up. After he and Mom landed this morning, Mom's first stop was the spa, while Dalton immediately came to see me: priorities perfectly encapsulated.

"Who did, Mom?"

"Yeah." We weren't exactly talking about my mother, but she lives rent-free in my head.

It's kind of exhausting, TBH.

"You know she loves you, right?"

"That's easy for the favorite child to say. You get the good Ella. I get the helicoptering banshee who criticizes how I breathe, chew, and sit."

"Fair. Let's ignore Mom's craziness. This week is about you." We cheers with the Perrier.

There's a soft knock on the door. I open it to find an anxious-looking Bardot.

"Hey, Bardot." I swing open the double doors, inviting her into the suite. "Welcome to Crazy Town."

Bardot looks around the room apprehensively, as if sizing it up. We first met earlier this year, when Mom and I flew to Paris "just for fun" on a shopping trip that actually turned out to be Mom lobbying Amélie to make me Queen Deb. While Mom and Amélie did God knows what, Bardot and I went out for coffee and bonded. She understands what it's like jumping through hoops to please the unpleasable.

"Everything okay?" I ask.

"Yes. Totally." She sits down and nervously pours herself a glass of water, her eyes sweeping the suite. "How's Paris been for you so far?"

"Dreamy as always. Lottie and I hit some boutiques in the Marais, spent an afternoon being lazy by the canals, normal stuff. I'm glad I came a few days early."

"Smart. Everyone else arrives today. Lots of balls in the air." She takes a deep breath. "I need to talk to you about something. I just spoke with Amélie, and—" She stops herself, changing tracks. "So, you know how we have that new girl, Piper Woo Collins, coming?"

"That's right," I say warily. As if I could forget the girl who took my spot at Columbia.

"Yes. Um. Well—"

Bardot is interrupted by a knock at the door. Dalton swings it open to find my assigned cavalier, Face Wellington. My heart leaps.

Confession. I have the world's biggest crush on Face.

Miles "Face" Wellington. Lottie's distant, distant cousin. Low-level British royal and first-year at Oxford. (Sorry, *fresher* at Oxford.)

I first met Face at Glastonbury three summers ago, when

Dad was performing on the Pyramid Stage. Dad might be in his eighties, but he was jumping around onstage like he was twenty-two and the crowd was massive. Face was impressed that *the* Otis Buckingham was my dad, while I couldn't believe that Face was even more gorgeous in person than on Insta. We got to talking, which led to flirting, which led to exchanging numbers and a make-out session. Next time I saw him, out at Annabel's last summer, we kissed again. It's not like we're *dating* or anything, but I can't help but hope being around him in the city of *amour* will jump-start something more serious.

Though I'd settle for making out with him again. He has the softest lips.

Plus, I'm always extra happy to see his gorgeous (yes) face. The only thing sharper than Face's sartorial choices is his cut-glass jawline. Rumors are he has a modeling contract in the works.

"Hiya, Chapin," Face says, strolling through the door with a lopsided grin from ear to ear. "Nice digs."

"Not too shabby, right? When did you get in?" I stand up and move across the room to give him a kiss on each cheek, Eurostyle. As my cheek touches his, my heart flutters at the proximity. God, he's gorgeous. I remember the feeling of his mouth on mine, the softness of his hand sliding up my back. He holds my gaze for a millisecond and my body goes into high alert.

He and Dalton politely shake hands before Face installs himself on the couch, manspreading like he owns the place. He notices Bardot, and the grin reappears.

She blushes. "Hi. I'm Bardot."

"Of course I know who you are," he says smoothly. "Thank you so much for all your hard work putting this together, Bardot. All the cavaliers appreciate you." Impeccable manners, too.

Bardot tucks her hair behind her ears, proud. "I appreciate *you*." She takes a deep breath and launches back into whatever she wanted to say before the disruption. "I know you're all busy, so I won't stay long. Chapin, I just needed to talk to you about something quickly. Obviously, this suite is massive. So, because Piper is new and needs some help learning the ropes, Amélie thought it might be a good idea—" There's yet another knock on the door.

"Hold that thought," I say, popping up to answer. "It's probably Mom, glistening with essential oils after her two-hour massage 'journey.'"

But when I swing open the door, it's a girl I've never met before.

Oh shit. It's Piper.

"Hi!" Piper says brightly. "I'm Piper Woo Collins. You must be Chapin Buckingham?"

I reflexively close the door a little. Why is the new girl banging on my hotel door? I look back at everybody. Face and Dalton are examining Piper with interest—okay, let's nip *that* in the bud—while Bardot looks as if she's about to have a heart attack.

"Um, yeah. That's right. Hi. Can I help you?"

Piper looks confused. She points to her suitcase. "I'm your roommate. We're living together this week!" Oh. Hell. No.

CHAPTER SEVEN

Piper
Paris, France

Chapin's looking at me like I'm a bug to be squashed.

Behind her, a tall brunette jumps to her feet. She's got kind eyes, but her anxiety levels could power a fusion reactor.

"Piper! Welcome! I'm Bardot Sinclair." Bardot rushes toward me, beckoning with her hands. "Come in, come in!"

Chapin reluctantly swings the door open. I step inside tentatively.

"This *is* my room, right?"

Bardot and Chapin speak at the same time:

"That's right!" Bardot says.

"No, I think there's been a mistake," Chapin says.

Well, now I don't know what to do.

Bardot and Chapin look at each other.

"That's what I was coming here to tell you," Bardot says to Chapin, voice low. "The hotel is booked solid, and Amélie decided it made the most sense to put Piper with *you*, since you have the biggest suite, plus a second bedroom."

"What about Storey's room?" Chapin says, her voice dangerously close to a whine. "Can't you put her there?"

Bardot flushes. She clearly doesn't like confrontation. I can relate. "Once Storey . . . um . . . backed out, the hotel released the room. McRae's father took it for his in-laws."

"Well, why does she have to stay in the same hotel? Can't Amélie put her somewhere else?"

"It's really important to Amélie that everybody be in the hotel together."

"But—" Chapin protests.

"I'm so sorry," I say. "I can stay with my dad. He's in the hotel too."

"Actually," Bardot says apologetically, "your father is in a single."

"I don't mind sleeping on the floor. It's not a big deal."

"You may not mind, but the hotel does," Bardot says. "The French are a bit . . . finicky about hotel occupancy. That room is designated as a single, so . . ." She looks at Chapin pleadingly.

"I know it's not ideal. But it would mean so much to Amélie if—"

"Oh fine," Chapin says, resigned. "Let's not make a huge thing out of it. Welcome to the circus, Piper. Your bedroom is over there." She points to a door through the living room. I step toward it tentatively.

Just then I notice two guys sitting on the couch. They both look like male models.

The taller of the two stands up, looking at Chapin expectantly, as if he's waiting to be introduced.

"Hi," I say, extending my hand politely. "I'm Piper."

Chapin sighs. "Miles Wellington, meet Piper . . . what's your last name again?"

"Piper Woo Collins."

"Meet Piper Woo Collins," she repeats perfunctorily. I feel like I'm at a job interview.

"Hello, Piper," Miles purrs in a voice smooth as silk. British. "How do you do?"

"Um . . . good, thanks. I do . . . I mean, how do . . . how are *you*?" Should I curtsy? These people are all so formal.

The other guy steps forward. He looks like a cheerful male version of Chapin. "Hi! I'm Dalton. Chapin's brother." American. Very, *very* cute American.

While Miles makes me nervous, Dalton puts me at ease. Maybe it's his dimples. Or his wide smile. Or his broad shoulders, which look like they'll envelop you in the world's best hugs. I can't help grinning back at him. We clasp hands. The touch of his palm is warm and smooth against mine.

This doesn't seem to please Chapin.

"Okay, well, thanks, Face, thanks, bro, you guys can leave now, see you later, bye!" Chapin practically pushes them out the door, Bardot following.

Door closed, Chapin turns and appraises me.

"Where are the rest of your bags?" she asks.

I point down to the duffel bag at my feet. "This is it."

Chapin recoils. "You brought . . . a duffel bag? To *Paris*? What if everything gets wrinkled?"

I laugh. "It's all cotton. I'm sure there's an iron somewhere in this joint." Chapin stares at me. She's impossible to read.

"The literal last thing on earth I want to do is babysit you."

"Um, okay?" I try not to show how much her sharp words bother me.

"But we're here together and we might as well make the most of it. Go unpack, or shower, or whatever, and meet me in my room in ten. If we're going to be seen together, you should at least look presentable."

She turns on a heel and heads toward the bedroom on the other side of the room.

Okay, so Chapin is kind of an asshole. Hopefully this rooming situation doesn't completely suck. But if you're going to have a shitty roommate, it helps to be at the Ritz in Paris. I text Dad— **Found my room!**—before walking into my bedroom, soaking up the details. Heavy brocade curtains, a four-poster bed, intricate molding on the walls. The furniture looks like it was stolen directly from an antiques exhibition at the Met. The bathroom— I have my own bathroom!—is no less impressive. It's all marble flooring and gold trim, with a separate soaking tub and rainfall shower. The toilet has a freaking *bidet*.

Dad texts back—**Feels like I've checked into Buckingham Palace!**— and I laugh. I've already prepped Dad that we may not have a ton of time together this week with all the scheduled events. He's promised to wander around Paris on his own. I think he's got a list of places he wants to see while thinking of Mom.

Ten bucks says he ends up in front of Shakespeare and Company, just like in *Before Sunset*.

I quickly strip down, hop in the shower, and let the hot water run over my body.

I've never experienced water pressure like this. Our shower at home spits out droplets.

How the hell did I end up here?

After drying myself off with the largest, fluffiest towel in existence, then putting on fresh clothes, I find Chapin in her room.

Wall-to-wall racks of beautiful, color-coded clothing line the room. Underneath the metal racks, there are rows of sneakers in every shade of the rainbow. There's a view of the Eiffel Tower from her window.

"Wow. Cool sneaker collection."

Chapin looks at me suspiciously, as if trying to figure out if I'm being sarcastic. Once she realizes I'm serious, her face relaxes. "Uh . . . thanks. That suitcase was *so* jam-packed." Huh. I guess talking about sneakers is the way to access Chapin's nicer side.

"Are all these clothes yours too?" I walk along the racks, reaching out to gently touch the garments: eye-catching designer dresses and tulle skirts and frilly blouses and poofy gowns.

Even *I* recognize a Chanel jacket when I see it. "They're gorgeous."

But Chapin shakes her head no. "They're my mom's. And some stuff lent by fashion designers hoping I might be photographed in them this week."

That's right. Her mother is Ella Somerset. Of *course* her mom has a personal closet to rival Saks Fifth Avenue.

Chapin peers at me. "We're about the same height. What are you, a size four?" I nod.

Chapin begins plucking items off the racks, throwing them onto the bed haphazardly. I realize she's pulling clothing items for me.

"Oh no," I protest. "That's so kind, thank you, but I'm fine with what I brought."

Chapin looks at my clothes pointedly. I catch a glimpse of myself in a mirror. I wouldn't call myself . . . fashionable. But my clothes are clean, and the colors complement each other, and most importantly—they were cheap.

"You cannot wear *that* to La Danse des Débutantes," she says matter-of-factly, staring at my outfit in horror. "There is a certain *standard* here." It feels like she's quoting somebody else. She picks a cream-colored romper from the pile. "Here. This is The Row."

I don't know what The Row is. "Wow! Thanks!" I say, pretending I do.

She sees right through me. "Why are you even here?"

I hesitate. "Amélie invited me because she saw me in—"

"No, really. You *clearly* don't care about fashion. You look like you shop at the gas station. So why come? You don't belong here."

The brutality of her meanness stings. I could tell her about Columbia, tell her about Amélie's financial deal, tell her how I'm panicking about my future and this felt like one viable way to throw spaghetti at the wall, but something in me now feels mean too. "My mother died," I say abruptly.

ALEXANDRA BROWN CHANG

She freezes. "Oh."

"She had breast cancer, but even before she died, her life was just . . . tiring. She always dreamed of coming to Paris, but she never had enough money or time. And so I'm here for her. In honor of the life she could have lived if her dreams had come true."

To her credit, Chapin bows her head in respect. "I'm really sorry for your loss." Okay, so she's not a complete monster.

Chapin continues pulling clothes in silence. She holds up a flattering sundress. "My mother made me buy this, and it's not my style. You should have it."

"Borrow, sure, but I can't take—"

"It's yours." She places it gently on the bed next to me. "We're due downstairs in an hour. You can wear it to the welcome drinks."

Maybe I'm a sap, but I'm touched. "Thanks, Chapin."

She shrugs, then kneels on the floor, inspecting her shoe options. She picks up a pair of funky platform sneakers, staring at them with reverence. She then sighs, puts them back down, and instead pulls a pair of stilettos from the closet. She holds them with disgust, as if they're a pair of rats.

"What about you?" I ask.

"Huh?"

"You don't seem into this froufrou stuff, either. Why are *you* here? What do *you* want from La Danse?"

Chapin stands back up. She looks dazed. I suddenly get the sense this is a girl who hasn't been asked very much what *she* wants. I notice her outfit for the first time. She's highly fashionable, but

62

in the weirdest way possible: like she pulled together items from different styles and eras and threw them in a blender. Anti-couture. Anti-Ella. Anti–La Danse.

"My mom wanted it. And I wanted to make her happy." She clears her throat. "So you and I have that in common."

Chapin turns back toward the clothing rack. From behind she suddenly looks small and vulnerable. She pulls a cocktail dress from the rack and turns toward me, holding the dress against her body. Back to larger-than-life Chapin Buckingham: she of zillions of Instagram followers and magazine articles.

"That's nice," I say encouragingly.

"It's hideous. But it'll make Ella weep tears of joy." Chapin sighs heavily. She nods back toward the door. "Go change. If you're going to do this thing, you have to at least look the part."

I've been dismissed. I pick up the clothes Chapin laid out for me and head back to my room, feeling completely in over my head.

In my room, I close the door behind me. I walk over to the ornate mirror with the sundress, holding it against my body. Chapin's right. I have to at least try to look the part.

I expect the sundress to look strange on me, but incredibly, it fits like a glove. It feels weird seeing my reflection—it's still *me*, but a shinier, sparklier version. A version that *almost* looks like it belongs here. Amélie's words echo in my mind: *You will rise to the challenge.* This week has a purpose—I can't forget that.

Chin up, shoulders back, Piper.

Operation La Danse, commence.

CHAPTER EIGHT

Chapin
Paris, France

Ugh, let the festivities begin.

Downstairs, the seating area off the lobby is a buzz of activity: the entire hotel has been taken over by La Danse, with debutantes, cavaliers, and parents scattered throughout. I've never been part of a hotel buyout before—Mom and I usually sneak into hotels as discreetly as possible, often through a back door and freight elevator—and there's a strange freedom to being able to take over the lobby without fear of some lookie-loos gawking at us.

In the center of it all, Amélie confidently stands.

I can't remember a time when I didn't know who Amélie Bouchon was. Her presence was always in the background of my life, another irreplaceable family friend like Anna Wintour or Bryan Lourd or Paul McCartney. My mother has a habit of collecting useful people—whether for now or for fifteen years in the future. And from the time I was old enough to talk, I've been groomed as the Perfect Deb for Amélie and La Danse.

Right on cue, the elevator doors ding and my mother makes her grand entrance. The buzz of conversation drops down a level, as everybody turns to stare at her. She looks perfect, as always: a byproduct of her regular Paris glam squad. Normally, my mother goes for the Incognito Movie Star look in public—all hats and sunglasses, as if she's fooling anybody—but here she's dropped the protective mask. She might be the most famous person in this lobby, but she's certainly not the richest or most powerful.

I mentally cringe at my inner monologue. It's hard to undo a lifetime of Ella's programming: who's in, who's out, who's got money, who's lost it. She's obsessed with appearances, with rankings, with knowing where she stands (and making sure that's on top).

She opens her arms wide and squeals. "Amélie! You have *outdone* yourself!"

Every eye is trained on my mother as she and Amélie cheek-kiss. "Ella," Amélie says warmly. "Thank you so much for being here."

My mother glances over at me. Her mouth softens into her famously dazzling smile, but her eyes widen imperceptibly. For anybody else, it might look like a sweet mother-daughter moment. "Oh, there she is! Come over here, my love!" But I see the anxiety and impatience behind the gaze: *Come play your part. We have a show to put on.* Part of me thinks it'll never matter how much money and fame Mom has: She's always going to feel like that poor hayseed girl from the middle of nowhere who has something to prove . . . and I'm the one who bears the brunt.

I walk across the room, a brilliant smile plastered on my face. All eyes are on us. "Hi, Ms. Bouchon. Thank you so much for the invitation. I'm honored."

"Chapin, *ma chère!*" I obediently cheek-kiss her. "You look magnificent, as always," she says. Well, yeah, I'm wearing one of Mom's cookie-cutter debutante-delight dresses. What I wouldn't give for the Dries Van Noten set I snagged from a vintage store—a loose bohemian maxi skirt with a billowing top. Alas, my mom detests baggy clothing.

"*Bon.*" Amélie claps her hands together and turns toward the group at large. "Ladies. Gentlemen. Thank you all for coming, and welcome to La Danse!"

Everybody claps. Waiters begin passing out glasses of champagne.

As Amélie begins some boring speech, I look across the lobby, where my new roommate is standing next to a guy. He's cute, but really old, like in his thirties. They sort of look alike. Wait, Is that her *dad*? Gross. I take it back. He's not old—for a dad, he's a baby. Mine was already in his late sixties when I was born.

Piper leans toward her dad and the two of them laugh softly, whispering at each other.

The dad is all wide-eyed and rosy-cheeked and corn-fed. They're equally annoying and adorable. I wonder what it would be like to have that relationship with either of my parents. My dad's not even here; there's a fifty-fifty chance of him flying in from Germany at some point during the week. He's on tour, and of course that's more important than anything.

Even me.

Bardot walks around, distributing pieces of paper. She grins and rolls her eyes as she hands me mine. Thank God for normal people; she reminds me that this craziness is all so dumb. I'm not insane. It's everybody else.

As I hold the paper, I realize it's heavy card stock: a schedule of events.

"Bardot is distributing your schedule for the weekend. Now I know you are all glued to your phones these days. I probably should have sent this to you on TikTok! But at La Danse, we are old-school."

My eyes run down the page. Our schedule is jam-packed:

We've got waltz rehearsals; we've got etiquette classes; we've got ball-gown fittings.

Dalton is now standing next to me.

"This looks so boring," I whisper to him. "Think we'll be able to sneak away for a quality hang?"

But he's looking across the lobby, his eyes trained firmly on Piper.

"Sorry, what?" he asks, turning toward me.

"Nothing," I mutter, annoyed.

The waiter approaches me and I grab a glass of champagne, gulping it down over the protest of my taste buds. Thank goodness for relaxed drinking laws in Europe.

On the other side of me, Face materializes.

"This is ghastly, don't you think?"

"Yes!" I say, both grateful he's here and relieved he feels the same.

"It's you and me, Chaz. Thank *God* you're here, otherwise I would *unalive* myself."

I smile, trying to play it cool while rearranging my hair discreetly. God, he's so charming.

He looks at me and his expression turns serious. He takes me in, eyes sweeping head to toe. "Chapin Buckingham."

"Yes?"

"What on earth are you wearing?"

"You know . . . I mean . . . my mom wanted . . ."

"You look radiant," he says firmly. "You are the only girl I know who could be wearing a burlap sack and yet still be the most gorgeous person in the room."

"Oh stop."

"Never," he says. "You're going to win this whole damn thing," he whispers in my ear, offering his arm. I thread mine through his. Across the hall, Amélie looks at us approvingly. So does Mom.

Okay, maybe this thing is looking up.

"We will have a proper toast tonight at L'Avenue," Amélie announces. "But for now, *à votre santé*, and welcome to La Danse!"

Everybody cheers and sips their champagne.

"Waltz lessons begin in the ballroom in precisely one hour," Amélie says. "Enjoy your champagne . . . but not too much!"

Polite chuckles. "And yes—because our cavaliers ask us each year—every event is mandatory."

"Shudder," Face says. "See ya in there, Chaz." He drops my arm and wanders off, striking up a conversation with another cavalier. I try not to let my face show my disappointment.

But once Face is gone, I stew. I didn't expect him to take me in his arms and throw me onto the couch or anything, but a *little* acknowledgment of our history would be nice.

I refuse to show that it bothers me. I lift my chin, moving toward the side of the room where Lottie, Peach, and McRae are talking in low voices.

"Well, I heard that the family is *completely* bankrupt," Peach whispers. "It's all a mirage. Her father's about to be the Bernie Madoff of Europe."

McRae gives her a meaningful look. "If that got out officially, that might be one less deb to compete with, don't you think . . . ? No way Amélie would crown her."

Lottie chuckles, looking over at me. "These two are *so* bad."

I pretend to see somebody in the back rather than join them. I don't know which poor debutante they're plotting about bringing down because of her shitty parents, but I'm all tapped out on drama.

As I exit the lobby, heading back upstairs to change for waltz lessons, I catch the eye of a young hotel butler. He raises an eyebrow at me, and I swear I can read his expression: *This is all crazy, no?* I smile, nodding. *It's nuts.* He grins back at me, and I'm swept into the elevator in a wave of tipsy debutantes, my spirits slightly lifted.

CHAPTER NINE

Piper
Paris, France

Waltz lessons. My literal nightmare.

All the debs and cavaliers are together in the hotel's gilded ballroom, a cream-and-gold space with ornate chandeliers, mirrored walls, and towering floral ornamentations. Amélie and Bardot wind through the crowd, distributing biographies of everybody participating in La Danse, as well as all the high-profile guests.

"This is . . . fun," Dad says diplomatically, accepting a sheaf of papers from Bardot.

"It's like the French Revolution never happened," I whisper back.

I examine the debutante bios. Girls beam up from the glossy photos, their images ripped straight from *Vogue* photo shoots.

Underneath each photo, fawning accolades and CVs are printed. Ironically, my submission looks glamorous too: It's the photo of me from *Teen Vogue*. Thank God for that professional photo; otherwise my submission might as well have been a blurry selfie on a cracked iPhone 5. There are bios of the families, too. (Dad looks adorable in the photo I snapped of him at Bardot's request.) However, one person especially catches my eye: Sea's dad, Phillip Reilly, CEO of a venture capitalist firm focused on environmental, social, and governance strategies . . . a.k.a. *exactly* the type of company that might invest in my polymer.

My heart skips a beat when I realize Mr. Reilly is looking straight at *me*, holding his own sheaf of bios. We exchange polite smiles, and a thrill goes through me. Maybe Amélie was right. Maybe this *is* the opportunity I've been waiting for. There are only so many debs here, and this rich-people world runs on connections. Maybe someday I'll see him again, not in a ballroom but in a boardroom.

All around me, debs flip through the pages, gossiping.

"I haven't seen the Mullers since we sold our chalet in Gstaad!" one debutante squeals. I flip through the bios until I find her face: Peach Davis, a frozen-food heiress from Montecito, California. Seb gave me a rundown on each deb before I left Pennsylvania. It's rumored that Peach washes her face exclusively with Evian water.

I recognize the deb next to Peach: Her name is McRae Lawrence. She looks up from her papers and gasps, putting her hand on a gawky boy's arm.

"Ohmigod, George? You're the snowboarder who broke my clavicle on Buttermilk!"

George looks confused. He scrunches his face. "Wait . . . *McRae?*" He has an unplaceable European accent. German? Swiss?

"Yes!"

They hug.

"It's been a *decade*," she says. "My mom was so upset with you. I heard you're going to Oxford?"

"*Ja.* I wanted to study back in the States, but . . ." He shrugs. "You know."

"Believe me," she agrees, sighing heavily.

On the other side of me, two American cavaliers bro-hug.

"Thought I recognized you, dude," one says. "Halcyon, right?"

"Yup."

"Knew it." He points to himself. "Shattuck. Two years behind you, I think."

"What up, man." They slap five.

I'm struck by what a small world it is. Even the people from halfway around the world all seem to know each other, all seem to be buoyed by the same insider knowledge and close connections. The rest of us are out here slogging through the game of life; meanwhile these people are playing with cheat codes on easy mode.

"Not everyone attending the dinner has a daughter debuting or a son escorting," Amélie announces. "We've invited some of our top fashion contacts—editors, designers, anyone who's anyone. Some future La Danse families are invited as well, many of whom have children close to your age."

According to the bios, the cavaliers include Nicholas Kim, the son of a real estate magnate; Prince Felipe, a member of Luxembourg's royal family; and James Kuenta, whose father is the de facto president of a small island nation.

Dad looks at the sheaf of pages, flipping through the bios. "Zella de Perignon? Is that a real person? It sounds like a dessert."

I shake my head, amazed by the circus swirling. "Rich people have the weirdest names."

The girl standing next to me lets out a huff. She raises her profile haughtily and I realize she overheard us.

"Zella!" a handsome cavalier says—Adebayo Ogbu, I think his name is?—offering her his arm. I look back and forth discreetly between the photo and the willowy brunette, confirming. Oh shit. She glides across the room, only now deigning to shoot me a dirty look over her shoulder.

"Don't let her bother you," a guy's voice says in my ear. I turn and realize it's Chapin's brother, Dalton. He grins at me. "Zella's a pill."

My heart begins racing. "Oh. Hi."

"Hi back," he says lightly. He offers his arm. "May I have this dance?"

I look around wildly, part of me wondering if I can get out of this. I don't dance. Mainly because I *can't* dance. Rendering my entire involvement in this ball probably the dumbest decision ever, scholarship money or not.

"Amelie's blocked all the exits," he mock whispers. "You might as well suffer through with me. I promise it will only be *slightly* tortuous."

Dad laughs. Dalton notices him and goes into polite parent mode. "You must be Piper's dad. I'm Dalton Buckingham, sir. Piper's cavalier." Wait—Dalton's my cavalier?

Okay, maybe learning to dance won't be complete hell after all.

Dalton and Dad shake hands. "Tom Collins," my dad says good-naturedly. "Yes, like the drink."

A woman next to Dad turns, putting her hand on his arm. "My favorite cocktail," she coos. "I didn't realize you were one of the fathers. I thought you were a cavalier!"

Oh lord. This again. Everywhere Dad goes, he's catnip for flirty moms: single, divorced, young, old, it doesn't matter. Ladies like Tom . . . and it's gross.

Dad shoots me an amused look. "Nope. Just Piper's dad," he says politely.

"I'm Araminta Graham," the woman says, sliding her hand around Dad's bicep. "You *must* come join us. We're just about to have espressos at Café Faubourg. You will come, won't you? Don't worry, the kiddos will be fine."

Before he can respond, Araminta tugs Dad toward the corner. A gaggle of moms await, staring at him like famished vultures.

Dad looks back at me, alarmed.

"Bye, Dad!" I trill, following Dalton onto the dance floor. "Enjoy yourself!" Dalton and I stifle a laugh as Araminta pulls Dad into the debutante mom scrum.

I turn back to Dalton.

"Your dad seems cool," he says.

"He's the *literal* best," I agree. "If there were a Dad of the Year prize, he'd win, hands down."

"I'm jealous," he says lightly, and I suddenly remember that I'm talking to Otis Buckingham's son. Who—not to be ageist, but—is old enough to be Dalton's grandfather.

"What's your dad like?"

"Absent," he says. "Half the time it feels like me and Chapin against the world."

I nod. "I know that feeling. After my mom died, my dad and I had to figure out how to survive without her. It sucked."

"I'm so sorry," he says.

"Thanks." I glance down briefly, and then meet his empathetic gaze with a small smile. The energy around us stills.

We stare at each other, guards all the way down. He's got little flecks of gold in his eyes, which are now crinkling at the corner because he's smiling back at me, and good lord, Dalton is cute.

"I don't know how to waltz," I confess, suddenly feeling awkward.

"That's what lessons are for," he teases good-naturedly. "Don't worry, I'm pretty bad at it. We can make fools of ourselves together. Deal?"

"Deal."

There he goes again. Making me feel calm and safe. Dalton's basically like walking, talking anti-anxiety meds.

"*Bon!*" Monsieur Mathis, the waltz instructor, shouts. He's a small French man with a perma-scowl etched across his round face. "Cavaliers, place your right hand near your partner's left shoulder! Debutantes, left hand on your partner's right shoulder! *Allons-y!*"

Dalton and I face each other on the dance floor. One of Dalton's hands slides on top of mine, while his other hand rests lightly on the skin of my upper back. Our bodies slowly press together and now our faces are inches apart. I suddenly understand why *Dirty Dancing* and *Footloose* tried to make dancing seem scandalous. With the proximity to Dalton, I can smell his shampoo. It's dizzying being this close to him.

He smiles at me again, and I smile back at him, and I wonder what it would be like to kiss him and—

Stop, Piper! You're here to get through this week, take the money, and run. This is about college. Not about falling for some rich kid and ruining the ball and wrecking your future.

Eyes on the prize.

Across the ballroom, I see Chapin staring daggers at us. She does *not* seem pleased that I'm connecting with Dalton.

But as Dalton looks down at me, his eyes steady, I feel a warmth spread through my body. I've never had this feeling before.

Oh, God, I am in so much trouble.

CHAPTER TEN

Chapin
Paris, France

Anybody who's anybody goes to L'Avenue. It's one of those Parisian institutions where you're just as likely to see the former president of France as you are the Olsen twins. (Sometimes together.) Naturally, it's the perfect location for the welcome dinner for La Danse.

I'm in the back of a town car—Mom on one side, Dalton on the other—wishing I were anywhere but here. Mom has learned about Piper's room arrangements and is predictably annoyed.

"What were they thinking, forcing you to stay with that girl? We're not paying for you to share with her! It's obscene. If the news gets out that you're the only girl who has a roommate— and *that* roommate—the press will have a field day."

"They said there was nowhere else to put her," I say.

"I don't want to be rude, but that's not our problem." Mom pulls out her phone. "I'm calling Amélie right now."

I think about Piper swooping in and monopolizing Dalton for the entirety of waltz lessons and am tempted to let Mom run with this. But her tone is giving me a headache. "It's not that big of a deal," I mumble.

She looks at me, irritated. "It *is* a big deal, Chapin. I'm trying to protect this family's reputation."

"If the news got out, Chapin sharing her room would be *positive* publicity," Dalton points out mildly.

This gets through to Mom. He's speaking her language.

"Hmm. That's a good point, Dalty." Mom stares out the window, wheels turning. I'm sort of relieved that Mom's been diverted, half annoyed that Dalton was so eager to step in on Piper's behalf. "Chapin Buckingham, carrying on the grand family tradition of charitable works." I have to stop myself from snorting. *Grand family tradition?* The only reason Mom and Dad donate so generously is because it's a huge tax write-off. "Inviting the poor girl to stay with you . . . staying up all night, sacrificing your own chances in the hopes of mentoring her . . . reaching down the social classes to help lift up the impoverished and give her the chances you were blessed with," she continues, nodding. "It could play great. Very smart, Dalty! I'll call Tinsley." Her publicist.

"She's not a war refugee," I mutter. "I wouldn't call her *impoverished*." But Mom is already on the call.

"Hi, it's me. So I'm thinking, could we place an article somewhere—*People,* maybe? Or *Us Weekly*?—about how

Chapin is taking Storey's replacement and mentoring her?" Pause. "Mm-hmm. Mm-hmm. Exactly." She nods enthusiastically. "Something subtle. You're the best." Mom hangs up, looking triumphant. "Never underestimate the power of the press."

I almost feel bad for Piper. Famous people with their own publicists don't stand a chance against Ella Somerset's machine, let alone a rando from nowhere who barely knows how to use social media and thinks Banana Republic is couture.

The car pulls up to L'Avenue, where a sea of paparazzi awaits. Ugh. Several of the debs have already arrived: some alone, others with their families. Looks like Dad isn't the only parent who can't be bothered to show up until the last day. McRae and Lottie link arms, trying to get photographers to pay attention to them.

"How did they know we'd be here?" I ask suspiciously. Was it Amélie, or . . . Mom beams, adjusting her boobs and hair.

Of course. She called them herself.

She turns to scrutinize me and Dalton.

Dalton first: She scans him up and down, her face beaming proudly. "Ya look great, kid," she says in a silly, exaggerated, old-timey-agent voice.

Then it's my turn.

Her eyes sweep over my hair, my makeup, my clothes, searching for any flaw, no matter how tiny.

I hold my breath.

She smiles. Looks like I passed.

She pats my hand, pleased. "Wonderful, Chapin." She threads her fingers through mine and squeezes.

"I love you, honey," she says, sincerity etched across her beautiful face.

I'm surprised by the lump in my throat. "Love you too, Mom."

But as I gather my purse, preparing to exit, she continues.

"Make sure you stand up straight, and don't forget to smile. I don't want to see a *single* frame with you scowling."

Dalton and I exchange a look. His face is sympathetic: *You got this.* I discreetly make a silly face back, and we share a quiet giggle that Mom doesn't notice. I'm excited to hang with Dalton inside the restaurant—ever since he's been away at college, we barely get to spend any time together. Reconnecting with him will be another silver lining of this godforsaken week. That is, if he doesn't spend it mooning after Piper.

The driver opens the door, and Ella steps out, a sea of flashbulbs popping.

"Ella! Ella! Over here!"

Ella smiles as if she's the president, waving this way and that, gracefully gliding toward the front door of L'Avenue. Dalton and I make our way behind her, smiling dutifully.

But suddenly the flashes stop. Mom turns, confused, as a Parisian taxi arrives. Piper steps out.

She's wearing one of the pieces I lent her: a vintage silver YSL minidress. To me, the dress is a torture device, but somehow on Piper it seems . . . comfortable? She looks like she was born to wear it. Her sheepish *what the heck am I doing here?* smile only makes her look more endearing.

She pauses at the curb, clearly overwhelmed and a little lost.

She looks around nervously, and our eyes meet. I sigh. If Mom's going to place this article, I might as well try to sell it. I take a step toward her, propelled by duty. But before I can even move, the paparazzi go into overdrive.

"It's the new girl! Piper! Piper! Over here! Show us the dress, Cinderella!" Piper stands in the flashbulbs, dazed, looking this way and that. She clearly doesn't know what to do. "Piper, this way! Turn to the left!" She obeys, shifting her body slightly. "To the right!" She obeys again, with more ease this time. She's a natural. Huh. It's kind of . . . frustrating?

"Should we help her out?" Dalton whispers to me. He and Piper make eye contact, and she gives him a look like: *This is crazy—what do I do?*

Dalton leaves my side, holding out his arm as he approaches Piper. "Let's go in together," he says gallantly. "You're doing great."

Piper takes his arm, appreciative, moving alongside him as they approach the restaurant. I'm frozen in place, watching the two of them effortlessly command the attention of the entire horde of photographers.

Mom stands by the door, utterly unimpressed by the entire scene. Meanwhile, McRae and Lottie are now inside the vestibule, watching with extreme irritation. Through the window I see Amélie, taking it all in, looking intrigued.

"Snap out of it!" Mom whispers anxiously, motioning toward me even as she keeps a dazzling smile on her face. I realize I'm staring after Piper dumbly. But this time I can't fake a smile.

She took Columbia. She took Dalton. And if she's already

such a natural *on day one*, she's going to take Deb of the Year, too.

My initial instinct was right: This girl is here to steal every-thing from me. But I'm not about to go down without a fight.

I stomp inside the restaurant, Dalton and Piper's backs to me, as the cameras click, click, click.

CHAPTER ELEVEN

Piper
Paris, France

Okay, this restaurant is hella fancy.

Back in Pennsylvania, Dad and I usually survive on food bought in bulk from Costco—shout-out roast chicken in a bag! Every once in a while, we'll splurge on the Cheesecake Factory to celebrate something big, like when I won the science fair. But mostly, we eat at home, huddled over our phones, doing our best to make leftovers last at least two days—maybe three.

We're *not* hella fancy.

But this table is long and elegantly set, with candelabras and white tablecloths and gloved waiters who bow deeply at the waist and lovingly murmur things like "Duck a l'orange, *oui*, magnificent choice, *mademoiselle*."

All the debs and cavaliers are congregated at one end of the table, with parents banished to the other. Dad is flanked by two gorgeous moms who could easily be on a *Real Housewives* European spin-off (Dusseldorf? Vienna?), but rather than looking charmed, he looks panicked, his eyes wide as saucers. I've seen that look before, at school when he'd get accosted by moms after dropping me off. We lock eyes and he mouths *help* at me. I giggle, giving him a mock shrug.

"So, how does it feel to have all eyes on you?"

I turn and realize that I'm sitting next to Dalton. My pulse quickens.

"You mean, everybody staring me down, wondering how the hell I got invited, and waiting for me to fail?" I deadpan.

"Yes. Exactly that," he teases back. "I've known most of these people since I was in the womb." He nods his head around the room. "Nicholas and I went to preschool together. My mom and his dad dated in the nineties, so we summered together on Martha's Vineyard."

"Your mom, your dad, *and* her ex-boyfriend? Together?" I ask, eyes wide.

"One big happy family," he laughs. "It's funny. You don't realize how weird your world is until you see it through somebody else's eyes."

"I don't think your world's weird. It's just . . ." Now it's my turn to look around the room. Nicholas Kim, the cavalier Dalton mentioned, waits to eat any hors d'oeuvres until his professional food taster tries them first. Apparently, his family is paranoid that someone might poison them. And then there's Peach's mom, who travels with a personal parasol holder. He stands at attention, ready to open the umbrella at any moment, should she want to go outside.

I mean, I'm sitting at a table with not one but *two* members of the British royal family.

File this under: We're not in Kansas anymore. "Okay, yeah. Your world's weird," I laugh.

"What about you?"

"Oh, my world's super weird. It's just weird with fewer Chanel bags, I guess?" I chew on a cuticle. "I didn't really know what to expect here. I guess I thought it would be lots of frivolity. Just sort of a fun, romantic lark. But it feels like everybody's taking this *really* seriously. People keep staring at me, sizing me up. I expected to feel a little like an outsider, but I didn't expect people to be *mad* at me for attending."

Dalton nods, his face appropriately sad. "I'm sorry. These people can be cool, but they can be elitist and insular, too." He nods down the table toward a tall man with a wide smile. "Have you met Dr. Hughes yet?"

Before I have a chance to respond, a waiter swoops in with the first course: escargot sautéed in butter.

I stare at it as if it's a bomb.

Are they kidding me with this?

Far be it from me to play the hayseed card. It's not as if we don't have fancy restaurants in Pennsylvania. But *escargot*? Really? What's next, frog's legs served by a waiter in a beret with a cigarette dangling from his lips?

I gingerly try a piece of the escargot, swallowing it down with an ocean of water.

Not bad. Not *good*, though.

The next course isn't in fact frog's legs, but rather steak tartare.

I tear off a piece of rustic country baguette, chewing happily. "This is divine. They got me with the escargot but . . . yeah. This bread is to die for. I don't even mind the steak."

Except I realize everybody else is delicately sectioning their bread into tiny pieces, placing it on their plate, and buttering it. It's only after the bread is arranged just so that they nibble at it in tiny bites fit for a squirrel. Meanwhile, I'm shoving it into my trap like I just escaped from the zoo.

Manners, Piper. Elegance. Grace, you big dummy.

Dalton stifles another laugh. But because he seems genuinely delighted, it's as if he's laughing with me, rather than at me.

"I'm glad you're here, Piper."

"Why do I feel like I'm suddenly the sideshow?"

"Not even a little." He tears off a large piece of bread and eats it with his hands, like I did. "You're the star." I turn my head to hide my smile.

"Well, I feel a little more like the troll. Everybody here is just so polished. So good-looking. So *cool*."

"Not all good-looking people are cool," Dalton says, cocking one eyebrow.

My heart skips a beat.

"Ahh! *Freaks and Geeks!*"

He looks pleased that I caught the reference. "Right? Such a brilliant show."

"Right now I feel like Sam Weir in the cafeteria," I quip.

"Where to sit for lunch, the age-old problem," Dalton shoots back.

We smile at each other. I'm immediately put at ease. Sure, he might be, like, supermodel levels of gorgeous, but he's clearly a dork at heart, just like me. "I can't believe you love *Freaks and Geeks* too. Actually, I can believe it, obviously. It's a classic."

"Some of the classics have aged really badly, though," he says, frowning. "The *Seinfeld* diner is near my school, and holy God has that show's humor not held up." My heart stops. Is he referencing Tom's Diner on Broadway in New York?

"Wait, you go to Columbia?" He pauses too.

"Yeah. Why? Are you going there?"

I pause. Should I get into it? I decide to gloss over the issue. "Yes!"

"Nice!" Dalton looks genuinely pleased. "You're gonna love it. I'm biased, but I think it's the best school. I know it's gotten a bad rap the last couple of years, but people really *care*. Everybody's engaged; everybody's passionate."

I swallow my anxiety over my scholarship. "Well, now you have to tell me everything. What dorm do I want to avoid at all costs? What's the best place to eat? Do people really get freaky in the stacks?"

He laughs. "Dorm to avoid: Carman. Best place to eat, debatable: I'm partial to Koronet. Their pizza is fire, especially at two a.m. And as far as the stacks . . . yup." He shakes his head, somewhat bemused. "Apparently, my roommate's best friend got caught down there the week before Christmas. The librarian was not pleased." We share a giggle.

I feel eyes on me once again and look up. Oh no. I'm on the receiving end of a death glare from Chapin.

I smile back at her tentatively. Why is she glaring at me?

She looks away, scowling.

Okay, this is so awkward.

Dalton must see it, because he nudges me. "Hey. It's a stressful week all around. Don't let it bother you."

I nod gratefully. "The whole reason I'm doing this is to fund my scholarship. That's it."

He raises an eyebrow. "Fund your scholarship?"

I decide to shut up. No more nervous yammering, Piper.

"It's a long story," I say, faux world-weary. "For another time."

He smiles, sizing me up. I catch a glimpse of myself in his eyes—are they blue? Gray?—and I think: I can deal with Chapin's death glares as long as it means I get to keep spending time with Dalton.

CHAPTER TWELVE

Chapin
Paris, France

"This Piper girl is invading my life," I complain to Lottie.

We're sitting together at the end of the table, watching as Piper and Dalton laugh like lunatics.

"What are they even talking about?" I ask.

Lottie pops an oyster into her mouth from the seafood tower in front of us and reaches for another one. "Dalton's easy to talk to. He's probably just being nice." She piles mignonette sauce into the shell and slurps it. "Oh my God, these are so good. I like the fat ones."

I ignore her. "Why does he have to be nice to her? She's such a Pick Me. Pretending she's all nice and innocent. I see right through her."

Lottie stares at Piper dubiously. "I don't know, Chapin. She seems like a plain ol' bumpkin to me. I don't think the innocent thing is an act."

McRae leans over. "Oh, are you guys talking about the new girl?"

"Obviously."

"Yeah, I'd watch out for that one, Chape. Feels suspicious having her as your roommate. Like they're trying to have her spy on you or something. Learn how to *be* you. Have you ever heard of that old movie *Single White Female*?"

"See?" I say to McRae, who is now creating a horseradish tower on top of another oyster. "That's what I said!"

Lottie shrugs, clearly over this conversation. "McRae's just paranoid because of her dad."

"You should see some of these scammers our papers write about," McRae affirms. "If I were you, I would be locking my door at night. Or at least installing a guard there."

She studies the spread on the table, brightening up as she spies a basket of cheese bread. "Ooh, Zella, would you be a doll?" McRae nods toward the bread. Zella passes it with a sneer and a sigh, as if passing along a ticking bomb.

I study Piper darkly as I sip my drink. She leans over to Dalton, putting her hand on his arm and laughing like he's onstage at the Comedy Cellar. But McRae is overreacting. I don't think Piper wants to wear my skin or anything creepy like that. She's just overstepping boundaries.

I take a cab back to the hotel with McRae and Lottie, instead of with Mom and Dalton, but I barely hear their steady stream of gossip. Instead, I stare out the window as Paris passes me by. In the distance, between the trees, I spot the top of the Sacré-Coeur.

I don't know what I was thinking saying yes to this trip. I should have known it would only end in tears. I had a one-in-sixteen chance of making Mom happy, and a fifteen-in-sixteen chance of being a disappointment to her yet again.

Amateur move, Chapin.

But Mom didn't raise a quitter and is always saying my generation is too soft. When we arrive back at the hotel, I decide to try to salvage this disaster of a day. I go up to Mom's hotel room and knock on the door of her suite. After all, the whole reason I'm here is to bond with her, right? But she doesn't answer, so I text her.

You back at the hotel? Thought we could grab a cup of tea.

She starts to respond almost immediately, and my heart lifts.

Sorry, lovebug! Meeting an old friend in the Marais. Have fun xxxxx

I turn on my heel and stomp back toward the elevators, glowering all the way back to my room. Looks like tonight is full of amateur moves. I reenter the suite in a foul mood. It only gets worse once Piper comes in. She slinks in, tentative, without making eye contact. I try to ignore her, wondering if I'm being too much of a bitch. But once Piper walks into the common room in a sweatshirt, I'm about to explode.

She's got this hopeful look on her face, like maybe we can start braiding our hair and painting our nails. And she's wearing a freaking Columbia sweatshirt.

I'd almost forgotten. She's going to study science at my dream school. The one I didn't get into. The one Dalton goes to.

It's like she literally took my place.

I can't look away from her sweatshirt, that COLUMBIA taunting me in blue and white.

She sees my thundercloud face and sits on the edge of the couch, nervous. For some reason, the more nervous she gets, the more irritated it makes me. I like to think of myself as a charitable person, but there's nothing I want more right now than for her to fall off the edge of the earth.

"D'you wanna watch a movie?" she asks hopefully.

I stare at her, literally dumbfounded by her inability to read my body language, which is clearly screaming *stay the hell away from me*. But she's not getting the hint.

"Maybe some room service, too? I'm starving after that dinner. All I ate was cheese and bread. That escargot was . . . something."

My stomach rumbles traitorously, but the last thing I want to do is spend an evening suffering through Piper's attempts to bond. Hasn't she taken enough from me today without draining what's left of my emotional energy? I stand up, look her dead in the eye, and say, "I'll pass. Thanks."

Her cheeks flood with color, and my irritation surges over how annoyingly charming she looks even when she's hurt, like a tiny kitten on the side of the road in need of saving. I turn away and head back into my room, leaving her to sit alone in our common space. Icing Piper out doesn't feel as satisfying as I thought it might, but I'm almost too tired to care. I change into a criminally soft cashmere set and collapse into bed. It's not even eight thirty, but I can feel myself drifting and I happily submit. Sleep feels like the only way to escape this nightmare of a day.

CHAPTER THIRTEEN

Piper

Paris, France

If I'm going to succeed at this, I need to start thinking more like these girls.

It's clear that Chapin hates me. Last night, she totally rejected my olive branch. I get it: She clearly doesn't want me hanging out with her brother. But it's not like Dalton and I were making out half-naked at the table. We had moved onto the world's dorkiest conversation about which *Star Wars* trilogy is the best of the three. (Original, obviously.)

But fine. No winning over Chapin. Stay away from the brother. Got it and got it.

It's clear that these girls all have their eyes on the prize, and I need to as well.

I don't need to be best friends with Chapin. This week is about kicking ass at La Danse, period.

I've succeeded in life by being methodical, by employing the scientific method. Just because I'm in the land of titles and tiaras doesn't mean I can't make it work for me here, too.

First, the problem: How can I make it through the week to impress Amélie and lock down my scholarship?

Then, data gathering: Observe the other girls, noting their strategies, behavior, and styles.

The hypothesis naturally follows: If I emulate the qualities and actions of past winners, I increase my chances of winning Deb of the Year. Of course, I will never be Chapin, or McRae, or Zella. If I try to become them, I'm only setting myself up for failure. But if I allow my own strengths to shine through— sensible, meticulous, hilarious science puns—perhaps I will please Amélie and secure the money I need for Columbia?

I will continue to test this hypothesis by implementing these strategies all week, carefully noting what works and what doesn't.

And, finally, I'll analyze the results and pivot as necessary. Too much eye contact with Dalton pissing off Chapin? A tangential problem—but one that could negatively sway Amélie's opinion of me. Solution: Keep my interactions with Dalton to a minimum, solely during official activities.

Luckily, most of the other girls seem determined to ignore me, so all evidence points to winning Chapin over—or keeping her from hating me—as my sole battle.

I got this.

. . . Except that this morning's activity is yoga, which I suck at. I did a free yoga class at the Y with Seb once. I accidentally took down the girl next to me in a failed attempt at Warrior Three. I can't imagine Amélie crowning me Deb of the Year if I accidentally hospitalize one of the other debs.

It doesn't help that, after I take the elevator downstairs and step into the scrum of debs and cavaliers, the first person I make eye contact with is Dalton.

"Hey!" he says, sidling over to me. Last night we were sitting side by side, so there wasn't a ton of eye contact. But right now we're face-to-face. And I never noticed just how deep his eyes are, how dark his pupils are, how long his eyelashes are ... *Focus, Piper!*

"Hi," I say, blushing. I look around furtively, trying to catch a glimpse of Chapin. She's already here, in the corner surrounded by McRae, Peach, and Lottie.

"So are we really doing this today?" Dalton asks, his handsome face sliding into a frown.

I shudder. "Do we have a choice?"

Dalton clocks the panic on my face—somewhere between *please don't make me* and *I'd sooner parachute off the Empire State Building.*

"Same," he says, nodding. "I don't know where Amélie comes up with these things. Every year is a new and fresh way to torture the cavaliers and debs."

"You've done this before?"

"Unfortunately, yes. The New York set is basically cherry-picked from two or three schools: Spence, Trinity, Collegiate. Ditto in the UK: Eton, Harrow, or bust. Over in Switzerland, it's Aiglon, Rosenberg, or Le Rosey, obviously. Hang round this crew long enough and you'll find out just how incestuous we are."

"As *unappealing* as that sounds . . ." I joke.

"Last year, she made them all go get facials with Iván Pol, who created the Beauty Sandwich."

I frown, feeling like I must not have heard him correctly. "Sorry, did you say the Beauty *Sandwich*?"

He laughs, nodding. "Yeah. Iván is this super-famous aesthetician who whips people's skin into shape like he's a drill sergeant. He sells some crazy expensive cream that my mom flips for. It's like a thousand bucks."

My eyes widen. "A thousand bucks for skin care? That is literally insane."

"Amélie wanted everybody to look 'flawless and poreless'— her words—before the *Vanity Fair* shoot, so she flew the dude out from LA. Long story short, apparently the treatments hurt like a bitch, and since he can only do one person at a time, after he'd tortured his way through half the cavaliers, the other half mysteriously came down with 'colds' and needed to skip, which Iván allowed because he's also a total germaphobe."

I shake my head. "You rich people are so weird."

He laughs. "Can't dispute that."

"The Beauty Sandwich. I can't decide if that's delicious or disgusting."

"How about both?" he quips. Dalton inclines his head toward a side entrance, behind the concierge desk. His eyes light up. "You wanna . . . ?"

I follow his line of sight. Several concierge staffers are working the phones, while an adorable French bulldog—the hotel's iconic mascot, named Clementine, I learned while perusing its Wikipedia page—sleeps soundly on the floor. The streets of Paris beckon, blissfully free of hot yoga.

"*Ditch?*" I look at him dubiously, making sure I understand.

"Amélie would murder us." I *cannot* afford to piss her off.

Dalton laughs. "Nah. She'll never know. She's so busy this week running all over town trying to lock things down at the last minute. The person in charge of the pre-events is Bardot, and she'll turn a blind eye." His dimple pops. "Trust me, I'd never screw you over with something as vitally important as a debutante ball."

"Okay, now I feel like you're just making fun of me," I tease. "But isn't it important to be, like, networking? Schmoozing? I don't know what you fancy, famous people call it."

"We call it breathing," he deadpans.

A few more people arrive on the elevators, and the lobby swells even further.

"I say we make a break for it," Dalton says.

"Wait, you're serious?"

"Life's too short to waste your first week in Paris solely focusing on making Amélie's sponsors happy."

I look between Dalton and the door. I don't think I've ever skipped out on a mandatory event in my life. Just ask my perfect attendance record. Ditching might not be great, but it might be preferable to making a complete fool of myself in front of everyone and irritating Amélie. What are the odds anyone would even notice I'm gone?

Besides. Isn't seeing Paris at least half the reason I'm here?

I gather my resolve.

"Okay," I whisper, "let's do it."

He nods toward the crowd. "I'll say I'm grabbing a quick coffee. And then you say you forgot something in the room. Let's meet back in the lobby in ten minutes."

"You've clearly done this before."

"You can't go to a private school in New York City and not know how to ditch without getting caught," Dalton says, smiling.

We lock eyes and . . . *break*. Dalton goes one way. I go another.

"Oh crap!" I say loudly to nobody in particular. "I forgot my thing in my room! Be right back—I'll just meet you guys there." Everybody ignores me.

I race upstairs to change out of my workout clothes, my heart pounding. The second I'm in my room, I pull out my phone to FaceTime Seb.

He answers on the second ring. "*Piper?* Are you okay?" His tone is so incredulous, you'd think I was calling from the moon.

"Better than okay. I think I'm . . . about to go on a date?" I whisper into the phone, even though I'm alone in the suite. Suddenly I realize the time difference back home.

"Seb, I'm so sorry!" I say. "It must be, like, three a.m. your time! I'll call back later."

"No, tell me everything! This is too good to miss," he says breathlessly. "Name, height, Myers-Briggs."

I laugh, propping my phone against a pillow on the bed as I

begin rifling through the outfits Chapin's lent me. Racks upon racks line the walls, miraculously appeared from seemingly nowhere. I don't think these are Chapin's castoffs. I stare at them confusedly, before realizing these are items designers have sent . . . with *my* name pinned to them.

Wait, designers want *me* wearing their clothes? Wild. I try to refocus on Seb.

"Name: Dalton. Height—" But Seb cuts me off before I can say *easily over six feet.* He's clearly got the attendees memorized.

"Sorry, did you say Dalton *Buckingham*?"

"Um. Yes?"

"Piper, you did not. I cannot. Dalton freaking Buckingham?"

"He's actually really nice," I say, feeling self-conscious. "He's not at all what you'd think." I pull out a sundress with a note pinned to it:

> *For Piper! Shine bright this week!*
> *xxx Your Friends at Christian Siriano*

It's canary yellow and feels fresh, like a lemon drop.

"What I'd *think*," Seb says dramatically, "is that you're vibing with a next-gen Kennedy as if you're Cinderella at the ball."

"Eh, pass on the Kennedys, thanks. But I mean, aren't I . . . literally . . . Cinderella at the ball?" I lower the lemon dress and instead pick up a cornflower-blue lounge set. Much more me. Relaxed. Not trying too hard. Plus, better for my complexion. *See, look at me? Thinking like the other debs!*

"Hello! Earth to Piper! Also, I love the yellow dress," Seb says through the screen.

"Sorry," I startle. "I'm just . . . ahh!"

"In your head."

"Clearly."

"Well, I don't blame you. You're not just in your head, you're in *over* your head. A Buckingham? Rich even for my blood, babe."

"His sister is my roommate," I admit.

Seb practically hyperventilates. "Okay, back the hell up. You're roommates with Chapin Buckingham. You're dating Dalton Buckingham. And you're basically blowing up like Kylie Jenner on Insta. We are officially in the upside down." His face is pure glee. "Are you registering this? Take it in, Pipes. This. Is. Real. Life."

But the more excited Seb gets, the more self-conscious I feel. "Chapin basically hates me—"

"Okay, gonna need the backstory on that."

"And I don't even know if Dalton is a date—"

"Spill and let Dr. Seb diagnose it."

I catch Seb up to speed on everything, from Bardot springing the room sharing on Chapin, to the butterflies I get when Dalton looks at me, to the mutual hot-yoga ditching. As I talk, he nods enthusiastically through the phone like a deranged bobblehead on the dashboard of a car speeding down a dirt road.

"And he invited you?"

"He practically demanded it."

"Oh, it's *so* a date. That boy's into you. And why wouldn't he be? You're amazing—"

"For a normie."

"You're gorgeous—"

"In a bland, dishwater kind of way."

"And you're self-deprecating as shit—in a hilarious, *who couldn't love you* kind of way," he rushes to say before I can come up with another retort. "He's the lucky one. And he's also officially been waiting too long as you armchair diagnose a micro relationship that's point-three seconds old."

I spring off the bed, realizing Seb's right. I've been so excited to catch up with him that I've lost track of time.

"Wear the Christian Siriano dress!" he exclaims. "Make sure you steal all those clothes and bring them home with you!"

"I don't know," I falter. "This feels like billionaire cosplay."

"Piper. It's okay to enjoy dressing up. It's okay to be the belle of the ball and play princess for one week. It's not gonna get your Mensa card revoked, I promise."

"I really wish you were here with me," I say, pausing, suddenly wistful.

"Oh, hush now. I'll be there in spirit." Seb sees my eyes welling with grateful, dorky tears. He helpfully rushes to change the subject. "Besides, you never answered my question."

"Which was?"

"Myers-Briggs, duh."

"Oh." I consider the question. "Hmm. ESFJ?"

"Which is?"

"I don't know, I was just pulling letters out of my ass. Whatever's the best all-around one who makes everybody feel safe."

"That's not him, babe. That's you," Seb says, blowing me a kiss before hanging up.

I take a second to center myself, feeling grateful beyond measure, before getting dressed. I race to meet Dalton downstairs as Paris awaits.

CHAPTER FOURTEEN

Chapin
Paris, France

The hot-yoga studio is just around the corner from the hotel, so we all line up and traipse there in a line behind Bardot like some kind of sore, muscle-plagued kindergarten class. Of course, like kindergartners, we're unruly, and within a couple of blocks everybody has split up into groups of twos or threes.

I walk with Lottie and McRae, glazing over as they talk about whether Sea Reilly's going to take over her dad's company someday or leverage his connections to marry rich.

"I mean, why not both?" I suddenly interrupt, feeling irritated. "Harvard Business School is better than any dating app. Two-income entrepreneur family for the win."

Lottie shrugs, but McRae nods eagerly. "You're so right, Chape."

"What do you think of this whole Piper smoothie thing?" Lottie asks me, holding out her phone.

My groan is probably audible all the way over on the Left Bank. "What. The Hell. Is a Piper smoothie?"

I take her phone, looking at the Erewhon Instagram account, where—sure enough—all the fangirling over Piper on social media has led to my roomie getting her own freaking smoothie named after her. The literal dream.

I forcefully thrust the phone back to Lottie.

"I think that Piper has been famous for three seconds, and she's already overexposed. Common mistake, actually. Mom always talks about how celebrity is all about longevity."

McRae leans over, sniffing at the phone. "I bet she doesn't even know how to pronounce Erewhon."

I snicker, then sigh. "Ella's gonna be so mad."

"Why?" Lottie asks.

"She's spent a year on the wait list, trying to get a smoothie named after me. *And* she spent ten thousand dollars to get on it! And here Piper just scores one without even trying!"

"No," McRae gasps.

"I know."

I pull out my own phone and look at the Erewhon Instagram page again as we walk closer to the studio. Fleetingly, I recognize the irony of walking some of the most beautiful streets in the world buried in my phone instead of actually paying attention to my surroundings. But then I see the caption accompanying the post:

The Piper Smoothie

In honor of everybody's favorite scientist-slash-debutante, it
features a blend of strawberries and bananas, coconut water
for electrolytes, and spirulina protein powder—a nutrient-rich
superfood—plus a sprinkle of reishi-mushroom extract for
enhanced brain function and green algae supplement chlorella
powder, with more chlorophyll than any other plant food.
A portion of the proceeds will be donated to Girls Who
Code, Piper's favorite charity (as insisted upon by her bestie
Seb, who's cheering Piper on this week from afar). Go, Piper!
Available this week for a limited time.

I cringe reading the caption, die, come back to life, and cringe again.

Incredibly, even though Erewhon only posted this a few hours ago, they already have thousands and thousands of likes and comments, everybody applauding Piper. The accompanying photo is of Piper's magazine spread.

McRae shakes her head in disbelief. "I do not get the press obsession with her. And I should know!"

I click onto Piper's bestie's Instagram page, where Seb has an enthusiastic post crowing about how Erewhon corporate DMed him trying to get in touch with Piper. God, this girl wanders into everything.

"She's so basic," Lottie agrees. "Just like her smoothie."

"I don't know," I counter. "She's an award-winning scientist with her own spread in *Teen Vogue*, she's got Erewhon *and* half the brands in Paris tripping at her feet, and she's somehow managed to leapfrog over every other eighteen-year-old in the world to find herself here with *us*. Seems to me like there's got to be *something* interesting about her—even if it's just that she's the most calculating sociopath any of us have ever seen."

McRae and Lottie nod as we all stare wonderingly at Piper's photo on my phone.

"That's true," Lottie says, suddenly looking extremely jealous.

"This girl isn't as boring as I thought," McRae says. "She's competition."

"She's a lot of things," I begrudgingly agree, "but boring isn't one of them."

CHAPTER FIFTEEN

Piper
Paris, France

"I still can't believe we ditched them," I laugh, as Dalton and I walk across the Jardin des Tuileries toward the Louvre.

"They're not even gonna notice we're gone," Dalton assures me. "Trust me, I would never steer you off course for something actually important."

"Only for the fake important stuff?"

Dalton pauses to let a toddler on a tricycle have the right of way, as the *bébé*'s nanny shoots him a grateful but apologetic glance. "You strike me as somebody who knows what matters."

I don't know what to say to that. I blush, hugging myself and taking it in as we continue on.

"How many times have you been to Paris?" I ask him.

"That's a tough one. I can't remember. Scores of times.

Chapin and I traveled a lot as kids. My mom was always off filming something, or getting invited to some fashion show or awards show. She might have her issues, but at least she always took us with her."

We're now just beyond the entrance to the Louvre's courtyard. He inclines his head toward the museum. "First time in Paris . . . you gotta see the Louvre. You game?" I look at the lines to get in, snaking every which way.

"That would be awesome. Not sure we have time to brave that line, though. We have to be back in time to prep for the boat ride tonight."

Dalton smiles. "I got you."

Instead of taking his place at the back of the queue, Dalton walks around the line, avoiding it entirely.

"Didn't take you for a line skipper," I say teasingly.

"Don't worry, I'm not pulling the nepo-baby card! We're members. Mom loves coming here when she's in town. Chapin, too."

We quickly enter through the nonexistent member line, easily shaving off an hour.

As we step inside the museum, I take it in, amazed.

"Best museum in the world," Dalton says proudly.

"Better than the Met?" I ask.

"The Met is fantastic. But pound for pound, the Louvre can't be beat. The old masters alone!" He pauses. "Is there something you want to see? The *Mona Lisa*, obviously."

I nod. "That would be great. But there's actually another painting I'd love to see first. . . ."

A few minutes later we're standing in front of *Liberty Leading the People*, the iconic Delacroix image with the goddess of Liberty holding the flag of the French Revolution. After my mother died, I found a postcard of the painting in her things—the backstory lost forever. Maybe she always hoped to see it; maybe it was just a gift from somebody meaningful to her.

I don't know. I didn't know about it until it was too late to ask her.

"It's bigger than I expected." I stare up at it, taking it in. "See how all the social classes are mingling? It's everybody from the bourgeoisie to a student to the lowest of the low, fighting along-side each other."

"The great equalizer," Dalton says. "Background be damned."

"Background be damned," I echo. We smile at each other and continue on, walking slowly side by side through the gallery.

"You know, a week ago I was inside the King of Prussia Mall, piercing ears at Claire's and eating leftover cookies with my bestie, who works at Mrs. Field's. And now I'm inside the great-est museum in the history of the world, in the shadows of iconic masterpieces, with . . . you."

"Life is funny," he says softly. "I'm glad we met."

I blush again. Dalton is the easiest person in the world to talk to, but with a spotlight on our connection, I suddenly feel shy.

"Although even if we hadn't met here in Paris, I bet we would have crossed paths in New York," he says. "What do you plan to major in?"

I suddenly realize that, unlike probably everybody else at La Danse, Dalton hasn't bothered to slavishly study the bios of everybody to figure out who might be helpful to him.

"I'm into science. Planning to study chem."

"*Chemistry?* Damn. That's impressive." He shakes his head, laughing. "I had a couple of friends switch from premed last year because they couldn't handle organic chemistry. Grant's parents were cool with him switching to econ. But McDowell's parents blew a freaking gasket when he told them he was gonna study art history instead."

I laugh. "I mean, yeah. That's a brutal bait and switch."

He pulls out his phone. "What's your Insta? I'll find you."

I give him my handle, then find his and click request on his private profile. Immediately, a notification pops up. Dalton's approved my follow request and has followed me back.

My stomach flutters.

"Public profile?" Dalton asks, scrolling through my photos right in front of me. "Living dangerously." He holds up a photo of a chemistry beaker. "And I see you weren't kidding about the science thing." He scrolls to another photo. "The International Science Fair? Sorry, why didn't you lead with that? That's awesome! You're gonna kill it at Columbia.'

I see another notification on my phone: I've been tagged by some fancy grocery store in California. Oh, and another tag by Seb! Something *else* to do with the grocery store. Why the hell is a grocery store on Instagram?

We walk into another gallery and stop in front of a series of Monets. "I have a confession to make." He looks at me expectantly. "I may not be going to Columbia."

His face falls. "Why not?"

"My scholarship was revoked."

"Oh no. What happened?"

I catch him up to speed on the benefactor drama, watching his face display genuine disappointment. "I'm so sorry you're dealing with that, Piper." He nods, looking thoughtful. "So this really is the chance of a lifetime. Forget the dresses and pretty photos. This is about shoring up your future."

"Exactly."

Guilt flashes across Dalton's face. "If I'd known that, I would never have pressed us to skip hot yoga."

I feel panicked. "Wait, do you think they *will* notice I'm gone? Amélie has been very clear that she doesn't want me creating any trouble."

He shakes his head no. "Bardot really is cool. You'll be fine. I just . . . you've got so much riding on this. It's so much pressure."

I cock my head, scanning him. "Said like somebody who understands pressure."

He laughs, but for once, the mirth is gone. "Ha. Yeah. Busted." He looks down at his hands. My gaze follows his eyes down to his fingers. His hands are strong and sturdy. The kind of hands you'd want to hold. "My mom puts a lot of pressure on us. On . . . Chapin, I guess, if I'm being honest."

I nod, not saying anything. Just giving him the space to open up. We sit together on a bench in front of a Van Gogh.

"Sometimes I feel guilty. Our mom treats me like the sun and the moon, but she's hard on Chapin. It's not fair to her." He shrugs.

"You're a good brother," I say simply.

He allows himself another microsecond of soaking in the frustration before jumping to his feet. "Sorry. What do I have to complain about? Hey, I saw a carnival in the Jardin des Tuileries. Wanna check it out?"

Twenty minutes later, we're on a swing ride together.

Dalton and I sit next to each other, our knees pressing together. He looks over at me and smiles, and as the swing rises into the sky, I have a feeling of weightlessness.

Like maybe I could be anybody I want to be.

Like maybe Paris is the place for new beginnings.

CHAPTER SIXTEEN

Chapin
Paris, France

This is torture.

I stand on the mat, twisting my body, trying to become one with the poses, but in reality I'm just pretzeling myself awkwardly as sweat pours off me like a waterfall.

I don't get yoga.

Mom loves it, of course. Every pose is an opportunity for perfection, for mastery of her body, for a chance to be the best at calming her mind. Even yoga somehow becomes a competition.

I glance around me, at everybody in neat little rows in their perfect little outfits. The same leggings. The same sports bra. The same pert ponytail. McRae has a determined look on her face, one hand by her ankle, the other extending insistently toward the ceiling. Lottie and I lock eyes. She smiles at me cheekily—*this is so boring*—and I feel relieved. Thank God, it's not just me.

Bardot is in the back of the room, frantically tapping on her phone as she oversees us. I wish I could join her. I'd much rather be scrolling than salabhasana-ing.

I wipe more sweat from my brow. Why do people voluntarily pay for this?

Part of the problem is it's hard to calm my mind. After my dad met with Maharishi Mahesh Yogi, he came back from India swearing that the key to happiness was Transcendental Meditation. But it just left me feeling itchy—how was I supposed to achieve happiness by repeating the same damn phrase over and over? It didn't matter if it was some phrase that was supposed to be unique to me. It was mind-numbing, not mind-calming.

Mom got really into meditation once, too. Although hers was different from Transcendental Meditation: some offshoot where you chant the same collective phrase over and over and over and over and over in unison for, like, thirty endless minutes. She once invited me to a group chant, where a bunch of rich Upper East Siders introduced themselves in a circle and then chanted together while staring at a scroll as if trying to summon rain. I'm pretty sure I saw Orlando Bloom.

I didn't go back after that. The next time she invited me, I passed and went to the Museum of Natural History to commune with the rare earth minerals instead. See? I can be spiritual too!

The thing I find hilarious about this yoga studio is how freaking nice it is. Isn't yoga supposed to be all about getting back to the earth, getting in touch with your body, renouncing the unimportant things? This studio is so fancy you could mistake it for The Row's boutique in LA—a courtyard with a reflecting pool and all. A bit ironic, methinks.

Plus, it's hotter than St. Tropez in August.

Finally, we're in the last pose: savasana. Everybody else seems thrilled and blissed out as they lie on the floor, settling into a sleeping pose. But I'm still squirming. The floor is hard. My back is uncomfortable. It's hard for me to settle my breath.

I do my best to pretend I'm into it—it's just expected that you'll be into yoga among my set—but yeah, I hate it.

And once we're done, I spring to my feet.

I pull out my phone and scroll through Insta stories.

Scroll: An Outfit of the Day photo from Margarita this morning in her room, the Eiffel Tower slightly visible out the window.

Scroll: Face looking absolutely delectable in a suit somewhere in London, posted a few days ago.

Scroll: Oh wait, somebody posted a video of Dalton in the Jardin des Tuileries. I cannot with these creepy Dalton fangirls. Like, post a celebrity, fine, they signed up for that life. But celebrity *kids*? It should be a no-go zone.

I zoom in on the video. It looks like he's stuck on a swing ride overlooking Paris, laughing hysterically. I smile, both glad and jealous that at least he's having fun on this trip, even if it's without me.

Wait.

I stop, frowning.

Oh hell, no. He's with *Piper*?

I rewatch the grainy video, as if my eyes are fooling me.

No, that's definitely my brother and my clodhopper roomie, laughing shoulder-to-shoulder on a swing ride in the Jardin des Tuileries, Paris at their feet.

I replay the video again, scrutinizing Piper's face. She's smiling at Dalton a little too adoringly. Dalton seems oblivious, which is par for the course.

I look around the yoga studio to confirm this is happening right now. There's Face, there's Peach . . . but yeah, my brother and Piper are AWOL.

"Have you seen this?" I demand in a whisper, holding the phone out to Lottie.

She leans over, watching the video of Dalton and Piper. "Aww. They're kinda cute together." Then she shudders. "Yikes. Stuck on a swing ride? Nightmare. Only thing worse would be getting stuck upside down. That's why I'll never go on a roller coaster."

"Cute?" I demand. "They're giving me the ick."

Lottie points at my phone. "Oh look. Piper got verified. Guess that Erewhon smoothie matters after all."

I pull the screen back, staring at it. I click through, disbelieving. There it is, that little blue check mark. Piper, verified. *Piper.* Who's never even done a step and repeat.

We're officially in a parallel universe.

McRae leans over on the other side of me, shakes her head. "Tsk, tsk. Don't sleep on the roomie. I don't know why you're surprised. I *told* you."

Lottie looks world-weary, stretching her limbs this way and that. "It's always the quiet ones you've got to watch out for."

"You better shut that shit down," McRae says. "And fast."

Don't think, just do. Before I can talk myself out of it, I DM the Instagram story of Piper skipping hot yoga to Amélie.

McRae catches it. "*Now* you're thinking." She smiles.

CHAPTER SEVENTEEN

Piper
Paris, France

Tonight's event is a spectacular boat party on the Seine with drinks, dinner, and a waterfront tour of Paris: apparently an annual La Danse tradition to welcome the debs and cavaliers.

La Danse has a lot of traditions.

I step onto the dock tentatively, trying to navigate it in my pumps.

I genuinely can't remember the last time I wore anything other than sneakers. The knowledge that I'm going to have to wear heels at the ball completely freaks me out. I've got my eyes on the prize, so I'll do it—and have secretly been practicing—but in the meantime I'm just praying I can make it through without a total wipeout.

A warm breeze catches my dress, and it flutters in the wind.

I look down, feeling self-conscious. I'm wearing a yellow cap-sleeve Valentino gown that fits better than anything I've ever worn. Newsflash: Designer stuff looks better than Kohl's off the rack! Groundbreaking!

But the real reason I feel anxious is because I've decided to incorporate a tiny piece of myself: a gold belt chain. It's from Claire's and has little butterflies on it. I thought it was cute, sort of a nod to my background. I impulsively brought it with me while packing. High-low fashion, right? Isn't that what influencers are always championing?

I know the whole point of this week is to impress, but I'm starting to realize there's a thin line between effortlessly dazzling and embarrassingly trying too hard. I thought I looked good in the mirror back in Chapin's suite, but now I worry I'm too out of place. In the Sprinter van on the way here, none of the other girls said anything to me, so I sat by myself in the last row, looking out the window.

It might have been my imagination, but I feel like Chapin intentionally went to get in the *other* van when she saw me in this one.

I didn't mind the other girls ignoring me, though. It gave me a chance to reflect on my day with Dalton. In my wildest dreams, I couldn't have invented this week.

To spend the day wandering around Paris with him, ending up in the Jardin des Tuileries together . . . it was one pinch me moment after another.

We were only stuck on the swing together for a minute or two, but it was exhilarating.

First we shrieked. Then we started laughing—me at his fear, him at mine. And then Dalton said, "I gotta capture this." He took a video of the two of us cracking up: "The ride just broke down!" For a second I worried he was going to post it to Instagram—the last thing I want to do is draw attention—but he put his phone away, smiling. "I'm not posting, don't worry." On the face of it, it wasn't a big thing—just a casual, tossed-off video between friends—but to me it feels huge. Every hour of this Parisian journey has felt increasingly surreal.

Journey. Blech. What am I, a contestant on *The Bachelor*?

Let's rein it in, Piper. A little more practical, a little less fantasizing. Eyes on the prize.

Dalton wasn't in either van tonight, so I don't know what his deal is. Maybe he decided to take a car with his mother. Maybe something came up. Or maybe he actually didn't have an amazing time today and now he's horrified about leading me on and in fact is already on his way home to New York City where his girlfriend—probably a premed supermodel who volunteers with the elderly when not fostering kittens—is waiting for him.

I mean, I'm just spitballing here.

As I step onto the dock, I look this way and that, trying to orient myself. I can't find my dad. In fact, I haven't seen him since this morning. We both knew we'd barely see each other here, but, we've been like two ships passing in the night: me running from one highly scheduled event to another, and him kidnapped by the moms and adopted as one of their own while they explore Paris.

I send him a text: **just checking in**

Almost immediately, he texts back.

Yes, hi honey, sorry. The parents took a cab from the hotel. We'll be there in five minutes.

Everything okay? Are you having fun?

Is everything okay?

Am I having fun?

I wouldn't call this *fun*, per se. More highly stressful, highly glamorous, but above all: a job. This is as much a performance as my time onstage presenting at the International Science Fair.

I'm realizing now it's not about looking pretty for the cameras. And it's certainly not about bonding with the other girls (or, ahem, Dalton). It's about showing up, hitting your marks, and playing the part.

And my part this week needs to be that of the perfect debutante.

After all, my future depends on it.

As I step onto the boat, Amélie appears from seemingly nowhere. Her eyes are narrowed, her lips are tight.

"What are you wearing?" she says by way of greeting.

I look around, confused. "Um, hi." We technically haven't yet been officially introduced. "Me?"

She exhales, irritated. She pastes a smile on her face, as if she suddenly realizes people may be watching us, though her voice is still low. "Yes, you. Piper."

I take a tiny step back. Of course Amélie knows who I am. Why wouldn't she? Still, I feel taken aback, exposed, small.

I smooth down the sides of my dress, full of shame, worried that I've gotten it wrong. Of course I couldn't pull off a dress like this. Of course I'm cringey. Of course Amélie would think I made the wrong choice. "I—I'm sorry," I stammer. "It appeared in my room. I think it's Valentino? A lot of brands have been sending me clothing—I guess they want me to be photographed in them? Like for publicity? And so I chose this one—I thought it looked pretty. But I'm so sorry, I didn't know it was wrong. Should I have worn something black, maybe?" I look around the dock at the other debutantes streaming in. McRae is wearing what I'm pretty sure is Chanel. Lottie's clad in something so futuristic and over-the-top that it makes me look like a medieval milkmaid in comparison.

Amélie's eyes roll to the top of her skull. I can't believe she's rolling her eyes at me. "Not your dress, Piper. Your . . . *that.*" Amélie points, disgusted, at the Claire's accessory I've strung around my waist.

"Oh. My gold chain?"

"The word 'gold' is doing some extraordinarily heavy lifting there. But yes. Your chain."

Amélie shudders as if the mere sight of it is physically revolting. "It looks like you plucked it from the waste bin at the Salvation Army." She continues picking me apart with her eyes, scanning me from head to toe. I hold my breath, feeling as if she's x-raying my insides. Is she gonna see the street-food hot dog I scarfed down for lunch? (You can take the girl out of suburban Pennsylvania . . .) This must be what it feels like to ride an elevator with Anna Wintour.

"I know you skipped hot yoga to traipse around Paris with Dalton Buckingham," she says.

My heart stops. How did she find out? Is she going to kick me out?

My eyes start to feel tight. Oh shit. I'm gonna cry. In front of Amélie Bouchon.

Amélie looks panicked. "No, no, no. We are not doing that here. No tears. No tears! There is press everywhere. Are you kidding me? We had a deal, Piper. *Absolument non.* Pull yourself together immediately."

"I know," I whisper. "I'm sorry."

Amélie sighs heavily. I want to add, *Sorry I'm not a punching bag! Sorry I'm a human being with feelings!*

"You are expected at *all* events—no exceptions." She clocks the photographers and tries to hide me from a nearby bank of them with cameras in hand. "I do not want *any* canoodling with your cavalier." My heart sinks. She glares at my chain. "And *that*. Just . . . take it off." With extreme effort, she manages to add, "Please." Her head turns, and a brilliant smile lights her face. "Carmelita! You made it! Thank God they were able to send the plane."

Amélie swans off across the boat, arms aloft. She pulls a gorgeous brunette into her embrace, triple (!) cheek kissing. And here I thought two cheek kisses was enough.

I turn back, surveying the boat as I remove the chain. I take a few steps through the crowd, suddenly feeling incredibly lonely. Despite my promise to Amélie, tears prick at the corner of my eyes yet again.

Observation: Attempt number one to fit in was a failure.

CHAPTER EIGHTEEN

Chapin
Paris, France

Now, *this* is the life.

We're all on a *bateau-mouche* on the Seine, the lights of Paris twinkling at us as the sun fades into a purply dusk. The boat itself is dotted with string lights, loudspeakers blasting French classics from the era when my grandmother was young. (Édith Piaf on a party boat? Really?)

I know it's all cheesy, like the lowest common denominator of what a tourist thinks is cool in Paris but . . . I secretly love it. When else but on a Parisian party boat on the Seine can you let your inner *Non, rien, rien, non, je ne regrette rien!* freak flag fly?

Across the boat, Face stands with a group of the other cavaliers, laughing and giving one another shit. Face nudges one of the guys with his shoulder, and the guy—Mathieu, I think? loses his balance for a second.

"Yo, watch out! I almost fell into the water!" the guy bellows, looking at Face angrily.

Face reaches out and puts his hand on the guy's shoulder. "Sorry, mate."

Mathieu shrugs Face's hand off rudely. Face puts his hands up in the air in a *my bad* gesture, and the tension in the group seems to fade.

I watch him, melting. God, he's hot. Oozes charisma.

Predictably, the debs have fractured into groups: McRae, Lottie, and Peach are in one corner, just beyond the boys, sitting on chaise loungers while giggling and looking at their phones. On the far side of the boat, by the bar, all the parents have gathered, mostly split along gender lines into moms in one corner and dads in another. The sole exception seems to be Piper's dad, who's in the center of a scrum of moms, appearing faintly bewildered.

I look around for Piper. Amélie is with her, giving her a full dressing down. She never responded to my DM, but I could tell she saw it.

After a minute of stern discussion, Amélie leaves her standing the middle of the deck for another attendee. Is Piper . . . crying? Yep. She wipes away tears before removing something shiny from her waist. For a fleeting second, I feel bad. My stomach clenches. Shit. I caused this.

But then I remember Piper outside the restaurant, dazzling in the light of the flashbulbs, and my mother's angry, disappointed face. I think of her landing an Erewhon smoothie. My sympathy dissolves. There can be only one Deb of the Year. And it's got to be me.

Speaking of my mother, she's lounging in another chaise across the deck, near the front of the ship. Amélie and several high-profile parents are dotted around her as my mother regales them. "And then George said to me, you've got a better laugh than Julia!" she trills. No doubt stories from her latest film set.

Mom catches my eye and beckons me over. For a second I think she might actually want to hang out with me. But then I catch the look on her face and realize what's going on.

Sigh.

Time to perform.

I take a step toward her and—*bam.*

I face-plant in my towering Manolo heels.

Everybody stops, the deck of the boat going silent. Slowly, a few titters start. Time slows.

I lock eyes with Face, who's across the deck. He gives me a shocked look—*are you okay?*

I don't have time to respond, because my mother has made her way across the deck and is reaching out a hand to gently pull me to my feet.

"My darling!" she says, her hand reaching down to mine.

I shake myself off, trying to regain my footing.

"Are you okay, sweetheart?"

"It's these damn heels," I mutter. "I hate them."

Mom surreptitiously glances around, sizing up whether

people are still watching us. Yep. Still watching. She leans over and gives me a fragranced hug. "I know," she says, patting me on the back before pulling away. She gets an impish look in her eye, smiling down at me and winking. She whispers, "I hate them too."

A moment of connection.

"Let's just make it through the night, okay?" she says.

I nod. She's in a cheerful mood tonight. I've got Good Ella.

"Oh, get this," I say to her, hoping to make her proud. "I found this Instagram video of Piper skipping the hot-yoga event. Guaranteed to make Amélie furious. So I forwarded her the video." I want to show Mom how seriously I'm taking La Danse.

My mom looks surprised. "Piper posted a video of herself skipping an official La Danse event?"

"No, no, she didn't post it of herself—it was a video somebody else posted of her with Dalton, and—"

She frowns. "She was skipping an official event . . . to be with Dalty?"

"Yeah."

"Which means Dalton skipped the event—and *you* forwarded a video of it to Amélie?"

"Yeah, but—"

She sighs, exasperated. "I swear to God, Chapin. You're only as good as the company you keep. Your brother is a liar and you're a snitch? Not exactly Deb of the Year material, is it?"

I flush. I hadn't thought of that.

She literally scoffs at me. Good Ella's gone—and it's my fault.

I frown, my face feeling tight.

"Oh, please do not cry," she hisses. "Everybody's looking at us."

"Nobody cares," I shoot back. "Piper was just crying, and nobody noticed."

"When you're a Buckingham, everybody cares. Everybody notices. This isn't rocket science, Chapin. Jesus, it's like we arrived in Paris and you were suddenly lobotomized. You know how this works. You're under a microscope, now more than ever."

Mom throws an arm around my shoulder, squeezing me tightly as she makes eye contact with Amélie. "She's okay!" Mom trills lightly, smiling indulgently. "Teenagers." The money-eyed crowd around Amélie chuckles. *Teenagers.*

But as Mom turns back to me, her face settles into something much more serious. "I mean it, Chapin. Why are we even here? I could be doing much more important things, but I cleared my schedule to come and be with you."

I take deep, quiet breaths, trying to keep my confusing cocktail of emotions from showing. *Cleared your schedule? You were trolling around the Marais having fun while I was trying to hang out with you!* I think.

"Do the ball right, or don't do it at all," she says.

As she glides back across the deck toward Amélie, I think: *Fine, then. But I'll do it my way.*

CHAPTER NINETEEN

Piper
Paris, France

I recenter myself.

Focus, Piper.

Eyes on the prize.

So you had a stumble. So Amélie is temporarily annoyed. You can still salvage this.

What do people do at these things? They connect. They schmooze.

So schmooze like your future depends on it. I *have* to show Amélie I'm taking this opportunity seriously. Everything hinges on pleasing her.

I look for a group of friendly faces to chat with. Chapin's sending me death glares. Her besties, McRae, Peach, Lottie, and

Margarita, don't exactly give off warm and fuzzy vibes. And Dalton is nowhere to be seen.

You can do this, Piper. Courage!

On the other side of the ship, I spy a beautiful girl with kind, wide-set eyes. She's has tightly woven braids cascading down her back. I approach tentatively.

"Um, hi . . ." I say shyly. "I'm—"

"Piper!" she says, looking delighted. "I've been dying to meet you. I'm Chloe Hughes. From Atlanta. You're from Philly, right?"

I nod, smiling at her. "Close enough. From King of Prussia. It's a suburb about half an hour away."

"Okay, then I've got one very important question for you." She looks at me seriously. I can't imagine what she's about to ask. "Pat's or Geno's?"

I laugh, and her face drops its faux-serious demeanor. "Told ya it was serious."

"Hmm. Will you judge me if I say . . . neither?"

"Ooh. This oughta be good."

"Hear me out. The meat at Jim's is way juicier."

"Jim's, okay! Plot twist!"

"The bread is—I'm sorry—the best. And the cheese—"

"Most important part, obviously."

"—is to die for. Therefore, I conclude my case."

We both laugh. "Okay, I hear you," she says. "I'll give it a go next time I'm in town." We walk together toward the railing.

"You're in Philly a lot?" I ask.

"Every so often. My dad's a visiting lecturer at Penn, teaches a couple classes there."

I suddenly realize that I know exactly who Chloe's dad is: Dr. Ethan Hughes, a world-famous game-show host who also happens to have a PhD in game theory. "That's right! Dr. Ethan, yeah?"

Chloe smiles self-deprecatingly. "The one, the only."

I crane my neck. "Is he here?"

She shakes her head no. "Some of the dads ditched, apparently. Last I heard, they were hitting up a bistro near Sébastopol."

I laugh. "Ah, that's right. Mine shot me a 'have fun, see you tonight!' text."

Chloe nods. "Yeah, I saw him fleeing from the moms in terror. He's become the trophy they're all trying to win."

Ugh. Poor Dad.

Chloe inclines her head toward the crowd. "How're you doing with this? It's a lot, huh?"

"It's all good."

Chloe shoots me a look, like: *C'mon, you don't have to lie.*

I smile. "Okay, yeah. It's a lot."

She laughs. "These girls wouldn't know reality if it bit 'em in the ass. They were born with a silver spoon in their mouths and think it's because they deserve it."

"And you weren't?"

Chloe considers the question thoughtfully. "You know, I was born extremely lucky. I have loving parents who actually *want* to spend time with me. A beautiful house, all the trappings. Everything I could ever want. So I'm already ahead of the curve. The difference is, I realize how lucky I am. And I *know* I didn't earn it. I *know* it doesn't make me better than anybody else."

She stretches herself to her full height, looking impossibly regal. "I might be a goddess—if I do say so myself—but I never take it for granted." She smiles at me impishly.

I thread my arm through hers. "I love you, and I would like to become friends, please."

Chloe cracks up. "Done." She looks around. "Have you met everybody yet? My girlfriend, Margarita, is around here somewhere!"

I shake my head no. "This isn't exactly the most welcoming crowd."

"Okay, well, we're changing that right now." Chloe flags down a cavalier walking by. "Hey, Klaus. Have you met Piper?"

Klaus shakes his head no, like he'd rather be scraping grime off a dirty toilet than saying hello to me. Chloe shoots him a look and it seems to put him in his place. He affixes a begrudging smile and approaches, putting a hand out.

"Klaus Von Dalwigk zu Lichtenfels."

I freeze. Klaus Von . . . what? "Um. Hi. Nice to meet you. I'm Piper. Piper Woo Collins."

Klaus nods, looking at Chloe like, *Can I go now?*

Chloe rolls her eyes, and the cavalier continues on.

"Klaus Von . . . um, Von Dodo. That's a mouthful," I say diplomatically.

But Chloe cracks up laughing at my slaughtered pronunciation. "Von Dodo! Oh my God, that's great. I'm gonna use that." She points across the boat toward a towering, handsome cavalier who looks a little like Andrew Garfield. "And that's older brother Von Dodo. He's a count or something."

Across the boat, Amélie stands on a raised step, commanding attention despite being pocket-sized. She taps lightly on a champagne glass. Heads swivel.

Chloe tugs on my arm, dragging me closer to Amélie. "This should be good." Amélie clears her throat, smiling angelically.

"I would like to take this opportunity to officially welcome you all to La Danse des Débutantes!" The moms and dads burst into applause, quietly congratulating themselves. "You are the *crème de la crème* of society, and it is my honor and pleasure to shepherd your sons and daughters through the following week. Let it be a week to remember!" More applause.

Amélie turns serious.

"In all my years of stewarding La Danse, I have seen the rise and fall of trends. The gradual societal ebb and whittling away of dignity and grace. Young people today are often unfairly singled out in the press, accused of moral rot and degradation—"

"Keeping it uplifting, as always," Chloe mutters sidelong toward me as I stifle a laugh.

"—but however true that may be in society at large, that is not true here at La Danse! Here, we honor young people who have devoted themselves to a life of service. Who know that the true measure of somebody's character is not the content of their bank accounts but the content of their souls. Who believe that young people can make a difference, that while, yes, the world may be full of ugliness and despair—"

"She really should be embroidering this pep talk on pillows," Chloe continues.

"—here we can celebrate a life of beauty and meaning!

Despite everything, I firmly believe that young people remain our brightest future . . . and it's all due to you, *mes chères parents*, who have done so right by your children and have brought them here, tonight, for us all to be together."

Enthusiastic applause. I look around the deck. The mothers and fathers are rapt—yes! We *have* done right by our children! We *are* amazing!—but the other debutantes and cavaliers look bored. Lottie and McRae whisper to each other; Face and Dalton are chuckling at something on one of their phones. Only Chapin stands apart from the rest, observing Amélie with a strange look on her face, as if she's truly listening to her.

She catches my eye and comes to stand next to me as Amélie continues her speech.

"You okay?" she asks.

"Huh?" *Me?* Chapin cares how I am?

"I saw you sobbing in the corner."

I flush. "I'm okay."

Chapin shrugs. We turn to face Amélie.

". . . and these past few years, some have said to me, 'But Amélie, what is the place of La Danse now? How can you continue in this new world, where people must apologize for their very existence?'"

"Oh boy," Chloe says.

"Here we go," Chapin agrees.

Amélie brings herself to her full height. She's still barely clearing five feet. She raises her champagne class, enunciating every word proudly.

"La Danse des Débutantes did not stop in the aftermath of

tragic terror attacks, nor did it stop during a devastating global pandemic. So I am here to tell you tonight that cancel culture certainly isn't going to stop me. There is still a place for us. We matter! We exist! Because debutantes do not live their lives in fear! The ball must go on!"

The mesmerized mothers and fathers clap like seals, enthused. Chapin's mother, Ella, *woo-hoos* her approval.

Chloe's jaw is on the floor. "Well, damn."

Chapin looks like she's got a migraine. "Jesus fucking Christ. She'd better *pray* that speech doesn't go viral." She shakes her head.

Chloe laughs ruefully. "I mean."

But I'm surprised to hear Chapin taking Amélie down. Most of the other debutantes seem to have let Amélie's words wash over them without a second thought. Maybe Chapin's more of a real one than I realized.

I must be staring at her, because she smiles at me wryly. "I'm not wrong."

"Not at all," I say, smiling back.

Are we . . . bonding?

Dalton sidles up to the three of us. "Well . . . that was special."

I feel relieved. I'm glad that Dalton didn't think that was normal either.

He elbows me. "So remember what I was saying today about us all being totally normal? Not the best example." We share a giggle.

Chapin looks back and forth between the two of us. A thundercloud seems to settle over her. "Bathroom," she mutters.

"I'll come with you," Chloe says, leaving Dalton and me alone.

"I think your sister hates me," I confess.

Dalton laughs. "She definitely doesn't hate you."

"No . . . pretty sure she does."

"Chapin is a good egg. She's the best sister on the planet. But she's sensitive. That's all."

"She keeps shooting me these death glares."

Dalton looks like he's trying to keep from smiling. A little dimple pops on one cheek. "Yeah, she does that without realizing it. RCF."

"RCF?"

"Resting Chapin Face."

I watch after her as she climbs below deck, gingerly navigating the stairs. "She seems especially upset that I was hanging out with you."

He looks interested. "Oh yeah?"

I suddenly feel shy. "Yeah. I feel like I should try to explain to her that we were just hanging out. It's not like it was a date."

"No?" he says softly, and my insides feel warm.

I glance up to find Dalton looking down at me.

"Was it?" I ask.

His lips part into a little smile, and my eyes are drawn to them. "I don't want to assume."

Now he looks down a little shyly. "But I had a lot of fun with you."

"Me too," I say.

Somehow our bodies have pressed a little bit closer.

A gasp goes through the crowd assembled on the boat. Just beyond us, across the Seine, the Eiffel Tower lights up, shimmering and sparkling like a bottle of popped champagne.

I look between the Eiffel Tower and Dalton, feeling like this is the stuff dreams are made of.

"So, just friends, right?" he says softly. "Nothing more?" The silence crackles between us, electric. His lips are so kissable. It would be so easy to lean forward, for our lips to touch. I feel a warm feeling in my stomach at the thought of his mouth on mine. This is the magic I was seeking—the nineties rom-com moment of my dreams. My mother would be so proud. Jesse and Céline *Before Sunset*–level romance.

For one shining moment, everything is perfect.

And then I catch Amélie's annoyed glance from across the boat. She *just* warned me: no canoodling with my cavalier.

I step away from Dalton, creating space between us.

His face falls. He looks as disappointed as I feel.

I see Chapin returning from belowdecks, glaring daggers at us, and I step even farther away.

"Yeah. Just friends," I say. I clear my throat, my voice quiet. "Nothing more."

CHAPTER TWENTY

Chapin
Paris, France

Today, Bardot has arranged a trip to the Dior atelier for me . . . and for Piper. Dior was planning to dress Storey for La Danse— so I guess they're slotting in one deb for another.

We sit together in the back of the car provided for La Danse, Piper desperately trying to connect, me desperately avoiding eye contact.

As the car turns onto Avenue Montaigne, I look out the other window and catch Piper's eye. She smiles at me hopefully. I know she wants to bond.

But I can't. Sorry not sorry.

McRae was right. She's a Single White Female, out to capture my life. I *do* feel a little guilty about throwing her to the well-dressed wolves with Amélie—but I have to remind myself that she deserves it.

I turn away, staring out the window on my side.

As we pull up to Dior, there's a scrum of photographers waiting for us.

Our driver scurries around to open the passenger door on my side. I step out first. Piper slides across the seat behind me, exiting my door.

"What's the friendship like between the princess and the pauper!" a videographer calls out in heavily accented English. I ignore him, putting my sunglasses on and walking toward the boutique entrance.

"Peeper! You are dating a Buckingham now. Smile, *chérie!*" a photographer says to her.

Piper looks in his direction, smiling uncertainly.

Another videographer gets close to Piper. "How does it feel going from Denny's to Dior?"

I know what they're doing. They're throwing things at her—praise! Insults!—desperately trying to get some sort of reaction for the photo. They don't care if it's a smile or agony—they just want to elicit *some* response that results in a memorable photo they can make money off.

"Heard you got a dead mom! Wish your dead mom was here right now?" another shouts.

The color drains from her face.

I've spent my entire life dealing with snarling paparazzi. It's a lot even for *me*, let alone for a newbie like Piper. They are serious scum.

I suddenly feel weirdly protective of her. "C'mon," I mutter, putting my hand out to usher her inside ahead of me. "Ignore these assholes. Let's go."

Piper looks at me gratefully, but I keep my face neutral. You've just got to be poker-faced in front of the paps.

As Piper enters, the photographers lose interest. Apparently, I'm not on their call sheet today. Rude.

Just then, I catch a familiar face beyond the retreating photographers: Raphael, the hotel butler, speed-walking past the boutique.

"Hey!" I say, before I can stop myself. I smile against my will. "What are you doing here?" So much for being poker-faced.

He smiles back, coming to a stop in front of the entrance. "Believe it or not, I don't actually *live* at the hotel."

I laugh. "No, of course." Then I pause, feeling playful. "I'm so glad they let you out from time to time."

We grin at each other.

"Sadly, though, I am heading into work," he says. "Don't rat me out. Sometimes I take the scenic route."

I nod up at the Dior atelier, its white facade blinding and beautifully lit. "Not the worst neighborhood to stroll through."

Raphael stuffs his hands into his pockets. He's out of his butler uniform, instead wearing jeans and a casual button-down. He kind of looks like a rugby player. It's working for him.

"Aren't you a bit young to be working there, though?" I ask.

He shrugs. "I'm nineteen. Everybody's gotta work somewhere."

I nod, feeling a weird flutter of excitement. "I'll turn nineteen this fall."

"Cool."

"Cool."

"You work?" he asks.

"I just graduated. About to start school."

"Ahh. *L'université.* Back in America, or here in Paris?"

I flush. The dreaded topic. "Um, back home. New York."

We grin at each other again, and I can feel my cheeks getting red.

I catch the eye of Elizabeth Drake, the creative director, inside the boutique. She's smiling at me, but in that polished, refined way that implies *I am totally fine waiting for you, and also get here RIGHT NOW.*

I turn back to Raphael. "Sorry, I have an impatient designer waiting for me. I should probably head in, or she'll ban me from wearing this gown we've been working on for months. You know how it goes." Wow. Could I sound more pretentious?

Raphael puts a hand up. "I get it. Fashion is art."

"Fashion *is* art!"

Raphael grins and salutes me before turning on his heel and continuing to walk toward the hotel.

CHAPTER TWENTY-ONE

Piper
Paris, France

I don't know how famous people do it.

The cameras in your face, the photographers and videographers yelling horrible things at you . . . There isn't enough money in the world to persuade me that fame's a good bargain.

I try to force myself to be present, to put the snarling paparazzi out of my head. My heart rate slows down. The soft, enticing smells of the Dior atelier waft over me—a gentle perfume that whispers, *I'm so expensive.* I take in the space, letting the glamour seduce me. Everything is in shades of cream and white, the center of the room a vast two-story atrium with a winding staircase in the middle. Headless mannequins clad in white dot the perimeter, arranged in highlighted alcoves like art installations.

Yeah, this is lovely.

"Piper?" a tall blond woman with a moneyed Texas accent says. She looks like the wife of an oil baron. "I'm Elizabeth Drake." She glides forward and shakes my hand gently, scanning me up and down even as she smiles. This is something fancy people do, I've noticed: the subtle scan. I can practically see the wheels in her head turning, making invisible little calculations: cheap shoes . . . cheap jewelry . . . cheap clothing . . . not one of us. "I'm the creative director."

"American?" I ask, even though I know the answer. *Look at me! Small talk!*

"What gave it away?" she teases. "My granny always said you can take the girl outta Texas, but . . ." She smiles self-deprecatingly and makes a funny little face. Okay, I like her. "Now!" she says, clasping her hands together. "Where's Chapin?"

I look behind me. Chapin's still outside, talking to somebody on the sidewalk. Elizabeth's eyes follow mine. She nods. "We'll do you first. Follow me."

Elizabeth leads me up the stairs and deeper into the boutique, through several large rooms, until we're in a smaller back room. "This is my workspace," she says in a conspiratorial voice, as if confiding a deep secret. "It's a mess. Don't judge—I promise the finished result'll be worth it."

I wouldn't expect anything less. "You should see my workspace when I'm in the middle of a science project. This is nothing."

"That's right!" she says, delighted. "Our scientist! Now, I do apologize—this was all so last-minute, it simply wasn't possible for your dress to have as much creative input as, say, Chapin's. However! I've been able to get something started, and I think you're just gonna love it, if I do say so myself."

Elizabeth nods toward an assistant who has suddenly materialized with a dress inside a garment bag. The assistant places the bag on a display rack and then unzips it.

A beautiful lavender tulle dress cascades out, looking every inch the princess gown. I gasp. "Oh my God. This is gorgeous!"

Elizabeth is visibly pleased. "Oh good, I hoped you'd think so!" She points to various layers of stitching and detailing on the dress. "Now, this here pays homage to Pennsylvania." Over on the side, there's a pencil. "This is meant to suggest your academic prowess—formidable indeed. And over here"—she points to a mermaid—"this represents your Virgo zodiac sign." She pauses, a twinkle in her eye. "I hope you don't find that creepy. It was a bit difficult to dig and find that information."

"What's the internet for if not a little light stalking?" I joke. I look at the dress, awed. "May I?"

Elizabeth nods: *Of course, go ahead.*

I reach out and take the fabric between my fingers. It's soft in places, stiff in others. The delicate embroidery must have taken countless hours of work—and it shows. The dress is a masterpiece. I've never seen a couture gown up close, but it's surprisingly hefty. It feels incredibly well made.

Better dresses. Better lives.

Chapin appears alongside me. She nods at my gown approvingly—less telegraphing her approval to me than to Elizabeth, who smiles at Chapin.

"And now for you, *ma chère*." She speaks her French with a charming Texan drawl. The assistant appears again, this time with Chapin's dress in a garment bag. The assistant hangs up the bag, Elizabeth unzips it, and Chapin's creation unfurls.

"Holy shit," Chapin whistles. "This is some serious business, Elizabeth."

Elizabeth laughs, appreciating Chapin's unexpected swearing. "All in a day's work. Or, rather, two months' work."

Chapin's gown is a work of art: a stunning black strapless gown, with a loosely tiered tulle skirt. The semi-sheer corset has a hint of edge—an unexpected quickness and sharpness that befits Chapin.

"Wow," I whisper softly, awestruck.

Chapin seems to forget that she regards me as a mortal enemy. She smiles, looking genuinely happy for once. "Wow is right."

Chapin reaches out to touch her own dress with the same sense of wonder as mine. "You nailed it, Elizabeth. I was worried about looking like a cupcake up there, but—"

Elizabeth nods her head, smiling enigmatically like the *Mona Lisa*. Hey, a comparison I can now make because of personal experience! "A dress isn't couture unless it fits the wearer perfectly—not merely in shape, but in spirit."

I'm surprised by how moved I feel. Mom would've loved this.

Chapin reaches out and gathers her dress into her arms. "Let's go do this." She marches confidently toward the back of the atelier.

I look around, unsure. "Should I . . . ?"

Elizabeth smiles, plucks my dress from the rack, and leads me in the same direction Chapin went. "Let's get you into this. Now, don't be worried if it's not an exact fit. Chapin's had months of fittings—I've only had your Instagram photos to approximate your size." She leans forward conspiratorially. "And a few models that we projected using AI."

I laugh. "Who says fashion and science don't mix?"

"I'll help you into it. It can be a little tricky."

The idea of being half-naked in front of a stranger is mortifying. On the airplane I watched this fascinating documentary on the nineties supermodels, trying to get in the proper headspace, and, honestly, I don't know how Cindy, Linda, Naomi, and Christy did it.

"Mmm, that's okay. I got it," I say in a rush.

"Are you sure? It might be better if—"

"Really! I got it!"

Elizabeth seems to understand my embarrassment. She acquiesces.

"*Pas de problème*," she drawls. "Try it on and come on out. This is just a start. We'll nip and tuck it until it's perfect for you."

I glide into the dressing room, high on Elizabeth's infectious confidence, and the door closes behind me.

I got this.

But once I'm alone, everything falls to shit. I stare at the gown, faced with the size of it, and realize I'm not sure if I should step into it or pull it over my head.

Let's try stepping into it.

I place the gown on the floor, feeling sacrilegious—almost as if I'm desecrating the American flag—and then step inside it. I try to wiggle the gown up my body, but it's impossibly tight. It gets stuck somewhere around my right thigh. I manage to fit my other thigh inside it, but now my lower half is encased like a sausage—there's no way this is making it over my hips. After a full minute of tugging and twisting, I give up and step back out. My thighs are now red and mottled, having gone to war with the dress's sharp edges.

Let's try this again. You can do it, Piper!

I place the dress back onto the hanger, set it on the wall, and dive underneath the prodigious hem, as if I'm a young child hiding in her mother's skirts. I'm lost inside the dress, drowning in lace and tulle, desperately swimming toward the neckline at the top and my salvation. My hands make it through, poking through the top, but my rib cage gets stuck, leaving me resembling a high diver preparing to jackknife into a swimming pool.

"Shit, I . . . shit . . ." I mutter.

"Piper? Are you okay?" Elizabeth calls from just outside the door.

"I'm fine!" I call back, panicked, my hands and arms pointed at the ceiling.

I begin to feel sweaty. My hair is caught on something—a sequin? a microscopic button?—and I'm now well and truly wedged inside the dress with no hope of getting out.

"Would you like me to come in?" Elizabeth asks. "The dress has a rather difficult zipper."

"No, I'm fine!" I repeat. "I got it! I'm just . . ."

Elizabeth obviously hears the panic in my voice. "It's a fairly delicate dress, honey. I think it would be best if . . ." She begins to open the dressing room door, causing me to intuitively step back to protect myself . . . except I can't see where the hell I'm going, and the step causes me to crash into the wall. I tumble onto my side, arms still in the air, stiff as a board, and let out an unladylike "mmmphhauggh!" screech as I crash into the other side of the dressing room wall.

"Piper!" Elizabeth gasps. "*Camille, viens, vite!*"

I still can't see anything, but judging by the commotion and all the footsteps, I now have an audience.

I am gently lifted back to my feet as Elizabeth says, "Hold still, honey, okay?"

Ziiiiiip.

Suddenly everything gives way. The dress falls onto my body easily, my arms settle down into a normal, human position, and my head pops through the top.

Across the room, Chapin is in her gown—poised, perfect, a goddess—watching this whole affair with a look of utter disbelief and disdain.

"I should have mentioned the zipper," Elizabeth says, plastering a smile onto her face.

"Is the dress okay?" I ask hopefully.

Elizabeth grits her teeth. "It'll be fine. Just a small rip. We needed to do some alterations anyway."

I turn this way and that. It's not just a small rip, but rather an enormous gash down the side of the dress where the zipper attaches. I catch two of the assistants shooting each other an incredulous look.

"I shouldn't have assumed you knew about the zippers," Elizabeth says graciously. "They're practically invisible. A trick of couture. It's my fault, really." She's no longer gritting her teeth. She's being sincere.

She doesn't say it, but she doesn't have to.

She shouldn't have assumed . . . because I'm not one of them.

It's written all over Chapin's face.

CHAPTER TWENTY-TWO

Chapin
Paris, France

I know I'm a sap . . .

But back in the car after our Dior sojourn, I can't help but feel bad for Piper.

This girl is trying to steal my life, and I was starting to worry that she was actively trying to sabotage me.

But I'm starting to realize maybe it's not her fault?

Maybe she's just unforgivably rural. Because how can you not know there's a zipper in the side of your dress?

She's pressing herself into the window, staring out at Paris as it zooms by. We're in the eighth arrondissement, rows of boutiques and red awnings and tantalizing designer goods visible through the windows. Normally, I'd ask the driver to stop, maybe pop into one of the boutiques to see if I can find something fun, but I don't want to spend another minute with Piper.

Mom and I are supposed to hang out this afternoon. I text her:

2pm still good?

She replies almost immediately.

Stuck on a director call. Let's do tomorrow, okay, lovebug?

I don't respond, just put my phone away. Typical.

Then I hear sniffles.

Oh God.

Is Piper crying?

I sigh to myself. *This is a good thing, Chapin. The more this girl fails at La Danse, the better your chances are of winning and making Mom happy. You want her to crash out.*

But I'm not, like, a complete monster. I don't want her to be depressed. I just don't want her in my way.

"Are you okay?" I ask.

"Mmm," she says in return, not turning to look at me.

The car speeds up the boulevard, the two of us sitting there in silence.

CHAPTER TWENTY-THREE

Piper
Paris, France

The second we get back to the hotel, I race up to our suite, leaving Chapin behind in the lobby as she chats with some of the debs.

I cannot believe I cried in front of Chapin Buckingham.

As soon as we left the boutique, I felt the tears pricking behind my eyes, but I managed to hold it in. And then, as we drove back to the hotel, I caught a glimpse of the Musée d'Orsay in the distance, and everything crumbled.

Mom was dying to go there.

I miss her so much I can't breathe. I wish she were here to talk to. To share everything with.

She always had the best advice. She always knew what to do.

When I was twelve, my best friend Emma moved to Miami at

the end of the school year. I was devastated; we'd been inseparable. Every day after school, Mom would ask me if I was okay, and every day I'd say I was fine. I was in my asshole-preteen phase.

One day, I was lying on my bed, staring morosely at the ceiling, when Mom came in and lay on the bed next to me. She didn't say anything. She just pulled up Spotify and started playing "Cruel Summer"—which it was indeed. A minute or two later she opened her arms for me to crawl into, and I lay next to her and snuggled in silence. I didn't expect her to understand—what on earth would a mom know about best friends and heartbreak? We made it halfway through *Lover* before I finally asked her what I should do.

"I know it feels like you'll never find another best friend again, honey," she said.

"I won't."

"I promise you will. You're the most amazing kid I know! You've just been hiding in Emma's shadow. Now you gotta let that Piper light shine."

I absorbed this quietly. Emma was the star, and I was just . . . *there*. What if I didn't have any Piper light? What if hiding in the shadows was my destiny?

Mom looked down, scanning my face. She was so good at reading me. "It's okay to feel scared. But the future has something amazing waiting for you. I just know it."

I desperately wanted to be the girl Mom saw: cooler, bolder, with something to offer on my own. Maybe someday I'd get there.

A couple of weeks later, I met Seb at the community pool—we were both secretly ogling the lifeguard—and the rest is history.

Back in the suite, I pull out my phone and retreat to the balcony to call Seb. I don't want Chapin to come back into the living room and see me bawling my eyes out to my best friend. Better to call him from the safety of the balcony.

"Are you kidding me with your Eiffel Tower view? You must be in heaven," he says. But then he stops when he sees my tearstained face. "Oh God, Piper, what happened?" I burst into tears, then catch him up to speed on the dress.

". . . and then I tumbled over like one of those gross Gumby stick figures outside a gas station, crashing onto my side," I recall, feeling an anxious red flush spreading across my chest. My eyes feel tight. My head feels hot. I physically carry embarrassment in my body. Always have. "How can this place be so gorgeous and yet such a freaking mess? I'm making enemies, I pulled a damn muscle trying on clothes so expensive that selling them could feed a small country, and you're a million miles away. Everything is the worst."

"Hey," he says. "You know what those gross gas-station Gumbys do?"

"Rust in the sun?" I sniff, wiping my nose.

"They float back up. And that's you, Pipes. Sure, you get knocked down. Yeah, you made a fool of yourself at the Dior atelier in front of the creative director. Who among us hasn't?" I give a reluctant laugh. "But that's no reason to feel ashamed of yourself. You're a person. You're human. Nobody is perfect. Not even Miss Chapin thinks-her-farts-smell-like-roses Buckingham."

"You really are unbelievable, you know."

I turn to find Chapin at the door of the balcony, glaring at me.

To his credit, Seb goes as quiet as a church mouse, even though I know he's dying to introduce himself to her.

Chapin fumes. "And to think I was feeling sorry for you."

"I'm sorry, Chapin, he didn't mean anything by it—you obviously don't smell bad—"

"Oh, I couldn't care less about that," she says dismissively. "You think I haven't learned to grow a thick skin about insults and lies after eighteen years as Ella Somerset's daughter? Please." She's practically sneering at me. "But to think I've opened my room to you, shared my clothes with you, and *this* is how you repay me?"

I stare at her, confused. "Chapin, I have no idea what you're talking about. I'm so sorry."

"My sneakers!" she wails. "What did you *do* with them?"

CHAPTER TWENTY-FOUR

Chapin
Paris, France

The wounded look Piper is giving me is so well-worn by now, it could be my own personal meme.

"Why would I steal your sneakers?" she says in a voice so calm it makes me want to throw her off the balcony.

"I don't know? To punish me? To send them home to your weird friends?"

Said weird friend on FaceTime looks chagrined. "I'm gonna go. Call you later, 'kay? Love you forever." He hangs up.

"Chapin, I'm just trying to survive this week. Why the hell would I want to punish you?"

"For Amélie berating you about skipping yoga for the Jardin des Tuileries?" I point out.

She freezes. After several silent seconds she asks, "How did you know I went to the Jardin des Tuileries?"

Oh. Shit.

"Did *you* tell Amélie?"

I try to arrange my face in a *no, definitely not* look. "We all saw her yell at you," I point out. But Piper's face has significantly changed. She's no dummy.

"Why the hell would you *do* that?" she yells at me. Whoa. I've seen Piper be annoying, I've seen her be dorky, but I've never seen her be furious. "How did you even find out where I was?"

I'm a shitty liar. "Some Dalton stalker posted a video on Instagram," I admit, shifting uncomfortably before jutting my chin up. "Don't turn this on me. It's not my fault. *You* shouldn't have skipped."

"This is my fucking *life*, Chapin!" Her face is cold fury. "This isn't some stupid debutante ball for me. This is my only path toward college. I'm trying to work my ass off for a future you can buy!" She's practically purple with anger. "I'm not here to backstab you. That's not who I am."

"How am I supposed to know who you are? You're a complete rando, from the middle of nowhere, who mysteriously elbowed herself into a ball that girls spend years angling for!"

"Because you pampered assholes don't have any real things to worry about!" she yells before storming back into the suite.

I follow her back inside and close the balcony door, feeling increasingly unhinged. This isn't me. I don't lose control like this. Sure, my insides are a constant, stressed-out wreck and I pop Tums like they're candy, but on the outside I *glide*.

I'm a freaking *swan*.

Now we're alone inside the suite. I point toward my bedroom door, where the racks of clothes are clearly visible next to the bed. But underneath them, nothing. "See? No sneakers! They've been stolen!"

She storms into my room.

"I. Don't. Care. About. Your. Stupid. Sneakers," she says, clapping after every word like a deranged cheerleader.

"Stay out of my room!" I shriek.

Piper looks around, as if she's having a pep talk with herself, trying to calm down. She exhales noisily, an *arrgh!* of frustration.

"Let's approach this logically. When did you last see them?" she asks.

"This morning," I mutter. "Before we went to Dior."

"To Dior. Okay. Where I was with you the entire time, right?"

I look away, not saying anything. "Well, somebody stole them."

"Maybe it was one of the other debs. Maybe *they're* trying to backstab you. Take you down a peg to win the crown."

I consider this. "I mean, maybe . . . but everybody's been at the ateliers all morning."

"Okay, then who *hasn't* been at the ateliers? Who would want to take your sneakers anyway?" she demands. "Let's examine the possibilities, and *that* will be the culprit."

Awareness dawns.

My mom?

Ugh. Yeah. That tracks.

I flush, suddenly feeling dumb.

It feels like Piper's reading my mind. She doesn't look angry anymore. "Your mom?"

"Yeah, maybe," I mutter.

"She hates your sneakers, right?"

I can't believe my mom would do this. I mean, I *can* believe it, because she absolutely despises my sneakers—but resorting to stealing? When she could have just asked me? Then again, I would have put up a fuss, and we would have almost gotten into a fight, and then I would have given in to please her, and I would have lost my sneakers anyway *and* pissed off my mother. Lose-lose.

I suddenly realize Piper is staring at me. I guess my own wheels have been turning.

Out of nowhere, I'm seized with the sudden urge to confront my mother. That's not what I do. I let things slide. I make nice. But I am filled with such rage that I have to get it out of me, consequences be damned.

"Look. I don't know why you hate me," Piper says, "but I'm sorry for whatever I did. But you need to work out your shit with your mom directly. Don't screw *me* over in the process." I'm impressed by her backbone, to be honest.

"Be right back," I hiss. Piper looks alarmed.

As I storm down the hallway and enter the elevator, I try to calm myself down. What good will come of this? It's completely counter to my goals for the weekend.

But the second she swings open the door and smiles at me, the rage dam breaks.

"Did you steal my sneakers?" I demand.

Instead of the smile dropping, it widens. "Come in, darling," she says, trying to pull me into the suite.

I wave her arm off. "I'm fine here, thanks. You didn't answer the question, Mom."

"Honey, this is absurd."

"It's a simple yes-or-no question. Did. You. Steal. My. Sneakers?"

"I honestly haven't the faintest clue what you're talking about."

I give her *a look*. It's rage and hurt and disappointment. This week was supposed to be all about us hanging out together, me getting on her good side, and instead we've been two ships passing in the night, her constantly putting me last—and now, me outside her room, accusing her of shoe theft.

"I don't ask for a lot from you," I say quietly.

"Oh, for God's sake, Chapin, you don't have to be so dramatic," she says in a low voice. "It's for the best."

This is the closest I'll get to a confession from her.

"Where did you put them?" I ask, desperate, suddenly feeling like a helpless little girl. I remember being four years old and getting stung by a bee in Central Park. My mother was there— she must have been on hiatus—and I ran across the playground to her and flung myself into her arms, screaming. She held me, patting my hair as I wailed. "There, there. You're safe." It's my earliest memory.

A lifetime ago.

"This isn't like you at all. The stress of the week is clearly getting to you. You need to *calm down*."

"Fine," I say, turning on my heel and storming back toward the elevator. I call over my shoulder, "If you're not going to tell me, I'll find them myself!"

As the elevator doors close, I catch a glimpse of my mother's face. For the briefest moment, she looks stricken. And all I want is for her to hold me again and tell me I'm safe.

CHAPTER TWENTY-FIVE

Piper
Paris, France

Chapin comes back from her mother's suite upset, declaring that Ella has, indeed, stolen the sneakers.

I could just nod and turn away, but I remember her face when she realized it was her mother.

It was like she was a kid who'd just discovered Santa wasn't real.

"We were barely gone two hours," Chapin says. "I'll bet anything they're still in the hotel."

She heads for the door.

"Wait," I interject. "Let me help."

And now here I am, wandering from floor to floor, looking for laundry rooms and garbage chutes—anywhere that Ella might have disposed of Chapin's sneakers.

It only took me about fifteen seconds on our own floor to realize: This kind of hotel doesn't have a public laundry room or an elevator chute. Duh. It's not a Holiday Inn. There's no alcove with a vending machine, no ice chest humming in the corner. Just a RING FOR CHAMPAGNE button in every room and an insidious voice whispering in my head: *You don't belong.*

But I don't want to give up the game so early—especially not since Chapin seemed at least *mildly* grateful for my offer of help. Chapin is downstairs talking with reception. So I'm trying to find something by scouring the hotel itself.

I'm doing this for positive goodwill, I tell myself. *If I help Chapin find the sneakers, maybe it'll get back to Amélie.*

The floor I'm on doesn't seem to be residential; it's full of ballrooms and communal spaces. I hear voices to the right, so I decide to head that way.

"... Chapin ..."

My ears prick, snapping to attention as I follow the conversation.

I peek through the doors of a magnificent ballroom. Inside, there's a camera crew and a producer setting up.

Right. Chapin's got a big interview today.

I'm about to turn away when I hear Chapin's name again. I turn back.

"... let's be nimble. She's a debutante, not a rocket scientist."

Sorry, what now?

I press my ear to the crack in the wall, now fully, shamelessly eavesdropping.

"Chapin may well make a fool of herself," a camera operator

says, nodding. "I've done interviews with these types of girls before. Dumb as a box of rocks."

"If we're lucky, something will go viral," the producer replies, picking up notes and shuffling through them.

"Fingers crossed!" They both laugh. The crew disperses, and someone starts walking toward the doors I'm spying through. Shit. I hustle off back toward the elevators, not wanting to get caught. I turn the corner and jab the button, my thoughts racing. My instinct is to tell Chapin she's walking into a setup. But a tiny voice in my brain asks me whether Chapin would do the same.

Would she tell me . . . or let me fail?

The elevator arrives with a ding and I step inside, pressing the button for a random floor. As the car lurches, I examine myself in the mirror opposite.

For the briefest of seconds, I don't recognize myself. I'm wearing one of my gifted outfits for the week: a striped blue-and-cream matching set. I've been borrowing Chapin's conditioner, so my hair is softer and sleeker than usual. Without fully realizing it, I've changed my part slightly, to make it look more like the other girls'. Even my makeup—normally nonexistent—is starting to resemble Chapin and company's. I'm turning into a lemming.

But isn't that what I promised myself I must do to succeed? Observe the other girls, insert myself into their habitat, learn their customs, and behave accordingly? Play by their rules to win the game?

Maybe I keep it to myself.

The elevator doors open to the second floor, and I step out.

"Piper?" I startle and turn, finding the young hotel butler Raphael.

"Are you . . . lost?" he asks politely. It might be my imagination, but I feel like I can see a dimple pressing into the side of his cheek.

I flush, embarrassed, like he could tell what I was thinking. "Sorry, I just . . . sorry." I try to recenter my thoughts. "I was—actually, maybe you'll be able to help me!"

Raphael bows slightly. "At your service."

"Okay, so—you know Chapin? My roommate?"

"*Bien sûr.* Of course."

"Her sneakers have been lost. Well, not lost, stolen. Taken, I should say."

Raphael frowns, startling. "There's been a theft? Let me alert the hotel manager."

"No, no, not exactly," I hasten. "It was her mom, Ella—she hated the sneakers and didn't want Chapin wearing them anymore. . . . It's a long story."

He nods, face settling. "I think I understand." He frowns again. "Ugh. Chapin loves her sneakers, no?"

"Uh, yeah. I promised her I would help find them. I've been trying to figure out where somebody might dump sneakers, because there's gotta be, like, a laundry room or a garbage chute or something, right . . . ?"

Raphael puts a hand up to stop me. "I know just where to look. Follow me."

CHAPTER TWENTY-SIX

Chapin
Paris, France

"I am going to absolutely kill my mother," I groan, lugging a trash bag of sneakers behind me.

Piper, Raphael, and I are in the bowels of the hotel, each of us carrying a bag of sneakers.

"Jesus, how many sneakers do you need?" Piper asks, struggling under the weight.

We reach a freight elevator. Raphael uses a hotel key to open it for us.

"That's beside the point."

"So . . . a lot."

"A lot," I admit sheepishly. "But if my mother thought her little stunt was going to make me fall in line, she is completely mistaken. All I *do* is fall in line. I mean, I *am* the line. It's not like

I have a face tattoo! I took AP US History solely to please her! Like, come on. Let a girl live."

As the doors close behind us, I look at Raphael gratefully. "Seriously, thank you for this."

We exchange a smile. "It's my pleasure," he says.

"The housekeeper's not gonna get in trouble, will she?" That's the last thing I want on my conscience: some poor hardworking person getting canned because of my mom and me.

He shakes his head. *"Absolument non."* The elevator reaches our floor, and we all struggle off in a scrum of elbows and bulging plastic. "Believe me, this hotel has seen everything. A mother asking for help getting rid of her teenager's clothing? That's a Tuesday. *Ordinaire.*" He grins at me again, and my stomach does an unexpected but not unpleasant little flip. Huh. He's really cute.

As we get to the door of our suite, I struggle to find my key in my pocket. The bag slips and the sneakers fall all over the hallway. "Damn it!" I hustle to pick them up.

"Here, let me help," Piper says, producing a key and propping the door open with her bag.

She gets down on the floor to begin scooping up errant sneakers, but Raphael is already on the floor with me, resting on his knees as he drops shoes back into the bag.

Our hands both go for a pair of sneakers at the same time and our fingers brush.

I stumble to my feet before I can make a further fool of myself.

Raphael gently places the remaining sneakers just inside

our suite, without coming inside. He bows again slightly at the waist—"pleased to be of service"—and hustles off as I watch him go.

Inside the suite, Piper is nervously arranging sneakers.

"Sorry, I didn't know where they went—is this okay?" she asks, fluttering.

I put a hand up to stop her. " You've done enough. You didn't have to help."

Piper nods, looking stressed out. I watch her, suddenly feeling guilty. None of this is her fault.

"I'm sorry I took my frustration out on you. That was shitty and you didn't deserve it."

She looks at me, brow furrowed, like she's trying to decide something. She looks away and continues sorting sneakers in silence. But after a few more seconds, she turns to face me.

"Actually, Chapin? There is something I need to tell you," she says.

I look at her warily. "Okay . . . ?" Is this where she peels off my skin after all?

"So, when I was wandering around the hotel, I walked through the ballrooms. And I know you have that interview today—"

"Yeah, don't remind me. I haven't had any time to practice yet."

"Right. Well, that's the thing. I wonder if you're being set up?"

I stop. "What?"

"I heard them talking about you. Something about 'vapid

debs' and 'dumb as a box of rocks.' I think they're hoping you make a fool of yourself so they'll go viral."

My heart stops. "Oh."

Piper looks guarded, as if she's expecting me to start yelling at her. It makes me feel even smaller. Have I become like my mother? Cutting people down to make myself feel better?

"Thank you," I say. "And I'm sorry."

Surprise flits across her face.

"I've been nothing but a jerk to you these past few days, and here you are helping me, over and over. Seriously. Thank you, Piper. It means a lot."

Piper nods. "Yeah, you have. But I forgive you."

"No more asshole Chapin, okay? I promise."

She nods again, then turns back to the pile of shoes.

I sit cross-legged on the floor next to her and grab a pair of sneakers from the bag. I place them neatly in a row, next to the sneakers Piper is arranging.

Piper busies herself tidying up sneakers. But I can see her shoulders relax.

"This week is pretty overwhelming. I know it can be a lot," I say.

Piper sighs. "I feel like I'm constantly in over my head."

I clear my throat. "I'll finish putting my sneakers back later. But the interview isn't for another two hours. Wanna grab a coffee?"

She smiles. "I'd love that."

CHAPTER TWENTY-SEVEN

Piper
Paris, France

Chapin and I walk side by side down the avenue in silence.

I don't know what to say. And, seemingly, neither does Chapin. After all, we just screamed our guts out at each other and now we're strolling like we're besties.

I should pretend she's Seb. I never have trouble shooting the shit with him.

"So, come to Paris a lot?" I ask in a jokey voice.

I expect her to laugh—I'm obviously kidding—but she gives me a weird side-eye before responding. "Yeah, we're here a lot. It's your first time, right?"

"That's right."

Conversation attempt one: aborted.

"My mom always wanted to come," I say. "Paris was at the

top of her bucket list. It's nice trying to live it through her eyes."

Chapin's eyes widen. "That's right." She nods, her face softening as she remembers. "You told me about her. How long has it been?"

"A few years."

Chapin nods. "I'm so sorry."

"It's okay," I say.

Conservation attempt two: dead mom not exactly fertile ground.

We keep walking in silence. Maybe I should tell her about Columbia. With Dalton attending, it's an obvious connection to her family. "When we met earlier, you asked me why I was here."

She turns and looks at me curiously, as if to say: *Go on?*

"The truth is, my college scholarship fell through. I was supposed to go to Columbia, but there was this huge—well, it's too screwed up to explain. Suffice it to say, a rich donor threw a big-boy tantrum, and suddenly my grant was gone."

Chapin looks outraged. "What? Are you kidding me?"

"I wish."

"That's criminal! And they wouldn't give you money from another scholarship fund?" Chapin nods her head toward a café across the street. It's cute and charming and impossibly Parisian. We wait for a bus and several motorbikes to pass and then scurry across the street, enter together, and take a seat.

"The bursar's office was full of apologies. They'll work it out eventually, but it'll take a full semester, and I refuse to miss the first three months of college. That's when you meet your friends, bond with your professors, learn your way around campus, you know? The idea of sitting at home in Pennsylvania while I miss my first semester of college makes me want to . . ." I pull a face. "Anyhow, so either I go somewhere else, or I somehow figure out a way to make up the scholarship money. Which my family does *not* have."

She stares at me.

Conversation attempt three: world-famous teenage heiresses— tough crowd.

"You have other options, right?" she asks.

"I got into a few schools."

"With scholarships?"

I nod. "With scholarships. But those disappeared when I accepted Columbia's offer."

The waitress arrives to take our coffee order, and then Chapin turns back to me curiously.

"So how did that land you here?"

"Amélie offered to pay for my first year of college if I joined La Danse. And perform like a trained monkey."

Chapin's jaw drops. But then—finally! A smile. Small. But it's there.

I nod. "I know."

Chapin looks impressed. "Damn. Amélie Bouchon stepping up. That's pretty cool."

Our coffees arrive swiftly—Instagrammable works of art— but Chapin doesn't bother to photograph hers. She takes a sip. "I get it now. Why you came to Paris."

"Well, what about you?" I ask. "You're doing La Danse for your mom, right?"

She snorts, then takes a sip of her latte. She seems a tiny bit more relaxed. "Not that it matters. I know it's dumb, fooling myself that winning some stupid debutante ball will make her happy. This was supposed to be a bonding experience, and she's barely spent five minutes with me in Paris." She looks out the window, staring at the chic Parisians—and not-so-chic tourists—streaming by. "She's not a bad mom. I don't want to make her seem like some monster. She's actually pretty fun at times. We do love each other. She's just"—she sighs heavily—"busy. And complicated."

"It's probably not easy being a famous actress," I say. "Lots of pressure, I'm sure."

I'm trying to be understanding. But Chapin frowns at me again. "Try being the *kid* of a famous actress," she snaps.

The two of us sit in awkward silence.

"I wanted to go to Columbia," she finally admits, dropping it like a bombshell. "I got rejected. Sorry, *wait-listed*, as Dalton keeps reminding me. But it sure as hell feels like a rejection."

Oh shit. No wonder Chapin was irritated with me. It must feel like I took her spot. "I'm sorry. That must have been devastating."

She stares me down, as if she's trying to decide whether I'm being sarcastic or sincere. "I'll be fine. I got into USC, it's Mom's dream, she went there, blah blah blah. I just thought it would be nice to do my own thing for once. Follow my own dreams."

"USC is an amazing school!" I say, encouraging. "People go to jail for it!"

This makes her laugh. "Varsity Blues aside, it *is* a great

school. I'm super lucky. And their geology program is awesome, too—"

"Wait," I say, interrupting her before I can stop myself. "It's kind of funny when you think about it. We're both into science. We both sort of have mommy issues. Neither one of us really wants to be here. We actually have a lot in common?" I flush as I finish speaking, suddenly expecting Chapin to cut me down like she does. Like, who the hell am I, comparing myself to Chapin Buckingham?

But to my relief, she smiles. "Yeah. Fair."

"I came here against my will, if I'm being honest. Doing a debutante ball wasn't at the top of my to-do list. Not that I thought I was above it or anything. I just didn't think I would be able to connect with anybody here." I give her an apologetic smile.

"Can't blame you there." She smiles back at me, leaning in slightly. "You know, a lot of these girls are cool. Clueless, to be sure. Zero idea how the real world works. And Zella is a total ball fiend—"

"Ball fiend?"

"She's obsessed with scoring as many high-profile galas as possible during her gap year. The Met, Bal de la Rose in Monaco, amfAR in Cannes. She started dating the guy from that weird A24 movie last year—what's his name? the super hot one?—just so she could go to the *Vanity Fair* Oscar Party."

"Austin Butler?" I whisper, eyes wide.

"No, but I think they were in an HBO limited series together? Whatever. The point is, they're their own brand of weird, but they're not bad people. Most of the debs here were chosen by Amélie because they *do* actually give back—even if that just means starting a charity with their parents' money." She laughs self-consciously. "I mean, take McRae. Hedonism is in her DNA. She never even had a chance. All things considered, she's all right." Chapin downs her coffee and politely gestures at the waitress for another one.

"Do you know Chloe?"

"Of course! She's great!" Chapin says.

"We were chatting yesterday," I say. "She's really nice. Super funny."

"Oh yeah, she's a riot. Smart as hell, too. I think she's going to Yale."

I'm impressed. "Damn. Pretty, rich, *and* smart. And here I was consoling myself that all the debs would be vapid dummies."

"Well, they're not *all* Ivy-bound. Peach's grandmother founded the International Best-Dressed List, so she's got the stylish and rich part locked up, but smart?" Chapin makes a sassy face. "Let's just say she's not on any wait lists." We giggle, but then Chapin looks around guiltily, as if she suddenly feels bad. "Peach *is* a genius photographer, though. She's a total Demarchelier behind the camera."

"I love all this gossip! It makes everybody feel less . . . scary?"

Chapin absentmindedly taps her chin, thinking. "Let's see, who else? Oh, have you met Nihat Farou yet?"

I shake my head no.

"She was on *Turkey's Got Talent*. Ridiculously good voice."

I'm impressed. "Badass. What about the guys? Isn't Face

Wellington the second cousin of the king or something like that?"

Chapin's face turns pink. Is she blushing?

I raise my eyebrow at her. "Are you two . . . ?"

She blushes harder. "No! *No.* Definitely not."

"Because he's super gross," I deadpan.

She laughs. "Hideous. No, we're just friends. That's all."

"But it sounds like you wish it were more?" I ask playfully.

She buries her face in her hands. "I don't know! We made out once . . . okay, a couple of times . . . but he makes out with everybody? Ugh, he's just so *charming.* It was probably drilled into him at royalty school."

I lean in, intrigued. "Is there a royalty school?"

"Oh yeah, top secret." She lowers her voice. "Lessons on how to overthrow the prime minister, which pinky to pop when you're having tea, the whole thing."

It takes me a second to realize *she's* teasing *me.* I smile. Chapin Buckingham has a good sense of humor. Who knew?

For a fleeting second, I think that I could confide in Chapin about Dalton. Tell her about the butterflies I get in my stomach when he looks at me. And then I'm pulled back to earth and realize that would literally be the dumbest move imaginable. Against all odds, Chapin and I are finally starting to bond. But she's made it clear that her brother is off-limits . . . and besides, I don't think there's a sister on Planet Earth who wants to hear details about how smoking hot her brother is. Too weird, even for this bonding session.

Instead I change the subject. "You know, I initially thought this ball was completely horrifying, and my best friend had to talk me into it—"

"The smoothie guy from FaceTime?"

"Smoothie guy?"

"Your Erewhon smoothie?"

"Who's Erewhon?"

"Oh my God." Chapin laughs. "Forget the smoothie. I meant your best friend. Seth?"

"Seb!"

"He seemed cool."

"He's the best. But yeah, he pushed me to come here, against my will. But now I realize my assumptions were totally prejudiced. I assumed everybody was going to be a pompous, spoiled asshole, and instead I found—"

"That only *some* people are pompous, spoiled assholes?" Chapin cracks, interrupting me.

"You get it."

We laugh, finally vibing for the first time.

CHAPTER TWENTY-EIGHT

Chapin
Paris, France

I sit down for the interview, the lights hot on my face. My heart is pounding in anticipation of what's coming.

The interviewer is a tall blond woman with a thin, wolfish face. Her hair is slicked back into a ponytail so tight that I wonder how her head still has circulation. She beams at me. "Are you ready, Chapin?" Ah. British.

"Yes." I clear my throat, trying to calm my voice.

She hears the nerves. "Oh, don't be nervous. This'll be quite easy. You'll do great." She turns toward the cameraman. "Lighting good?"

He peers at his screen before giving a thumbs-up.

"So you'll just ask a few generic questions about the ball, right?"

She laughs, shaking her head. "Oh, no, no. I'm not the interviewer. I'm just the producer. This is going live in studio."

My heart goes into overdrive. "Live?"

"Don't worry, there's a five-second delay. Nothing to fret about. Very quick segment." I nod, beginning a deep-breathing exercise my mother showed me ages ago. Hmm. Maybe that yoga does come in handy after all.

As I sit in front of a backdrop, the producer affixes an earpiece in my ear. It's silent, no noise, no buzzing, no chatter. I look up at her, clueless.

"You must have done these a million times, no?" she asks me.

I shake my head. "I've done interviews but not, like, *live on the news.*"

"Oh, it's fine, it'll be great," she says breezily. "Piece of cake. You face the camera, talk directly into it. You won't be able to see the interviewer, but people at home will see you, okay? And you'll hear the interviewer's questions in your earpiece. Just speak normally. Very easy. Very routine."

The producer stands behind the camera, frowning as she listens to something in her ear. I spy a tiny earpiece. She nods, muttering, "Okay, okay, got it." She looks at her watch. "Ten seconds, Chapin."

Oh God, here we go.

The producer makes eye contact with me and then a wide smile lights up her face from ear to ear. She nods exaggeratedly and then points at me, mouthing the words: *You're live.*

Suddenly I hear a voice in my ear. It's Darleen Channing,

the news announcer in New York, or London, or wherever. I've seen her once or twice on TikTok, when her segments have gone viral.

"And, turning to lighter news, the world of debutante balls is rarefied air. Think gorgeous gowns, shining tiaras, and impossibly luxe dances. But it's not solely confined to the old world and *Bridgerton* on our TV screens—it's happening right now. La Danse des Débutantes is one of the world's most prestigious debutante balls, taking place this weekend in Paris. Today, we have Chapin Buckingham with us, one of the esteemed debutantes herself. Welcome, Chapin."

The producer points at me from behind the camera lens. *You! You're on! Go!*

I am the daughter of Ella Somerset. I've had cameras in my face since the day I was born. I can do this.

Activate.

"Thanks so much, Darleen," I say smoothly, my voice elegant. "It's a pleasure to be here with you."

"Now, Chapin, you're no stranger to the limelight. Ella Somerset is your mother. Were you expecting to be selected as a debutante, or was it a surprise?"

"It was not just a surprise but an honor," I say smoothly. "I've been dreaming of this debutante ball since I was a child, ever since I first heard about it. But I never could have imagined I'd be lucky enough to get picked. It's truly an incredible group of young women. La Danse des Débutantes is devoted to giving ba—"

"But aren't debutantes hand-selected from the same small

group of wealthy families over and over?" Darleen says, interrupting me. I can't see her face, but from the tenor of her voice, I gauge that she's frowning to look serious. "You, yourself, have enjoyed immense privilege since you were a child. In this day and age, where such a spotlight is shined on wealth inequality, doesn't it feel a bit antiquated and nepotistic to reward people whose sole accomplishment is being born well?"

I blink back my surprise and transition seamlessly. "You're right that wealth inequality is, indeed, an important issue. That's why I'm humbled by the mission of La Danse, which is to highlight charitable causes while giving back. My personal cause is—"

"And, of course, La Danse came under considerable fire when Storey Ricci was booted from the guest list after shoplifting from Sephora. Does that say something about the caliber of the individuals chosen?"

God, she really is trying to railroad me, isn't she? She clearly has something against the entire institution. Which—fair—I mean, I do too. But my distaste comes from an informed place.

She's just being prejudiced.

"I don't think it's fair to tar and feather an entire group based upon the actions of a single individual," I say primly, deciding to go for the jugular. I affix the same disappointed look on my face my mother has used on me my entire life. "You of all people should know that, judging by the anchor scandal on this very network last year. Or would you say that *that* single regrettable incident reflected upon the caliber of *you* and *your* other hardworking colleagues?" There's a moment of awkward silence as I reference last year's firing of their top news anchor for sexual-harassment allegations. What I wouldn't give to see her face right now.

But then Darleen comes back stronger.

"These debutante balls, of course, are centered around young women and their cavaliers coming together for a week of events, culminating in a big dance—the ball itself. But it's been reported that the haute couture gowns cost an astronomical figure: up to twenty-five or thirty thousand dollars in some instances. Is that true?"

"Can I just say . . . ?" I fight to stifle a sigh. "You know, these days I think there's a considerable lack of nuance. We live in this world where people want to believe things are black and white, either/or. But multiple things can be true at once, and that's one of the most revelatory things about the ball and the company I've found myself in. Yes, these gowns are quite expensive—because they're works of art. Rather than fast-fashion garments made by exploited, often-underage workers in impoverished countries only to be thrown in the trash after a few wears, they're handmade designs, crafted with as much intricate love, care, and skill as Picasso put into his own masterpieces. These gowns are symbols of the arts, of beauty, of the diminishing craft of dressmaking, and after they are worn, they're archived and put into museum collections alongside other celebrated works of art that demonstrate that just because something isn't quote-unquote serious doesn't mean it's any less important or valuable. These dresses provide food and rent for literally scores of workers in these dressmaking ateliers and are no less wondrous than the sculptures and oil paintings you find in the Met in New York or the Louvre here in Paris. I wish we lived in a society that could hold space for fashion as an art form and give it the respect it deserves."

I take a deep breath and continue. "And furthermore, I'm a bit disappointed in the implicit and rather tired narrative that a debutante can't also be intelligent and well-spoken. Not that it really matters, but these are some of the most well-read, well-rounded young women I've had the privilege—yes, *privilege*—to meet in my entire life. Finally, let's address the fact that fashion is often villainized as frivolous and shallow—not such a coincidence when you consider it's an industry associated with women. Every industry is heavily commoditized, and yet *fashion* bears the brunt of this judgment. So thank you for the question, Darleen. Thank you for giving fashion and the debutantes their proper due."

Darleen is stunned into silence. Finally, she speaks.

"Um, yes . . . Chapin Buckingham, thank you so much."

My earpiece goes dead, and the camera lights go dark. The cameraman and producer are both looking at me, slightly dumbstruck.

I pull the earpiece out and stand, offering it toward the producer sweetly. "That went well, don't you think?" I say brightly.

CHAPTER TWENTY-NINE

Piper
Paris, France

Inside our suite, watching Chapin's interview on live TV, I've been stunned into speechlessness.

"Hell, yeah," I say out loud.

Chapin bursts through the door of the suite. "Did you see?" she asks, breathless.

"Yes!" I exclaim.

"How did I do?" Chapin asks.

"Fucking incredible! Her face was priceless."

There's a knock at the door: It's Ella.

Chapin welcomes her mother into the suite, anxiety creasing her beautiful face. "So . . . ?"

Ella is hard to read. For a split second I think she's going to nitpick Chapin. But Ella opens her arms wide and pulls Chapin in for a hug. "You did wonderful, darling. Well done." Chapin melts into her arms.

After she disentangles herself from her mother, she's smiling. "Shit. That was stressful!"

"Grace under pressure." Ella nods, pleased. "Just like I taught you."

Chapin turns to me. "Credit to Piper. I nearly walked into an ambush."

"I didn't do a damn thing," I demur.

Ella eyes me warily but doesn't say anything. Instead she looks at her watch. "Well, that was delightful. Sadly, I must go. Zoom in fifteen with the president of TriStar, and my makeup is a disaster." She blows Chapin air kisses. "Congratulations, lovebug." Then she turns to me, as if she might hug me. She thinks better of it, instead sending a curt half nod in my direction. I'm not dismissed, but she clearly doesn't hate me quite as much as before.

Chapin watches her mother go, as if she wants to say something. For a moment I think I spot . . . is that sadness? But then she pulls out her phone, which is vibrating incessantly, and I wonder if I imagined it. She scrolls through notifications, chuckling and smiling. I see a few messages from people who saw the interview, all congratulating her.

I stand there awkwardly, unsure what to do. It's not like we're BFFs now. And Chapin is mercurial as hell. Finally, I make my way toward the elevators. "Well, I guess I'm gonna . . ."

"Wait," Chapin says, looking up from her phone. "I haven't thanked you properly."

"It's all good. You're welcome."

"No, I mean it. Not just a coffee. Let me take you shopping tomorrow. I meant what I said about fashion being an art form, and it's clear you need a crash course. You deserve to be here just as much as anybody else."

"Chapin. That's . . ." I feel touched beyond belief.

"I'm gonna help you win that scholarship," she says firmly.

I'm shocked. "But . . . don't *you* want the crown?"

Chapin looks sober. "You know how a near-death experience changes people? That's what that felt like. Screw this nonsense. Yeah, my mom'll be disappointed, but me just being here is enough. She knows how publicity works. She'll find a way to spin it into even more coverage for us. That's her gift."

I don't know what to say.

She smiles.

"You. Me. Avenue Montaigne. It's time for a shopping montage, people!"

CHAPTER THIRTY

Chapin
Paris, France

After an epic room service breakfast, I take Piper to Avenue Montaigne with the goal of building her fashion knowledge.

First up: Loewe.

As we enter, the shopkeeper looks us up and down.

Next to me, Piper stiffens. "Oh God," she whispers. "It's just like *Pretty Woman*."

But instead of frowning, the shopkeeper's face relaxes into a smile. "Chapin Buckingham! Welcome!" She then turns to Piper. "And hello, Chapin's friend. Please come in."

The shopkeeper leads us to the back and sits us in a large dressing room. Coffee is procured. Cushions are fluffed.

Next to me, Piper is frowning into her phone, her fingers furiously texting.

"Everything okay?" I ask.

She startles as if she's been caught.

"Hmm? Yes, oh, um—yes, totally." I give her a *talk to me* look.

She deflates. "This is overwhelming. I was texting my best friend, Seb, for help."

I laugh. "What help can he provide from America?" I glance at my own phone. "Besides, it's crazy early there. Unless he's the greatest early bird of all time, he's probably sleeping."

Piper flushes. "I don't know how to pronounce the store's name. Is it . . . *Lo-ewwww*?" She drawls "ew" as if she's seen something gross.

I gather all my strength to suppress a laugh. "It's hard to pronounce. I totally get it," I say, instead sounding suitably sympathetic. "It's *Low-ey-vay*," I say slowly. "The W is pronounced like a V." I rack my brain, trying to think of something to rhyme it with. "Sort of like . . . *low oy vey*? Except not, because that's a terrible example. *Low . . . bay-bay*? Ugh, no, still bad."

"*Loewe*," she pronounces carefully.

"*Ça, c'est parfait!*" the shopgirl says, returning.

The shopgirl looks at us expectantly. "Now, what can we get you into?"

She begins bringing out the new collection, one item at a time, so as not to overwhelm. I've been in the back of couture shops more than any eighteen-year-old should, but obviously this is Piper's first time.

I try to see it through her eyes as one avant-garde piece after another is displayed, remembering those magical times during my childhood when my mother would take me with her. She'd sit me on her lap, and I'd giggle as she'd make silly faces when the shopgirls left.

When did it all go wrong with my mother?

"Whoa, that's cool," Piper says, recapturing my attention. I look up to see a 3D top, shaped like a flower, that I'm pretty sure Zendaya wore once.

"Wow, that is cool," I agree. I feel inspired. "Let's try it on!"

Piper looks confused. "Wait . . . both of us?"

"Sure! Why not?"

Sizes are procured, and before I know it, Piper and I are retreating into separate dressing rooms.

"Are you ready?" I call out to her.

"No!" she calls back.

"Oh God. Is this another Dior moment?"

"No. This is a do-people-seriously-wear-this moment!"

I laugh. "Come on. Show me. One, two, three: go!"

We step out of the dressing rooms at the same time and stare across at each other.

The top is so whimsical, it looks like it could belong in the New York Botanical Garden.

"It's so unlike anything else," I say. "I totally get why Law Roach chose this piece."

After Loewe, we hit up a slew of other stores on Avenue Montaigne: Jacquemus, Paco Rabanne, Celine.

"I've literally never heard of any of these," Piper whispers as we pass by Loro Piana. "Like, who buys all these clothes?"

"Ella Somerset," I drawl, as we enter Loro Piana and are fawned over by yet another set of shopgirls.

At Rabanne, I'm poking around the boutique when I see Piper still, dazed, as if in a trance. I follow her gaze and see that it's locked onto one of their classic "Disc-o-Rama" dresses. I laugh, coming next to her. "It's gorgeous, isn't it?"

Piper nods, beguiled.

"Here, let's get a closer look," I say, tugging her by the elbow toward the dress. I pluck it off the rack and hold it out toward her.

She looks around, nervous. "Can we touch it? Aren't the salespeople supposed to handle the dresses?"

"It's all good. Everything here is *literally* off the rack."

Piper takes the hanger, holds the dress against her body, and goes to look at herself in the mirror.

"That's one of the most classic dresses of all time," I explain. "Audrey Hepburn wore it in the 1960s; Françoise Hardy was *très chic* in a long-sleeved version; it was in a James Bond movie. . . ." I rack my brain, trying to remember other examples. "Oh, I think Jane Fonda wore one in *Barbarella*?"

The shopgirl comes over to us. "Would you like to try it on?" she asks Piper.

She looks at me, as if scared to reply.

"Yes," I say firmly. "She would."

I recline in a chair in the dressing room, waiting for Piper to exit. This is so much fun: Now I understand why Mom likes to drag me shopping.

Piper peeks her head out of the dressing room, poking it through the curtains.

"Come out," I say.

She's blushing. "I feel dumb."

"Oh, come on, Piper, I'm sure you look incredible."

Her head disappears back beyond the curtain. I think I hear murmurs, and I could swear that she's giving herself a pep talk. I smile to myself. Okay, that's kind of adorable.

Piper exits from the dressing room. She's wearing one of the shimmery silver sleeveless dresses, the light bouncing off the mirrored discs in a kaleidoscopic prism. The shopgirl has smartly given her a bodysuit to wear under the dress, to make her feel more comfortable.

I gasp, exaggerating a tiny bit. "Piper, you look *amazing!*"

She stares at herself shyly in the mirror. "You sure?"

"Yes!"

"I'm not sure I can pull this off. I feel like a giant disco ball."

I laugh. "If you're a disco ball, then you're a super-hot disco ball." She looks back in the mirror, this time a bit prouder. "It's giving glittery space alien."

"Take me to your leader," she intones.

I groan. "And then you had to ruin it." We both laugh.

One of the sales associates hustles around the shop, looking for clothes in my size. I accept them gratefully.

"Thank you so much," I say.

Next to me, Piper is looking like Christmas has come early. "These are mine . . . to keep?" she whispers, shocked.

Before I can set her straight, the shopkeeper delicately jumps in. "We would be pleased to *loan* these to you for the week." She puts a lot of emphasis on the word "loan."

"It's a pretty standard thing," I explain to Piper quietly.

"Usually it's your stylist pulling clothes for you, but most of the stuff my mom wears on the red carpet is on loan."

"Ohhh, your stylist, of course," Piper says, as if she has her own stylist on standby.

We smile at each other. Another bonding experience: oil and water no more.

As we're walking down Rue Saint-Honoré to the Louboutin flagship, Piper looks at me sidelong. "I feel like you're *Devil Wears Prada*–ing me."

"How's that?" I ask.

"I never fully appreciated the artistry of fashion. I just thought, oh, cheap clothes versus expensive clothes, and that's that. Shein or Chanel, nothing really in between. And I figured that the expensive stuff was just exploitative pricing. Marking up because the fashion-obsessed rubes didn't know any better, and you could charge those suckers whatever you wanted." I pause. "It's sinking in how judgy I've been."

"Okay, ouch," I say.

"I don't think that now," she rushes to add. "It's fun seeing the whimsy of it all. It really is like living, breathing art."

"Exactly. Don't get me wrong: Some fashion brands *are* exploitative. And it's never gonna sit right with me that high-end labels buy up and trash all their old stock rather than dilute their brand by letting it go on sale to 'the poors.'"

"I'm sorry, *what*?" Piper looks scandalized.

"I know. It's awful. God forbid somebody find an Hermès bag at TJ Maxx—the horror! Although, to be fair, Hermès is amazing quality. Their bags are wearable art. But some of the other brands? Yeah, it's just a label slapped on mass-produced polyester and arbitrarily priced, like box seats at a sold-out concert."

Piper nods knowingly. "I always suspected that."

"That's what makes couture so incredible. It's made by hand, in an atelier, just for you. Wearable art. How lucky are we?"

She grins. "We are."

"Besides, half the fun of fashion is finding your own distinctive style. I'm a vintage gal."

Piper nods, looking thoughtful. "You know what's interesting? I think I like the loud stuff. The really fun, over-the-top, look-at-me creations? I find those so cool."

"Maximalist." I nod.

"I never thought that's the kind of style I'd gravitate toward."

"Well, now let's pull everything together. Step one, done. But step two: You've gotta learn how to walk in heels," I say as we enter the Louboutin boutique. "My least favorite thing."

Inside, the shopgirls seem dazed and preoccupied. Piper and I wander the aisles, picking up shoes and oohing and aahing. But nobody comes over to us. It's only once I have a pair of sparkly flats in my hand—give me comfort or give me death—that I realize something weird is going on.

I finally manage to flag down a sales associate. "Is it possible to get these in size thirty-seven?" I ask her.

She looks frazzled. "Yes, of course. So sorry to keep you waiting."

"Is everything okay?" I ask. "Everybody seems—" And then I see him. In the back of the shop.

Mr. Louboutin himself.

I gasp.

Piper hears me. "Is everything okay?"

My voice low, I nod my chin toward the back of the shop. "It's him. Christian Louboutin."

I must not have spoken as quietly as I wanted, because he looks up, locking eyes with me. "Chapin Buckingham!" he says. Weirdly, there's delight in his voice.

He comes over to say hello to us, giving me three kisses: right-left-right.

"Monsieur Louboutin," I say. "It's an honor."

"We've met before! Your mother and I are old friends."

We *have*? I don't remember. I simply smile and nod, etiquette lessons from my youth kicking in. "Yes, of course!" I turn to Piper. "Mr. Louboutin, this is my friend Piper Woo Collins. We're in Paris for La Danse des Débutantes."

His smile lights up his entire jolly face. "Of course. What a delightful event." He turns toward Piper, curiosity behind his kind eyes. "I believe I read about you. You were a later entry, but no less welcome! A very illustrious scientist, *non*?"

Piper blushes so deeply it can probably be seen from space. "That's right," she squeaks out.

He inclines his arm toward the shop. "Please, ladies, it would be my honor to have each of you select a pair of shoes for yourselves. My treat."

"Oh my God," I gasp, "thank you so much!"

Piper and I get to work, trying on a selection of shoes pulled for us by the shopgirls. Piper's a bit off-balance while trying on the higher heels, so I give her a tutorial in how to walk properly.

"Pro tip," I say. "Scuff the soles to make them less slippery." She looks horrified. "I know, I know, it probably sounds sacrilegious to purposefully scratch a pair of Louboutins, but this way you won't face-plant on marble. Trust me. I've been there more times than I'd like to admit."

"I feel like I'm Carrie Bradshaw in some sort of weird dream sequence," Piper replies. "I think the matrix is glitching. Me, in Paris, at a Christian Louboutin boutique, with Chapin Buckingham, learning to walk in heels. Definitely bizarre fashion Mad Libs."

I stifle my inner monologue—actually, Carrie Bradshaw was addicted to buying Manolos—and just smile and nod. "Yup. Fashion Mad Libs indeed."

Mr. Louboutin has been tinkering with the displays. He comes back over to see us in his shoes, smiling at Piper's visible awe.

"I must tell you, girls, I normally spend time with jaded celebrities, whose closets are already overflowing with my creations." He smiles at me. "I know you know something about jaded celebrities."

I laugh. "Oh yeah."

"So it's a treat to see you both here," he continues.

"Are you sure we can take a pair, Mr. . . . ." Piper struggles to pronounce "Louboutin" and stops herself. "Sir?"

"I insist. Have you made your selection?"

Piper nods, waggling her foot this way and that. She's wearing a pair of the classic So Kate pumps.

With a few swivels of his finger, a shopgirl appears, whisking the heels away to be engraved. When they return, the heel has the phrase *So Piper* on it. I think she's going to float away with happiness.

And with some hugs and kisses and well wishes for La Danse, we're gone, back onto the street, as if the entire thing was a dream.

CHAPTER THIRTY-ONE

Piper
Paris, France

When Chapin and I set off this morning, I was mentally prepared for maybe an hour of shopping. After all, my clothing purchases are mostly limited to H&M a few times a year for the sales—in and out in forty-five minutes, tops.

But five hours later, we're still at it. We've stopped for a quick sandwich at a cute little café, during which time I ravenously eat an entire baguette. I will never get over how impossibly charming even the random, throwaway spots are here in Paris. Even the pharmacies are chic. I half expect to see the cast of *Emily in Paris* filming in one.

After our lunch, my food coma sets in, and I'm ready to call it quits.

"Well, I guess we're all shopped out, huh?" I say.

We're walking back toward the hotel, bags swinging. I feel like Cher freaking Horowitz.

"Oh, absolutely not," Chapin says. "You're not getting away that easily."

She drags me toward a men's store named Erijan. It's got a garish Ferrari parked out front.

"Is that the Erijan Ferrari?" I ask. "I saw this on TikTok!"

"It's *one* of the Erijan Ferraris. They rotate them," Chapin says. "Some days it's the red one. Others, the yellow."

"Apparently, today it's the green."

"My dad is absolutely obsessed with Erijan," Chapin says, pressing a button on the wall outside the shop. I pull on the door, feeling more emboldened after our day of shopping, but Chapin stops me. "Oh, no, no, no. This isn't the type of shop you just *enter*."

"It's not?" I ask, feeling confused. "Well then, what kind of shop is it? Do you teleport inside?"

A male shopkeeper appears at the door, peering through the glass at us as if confused that customers would be so rude as to want to come inside. He unlocks the door, then opens it an inch or two, speaking to us through the slit like a reluctant neighbor. "May I help you?" He doesn't bother speaking to us in French first. Somehow, he instinctively knows we're American.

"We have an appointment," Chapin says authoritatively. "Under Chapin Buckingham."

As he does a quick head-to-toe scan of Chapin, his gaze softens. Apparently, he likes what he sees. Next, he does the same to me, taking in my hair, the monochromatic La Ligne set that

Chapin loaned me (which feels supremely like the outfit is wearing *me*), and my shoes. His gaze hardens again. Apparently, he does *not* like what he sees.

"I'll have to check," he sniffs, closing the door and relocking it in our faces. I can see him moving through the glass doors toward a table in the back, where an iPad rests.

"Is he getting a clipboard?" I ask, scandalized.

"Digital clipboard, but yeah." Chapin is very matter-of-fact about the whole thing.

"We have to be on a *list* to shop at a boutique?"

She shrugs. "That's like the new thing with all these boutiques. Honestly, I'm surprised this is the first time we're experiencing it today." She leans in, conspiratorial. "At Hermès in London, if you want to buy a bag, you have to get on a wait list. Then they'll text you a few hours before, and you have to scurry to the boutique, come hell or high water. It's common for people in Europe to book the next flight out, or in Paris to race to Gare du Nord for the Eurostar to St. Pancras. Just for the privilege of buying a bag that you might hate! If you miss your leather appointment, you're out."

"Wait, what? Why would you hate it?" I ask, confused. "Surely you wouldn't buy a bag you didn't love?"

"Because you need to buy a few different bags to prove to Hermès that you're worthy of the really good ones. The Kellys, the Birkins, what have you. They won't even let you spend your money unless you've demonstrated you're a worthy client. The Herbag bag is a pretty popular entry-level one." She shudders. "Hideous, in my opinion. Glorified burlap sack."

I'm scandalized. "Seriously insane. To have to beg to give them your money?"

Chapin shushes me. "Wait, here he comes. Watch, his whole demeanor is going to completely change now that he knows who my dad is."

Sure enough, the shopkeeper is all smiles, unlocking the door and opening it widely. "I found you on the list, Chapin! Thanks for stopping by—we're thrilled to have you with us today." He looks at me, expression turned from *ugh, who's this rando?* to *oh, hooray, an absolute delight!* "And who is your friend?"

"This is Piper," Chapin says grandly. I don't think it's my imagination that she's got a hint of condescending Ella in her voice now. I wonder if she even realizes she's doing it. "She's a very good friend of mine."

"Piper, welcome, welcome," he says, bowing at the waist. "Absolutely delighted to have you both with us."

As he escorts us into the salon, he's snapping his fingers at other shopkeepers, trying to mobilize them. "Coffee? Tea? Champagne? Water? What can we get you?"

"Some sparkling waters would be great," Chapin says smoothly. "We'd love to see the new collection."

"Of course, coming right up," he says, hustling into the back.

"What on earth is with the personality transplant?" I ask, amazed.

"My father is one of their best customers. He wore a hideous Erijan shirt once, and now he's in the club for life." She shudders. "Not my taste at all."

I laugh. "Then why on earth are we here?"

She smiles. "If you're going to get the full Parisian shopping experience, you have to shop at House of Erijan. Dictators, shahs, the occasional mobster . . . Erijan clothes them all."

"House of Erijan. It sounds like a bad reality show."

She walks into the back, and I follow. "They're known for their bespoke suits, but also for their insanely complicated perfumes. I'll be honest, their clothing isn't my thing, but their perfumes? Yeah. To die for."

"So that's why we're here?"

"That's why we're here," Chapin affirms. "Get ready to create your very own Eau de Piper."

We walk farther inside the store, entering into a massive foyer that reminds me of the Cheesecake Factory at the King of Prussia Mall. Marble everywhere. Dark wood. A sweeping staircase. The only thing it's missing is a twenty-page menu and a cheesecake display bigger than the Large Hadron Collider.

Suddenly a tiny, shiny man holding a tiny, shiny tray rushes over to us.

"I am Pierre," he says in a thick French accent, bowing deeply at the waist.

I look at Chapin awkwardly. "Um. Hi."

"May I spritz you?"

I back away, alarmed. "Oh, thank you so much, but—"

Before I can finish my sentence, he whips out a white paper from nowhere and enthusiastically spritzes the cologne all over it. As I cough, the air doused with the overpowering scent of leather and cigars, he waves the paper back and forth in a frenzy.

"*S'il vous plaît.*" He offers the paper toward me, thrusting it under my nose. "Gender neutral. *Very* subtle." About as subtle as an atomic bomb, I'd say.

"Mmm," I say unconvincingly, stepping away. "Very nice. Thank you."

"And you, Miss Chapin?" he says, turning toward Chapin with a deranged look on his face. "May I—"

But Chapin has already sprinted away, pretending to find something on the other side of the atrium supremely interesting. Pierre turns away, disappointed.

I walk around, investigating everything like I'm inside a science lab. I find myself in front of a gigantic, muscular mannequin—seriously, it must be seven feet tall—wearing an unsettlingly glossy dark green coat. I spy a sign saying it's from Erijan's gender-neutral line. Wait . . . is that . . .

"Is that alligator?" I blurt out.

Pierre appears from nowhere. "Not many people know the difference between alligator and crocodile. You have a very discerning eye." He slips on a single white glove and runs his hand lovingly over the alligator coat. I catch the price tag: one hundred thousand dollars.

Okay, he missed the point entirely.

Chapin reappears, her eyes wide. "You ready? I feel like we've soaked this up."

"Yes. Please."

We turn to Pierre. "Thank you," Chapin says grandly, inclining her head at him.

As we exit the store onto the boulevard, we start cracking up.

"I would rather wrestle a honey badger than drop a hundred grand on an alligator coat," I say, gasping with laughter.

"Or, worse, get it for free and then be obligated to promote the House of Erijan!" She shudders. "Pass."

"I think we should go back," I joke. "I forgot to create my Eau du Piper."

"The cologne is sinking in my pores," she gasps. "I need a shower ASAP."

"I need two showers."

Chapin and I burst out laughing again.

"You know," I confess, "you kind of reminded me of your mom back there."

Chapin is taken aback. "I did not."

"You did. You were all commanding and authoritative. It was kind of hilarious, actually."

I expect Chapin to start laughing again, but instead, she seems stunned into pensive silence as we continue on down the boulevard back toward the hotel.

CHAPTER THIRTY-TWO

Chapin
Paris, France

After Erijan, Piper and I walk back to the hotel, laden with bags.

I'm still mulling over her comment about me acting like my mom. I feel slightly offended. I mean, what was I supposed to do? Let the snobby sales associate walk all over me?

We make our way through a busy intersection with a towering Egyptian obelisk in its center. She looks at it admiringly. "Very Cleopatra."

"Yeah," I agree. "Iconic."

"I'll never get over how gorgeous Paris is," she says. "You'll be walking down the street and then, *bam*, there's a palace. You'll be crossing the road and, *boom*, hey, that's where Marie Antoinette used to live. It's wild."

"Wait," I say, awareness dawning. "Other than through the

windows of a car speeding by, I just realized all you've *really* seen of Paris is the hotel, the Jardin des Tuileries, and the shops I just dragged you to."

"Would we call it dragging?" Piper asks.

"Oh yeah. Kicking and screaming."

"Well, plus that restaurant the first night," she points out. "Oh!" she adds. "I saw the Louvre a couple of days ago too." But then she gets a weirdly guilty look on her face that I can't decipher.

I shake my head. "Unacceptable. We've got to expand your Paris education. And I'm not talking, like, hitting a museum— amazing though the Louvre might be."

"It *was* amazing," she agrees. "What do you have in mind?"

Fifteen minutes later, we're sitting at the bar at my favorite Parisian watering hole: Bar Hemingway, which just so happens to be inside our hotel.

Piper looks around nervously. "Are we allowed to be here? We're underage."

It's actually very endearing how nervous she is. I'm not used to that level of rules awareness and anxiety from my friends, who spend their lives assuming rules will snap for them like twigs in the wind. "Not here. The legal age in France is eighteen."

Piper is mollified, but only barely. She keeps looking around as if she expects the cops to bust out at any second and haul her away in handcuffs.

"I promise," I say. "It's legal. You're all good."

"So," she says, turning back toward the bar and picking up

one of the leather-bound menus. "What do you recommend?"

"At Bar Hemingway, there's only one thing to order, and that's the martini."

"Okay." Piper nods, looking excited. "Just like James Bond. And Serena van der Woodsen!"

Wow, she is such a dork. I suddenly understand more why she and Dalton have been spending so much time together. He can't stand "cool" girls.

"Have you ever had a martini?" I ask.

She shakes her head no. "But there's olive juice in them, so they're sort of sour, right?"

I stifle a laugh. "Yeah. Sort of."

We order two martinis from a cute waiter, who makes them with a flourish in front of us.

"*Et voilà.*" A dimple appears in his cheek as he sets the drinks in front of us. I can't help thinking of Raphael.

"*Merci,*" I respond.

"You have a good accent," Piper says.

"Well, you would too, if you learned French when you were a baby. My mother hired an au pair from Paris so I'd pick it up fluently."

"Wow. Fancy."

I shrug. "Fancy, or just trying really, really hard to make people forget she's actually from the middle of nowhere?"

"Touché."

"See? You've got a French accent too!" We both laugh.

I pick up my martini and hold it aloft, preparing to toast. "To making new friends, and to breaking old assumptions."

"Hear, hear," Piper says, smiling as our glasses clink together. "Very poetic." We cheers.

I take a sip of the martini and let the cold, briny concoction run down the back of my throat. It's delicious: smooth and complex.

But Piper shudders as if she's been smacked in the face.

"Not your thing?" I say, suddenly feeling protective of her.

"Martinis are an acquired taste—but alas, as the daughter of Otis Buckingham and Ella Somerset, I practically had martinis in my baby bottle."

Piper is still shuddering, her face puckering. "That's bitter as hell!"

I laugh. "Yeah, fair."

"People drink that *voluntarily*?"

"Well, now you can say you tried it. Let's get you something tastier." I peruse the menu. "Do you like sweet?"

"Who doesn't?"

"You'd be surprised." I set the menu down and wave over the bartender again. "So sorry, take two. Can we get her a raspberry Tom Collins, please?"

"You're joking me," Piper says.

"What?"

"My dad's namesake drink!"

"Oh," I laugh. "Right. Well, I guess you're getting the full Chapin Buckingham experience. There's a drink named after *my* dad at a bar in Tokyo. Except a Tom Collins is refreshing and delightful, whereas an Otis Buckingham tastes like peaty whiskey and regret."

The drink materializes almost immediately. I watch Piper's face as she sips it, keen to see how I've done. "Now *that's* good." She smiles. "Not even an ounce of regret."

I lean back, feeling victorious.

Piper reaches out with her fresh glass. "To second chances."

"I'll drink to that." We cheers again.

"Can I tell you a secret?" I say.

She nods, wide-eyed.

"I'll take Coke Zero over alcohol any day of the week. Except for an occasional, perfectly mixed martini. I especially don't get the obsession with champagne," I say.

"Yes! It's so . . . dry."

"Almost sour?"

She crinkles her nose. "Disgusting."

"Well, don't tell Lottie or any of the other girls. Actually, do tell them. Whatever. I don't care. They know all my quirks by now."

Piper studies me. "You're a really interesting person, Chapin."

I squirm, suddenly feeling uncomfortable. I don't mind picking apart other people, scrutinizing their strengths and flaws like I'm studying quartz under a microscope, but I don't love that analysis turned on me.

She must see my discomfort, because she looks away, downing her drink as if it's a shot rather than an expensive sipping cocktail. "Should we get back?"

We leave the bar in silence, each lost in our thoughts. In the lobby, I spy Face having a cup of tea alone. Before I can decide whether to take advantage of potential one-on-one time or to sneak off for a shower, Face sees me from across the way and waves me over.

"This was really fun," Piper says. "I know this is one of our only free days, so it means a lot that you spent it with me. Thank you so much."

For the briefest moment, my chest feels tight. In a parallel universe, I'm spending today with my mother.

"No, thank *you*. You saved my ass yesterday. It was the least I could do. Maybe we can try to hit La Galerie Dior before the end of the week. If we can sneak away from Amélie."

Piper turns and walks toward the elevator.

"Hey, Piper?" I call after her, before going off to see Face.

She turns back. "Yeah?"

"I had a fun day too."

Piper grins, makes a silly, pleased face, and then gets in the elevator.

"Hi," I say to Face, trying to keep my voice from wavering. I subtly try to smell myself without him noticing. Paris might be gorgeous, but after a full day of walking around the entire Right Bank, I worked up a serious sweat.

"Hello, you," he responds. He pulls me into a smooth hug, a kiss on each cheek.

"How are you doing?" he murmurs. His voice is low, conspiratorial. My heart begins a drum line like it always does around Face.

"Oh, good, good," I say, trying to sound breezy. "The week is flying by, don't you think?"

"Come. Sit." He takes me by the hand and leads me across

the lobby. My heart is now hovering somewhere around my throat. Face and I are holding hands. He plops down into an overstuffed chair and I follow suit next to him.

"I see right through you," he says, smiling.

"Oh?"

He nods. "Mm-hmm. I can tell you don't want to be here."

I laugh. "I'm not sure that exactly makes you a mind reader, Face."

He grins, reaching out and poking me on the leg. It's hardly a romantic touch, and yet my skin burns after his finger pulls away. My eyes move to his hands. They're long and thin, full of elegance. I can't help remembering what they felt like sliding over my skin. "Well, I'm here if you need to chat." He momentarily breaks eye contact with me, as if shyness has overtaken him. He studies his own hands. "You're a cool girl, Chapin Buckingham."

I clear my throat. "Likewise."

"I'm a cool girl?"

I laugh, embarrassed. "You know what I meant."

He pops back up and I follow suit. He leans in, giving me a slow kiss on each cheek. The scent of him lingers as the energy around us crackles. Before I can stop myself, I reach out and lightly pull him in. Our lips briefly touch.

"See you later, Chaz."

"Bye," I say softly as he leaves, hugging myself with longing.

CHAPTER THIRTY-THREE

Piper
Paris, France

"Waltzing is elegance! It is style! It is not clomping around like a herd of elephants!" the tiny, scowling French instructor screams.

The debs and cavaliers are all in the ballroom, apparently desperately failing as we pair up for our second round of waltzing lessons.

"Sounds like Monsieur Mathis could really use a week in Barbados," Dalton whispers to me.

His hand is resting gently on my shoulder, while our other hands are lightly clasped together. It's almost painful to be this close to him knowing he could be a much bigger part of my Paris experience if I weren't so worried about Amélie's warning to stay away from him. But since he's my cavalier, and this is an officially sanctioned event, I might as well lean into it. Because as much as I abhor dance lessons, they clearly have their perks.

"Again!" the instructor bellows, restarting the music.

As we waltz around the ballroom, I catch sight of Dalton and myself in a mirror. It's hard to believe this is real life when it's only been a week since I had a middle schooler yelling in my face because I wasn't allowed to pierce her nose.

"Wouldn't it be funny if we did something scandalous during the dance?" I whisper back to Dalton.

"What do you have in mind?" He cocks an eyebrow.

"Oh, I don't know. Suddenly all the debs break out into a flash mob. The Macarena."

"Cotton-Eyed Joe," he cracks.

"Now you're thinking."

"Please do not let me interrupt your private conversation!" Monsieur Mathis yells at us, materializing right in our faces. "Are we bothering you?"

"No, Monsieur Mathis," we reply dutifully in unison.

He looks up at the ceiling disgustedly. I can practically read his thoughts. A lifetime of training, and now here he is, babysitting. I silently curse myself. The last thing I need is word of my disobedience making its way back to Amélie.

"We will take five!" he says, resigned.

Dalton and I break apart, but even as we do, he casually fails to drop my right hand with his left. My heart begins pounding as we walk to the edge of the ballroom.

Every synapse in my body begins firing. I am acutely aware of the feeling of his skin on mine. Sure, we've been holding hands for the last half hour while dancing, but this is different. Dalton isn't holding my hand because our minuscule terror of a dance instructor will burn the ballroom down if he doesn't— he's holding my hand because he *wants* to.

And I sure as hell want him to.

Just friends, we said. Except now we're friends whose hands are still touching.

Dalton walks me over to two chairs at the edge of the ball-room, and we sit down together, our knees kissing. I'm sud-denly acutely aware of the proximity between us. The way his lashes frame his eyes perfectly. His lips, soft and inviting. The shadow of a dimple on the edge of his cheek. The way he's look-ing at me: full of curiosity and vulnerability.

It takes everything in me not to break every rule Amélie set out for me.

He's still holding my hand.

I clear my throat, nervous. I glance around the room, trying to avoid getting lost in Dalton's gaze, when my eyes lock with Chapin's. She looks down at our intertwined hands. Reflexively, I yank my hand away.

For a fleeting moment, Dalton looks disappointed, but it passes.

I'm saved from the moment when a small group of parents enter the ballroom, including Sea's dad.

"Came to see how everything's going," Mr. Reilly booms.

"He's a huge venture capitalist," I whisper to Dalton. "He specializes in environmental start-ups."

"Why don't you go talk to him?"

My heart thuds. "Just . . . go up to him? And talk to him?"

"Yeah! Why not?"

"I don't know. This isn't exactly a *Shark Tank* setting."

"Nah, everybody here knows what's up. The entire point of the ball is to network."

He has a point. This is part of the reason Amélie convinced me to come here, after all. I've been so distracted with La Danse I haven't spent much time taking advantage of the associated company. And it would feel like a squandered opportunity not to try to connect with someone who could fund my research. I guess this is a now-or-never kind of environment.

Dalton gently nudges me to standing, and next thing I know, I'm striding across the ballroom with my hand outstretched.

"Mr. Reilly! Hello! I'm Piper Woo Collins," I say, faking a voice that telegraphs *I am extremely confident.*

But instead of receiving me warmly, Mr. Reilly frowns back at me. "Hello, Piper." He shakes my hand, a lack of enthusiasm apparent.

Shit. He doesn't want to be talking to me. What do I do?

Suddenly Ella Somerset pops into my head. There's nobody more confident on the planet. She swans around like she owns it. I'll channel her.

Press forward. Have the confidence of a mediocre male showrunner! (Isn't that something Ella would say?)

"Mr. Reilly, I would love to pitch you my polymer," I say, trying to keep my voice from shaking. "I know that you're active in environmental start-ups, and I'm looking for investment."

Sea's dad looks at me witheringly, with a hint of pity. "I'm not sure this is the place, Piper."

My stomach falls out from underneath me. "Oh. Right. Sorry. Shit. I just . . ." Now I don't know what to do. I'm discombobulated.

"Good luck this week." Mr. Reilly turns on his heel and exits the ballroom.

I feel sick to my stomach. I thought I was being brave and confident, but I read the situation entirely wrong.

I return to Dalton on the brink of tears. He doesn't need to ask what happened. He sees it all over my face. He looks as if he wants to give me a hug. God, I wish he would.

"He rejected you?" he asks. "I'm surprised. People are normally chill here about that sort of thing."

I try to laugh it off. "Piper Woo Collins, here to make any situation fifty percent more awkward!"

But behind my light self-deprecation, I'm stewing in my failure. Even when I try to follow the rules, I don't fit in.

Will I ever?

CHAPTER THIRTY-FOUR

Chapin
Paris, France

The ball is tomorrow, and I've still barely spent any time with my mom, so after my Big Day Out with Piper, and following a deadly dull morning of etiquette lessons, I decide to take the bull by the horns.

Can we finally hang today? It would mean a lot to me

I wait for her reply to the text, terrified. It's as if I've just texted Face asking if he likes me, too.

Shockingly, Mom replies almost immediately:

I'd love that!

Two hours later, the two of us are at Le Comptoir, the Ritz's legendary patisserie, sipping cappuccinos and sharing a croissant. Or, at least, I'm nibbling on a giant croissant while my mother stares at it like it's a hairy rat.

"It's really good, Mom," I say, offering it toward her. "You sure you don't want any?"

Her lip curls in disdain. "I can't even imagine how many steps I'd need to work that off."

Ugh. I can't stand it when she drowns in diet-culture bullshit. I break off a giant piece. "Your loss. It's delicious."

"A moment on the lips . . ." she says, but cuts herself off when she sees my thunderous face. She knows better than to finish the phrase.

I decide to throw her an olive branch and change the subject. "So how has your week been?"

But she's now frowning at her phone. She doesn't even hear me.

"Mine's been great," I say, as if we're having a normal conversation. "Had my fitting at Dior. Went shopping yesterday on the boulevards." Still nothing. "Got abducted by aliens near the Concorde—they've discovered it's a portal to another universe."

"Oh, that's nice," she says absentmindedly.

I should find it funny, but I can't help but feel hurt. She's not paying attention to me at all.

Eventually, Mom puts her phone away. Her face is full of stress. For a moment I see her not as a mother but just as a woman—as a girl—as a friend. "Everything okay?" I ask quietly.

She sighs heavily. "We're waiting to hear back about my pilot. It's not looking good."

"Oh. I'm sorry."

She reaches over and pats my hand. "It's okay, lovebug.

Thank you. Sorry I'm distracted today. Tell me. How is the ball going for you?"

I pause. How honest should I be? I want to tell her what she wants to hear, that it's been great, but the words get stuck in my throat. It doesn't matter, since her phone buzzes again and she picks it up, frowning. "No. Absolutely not," she mutters as she texts back. Probably her agent.

I get it. Her career is important. But can't she be present with me for more than ninety seconds at a time? I've had enough.

"Actually, this week has sucked," I say flatly. I half expect her to keep texting and ignore me.

Instead she frowns and puts her phone down. "What? Why?"

My heart begins to pound. But the words spill out before I consciously decide to say them.

"This isn't me," I say simply. "I feel like I've been wound up like a trained circus animal this week. I only did this to be close to you."

Mom just stares at me, saying nothing.

"I don't care about impressing Amélie, or any of the famous parents, and especially not the *Daily Mail*. I don't care if I win Deb of the Year. I only care about you."

She blinks slowly.

"I did this to make you happy," I say. "To spend time with you. That's it."

Her phone buzzes again. Her eyes flicker down toward it.

"And I get it, you're busy. But . . . it kinda hurts that this is the first bit of quality time we've had, and you haven't been able to stay off your damn phone."

Her phone buzzes again. I know it's taking every ounce of self-control for her not to pick it up.

Her silence is weirdly emboldening. "I just want to feel like you love me for *me*," I continue, my voice small. "Not for who you want me to be."

She sighs. "Oh, *Chapin*." Her face is awash in guilt.

"I know, it's okay," I say in a rush. Uncomfortable Hallmark moments make me squirm.

But her face hardens. "Are you seriously laying this guilt trip on me now? This week, of all weeks?"

Wait, *what*?

I study her face again. It wasn't guilt. It was disappointment . . . in *me*.

"Do you know how hard it is to get a network pilot off the ground? In these conditions?" Her voice is brittle.

"I mean, yeah. It's always hard—"

"It's not hard. It's a goddamned *miracle*. I'm on the wrong side of forty. My last show was supposed to be my Primetime Emmy Award for Outstanding Lead Actress in a Drama Series—and it came and went with a blip. I have to battle upstream for every single role. It doesn't matter who I was fifteen years ago—all Hollywood cares about is your last project, period. For me to be *this close* to another opportunity, and to have you throw it in my face like this . . ." She shakes her head, finally picking up her phone. "Unbelievable."

I cannot believe the nerve of her.

Scratch that: I can.

I reach over, yank the phone out of her hand, and toss it

angrily into her purse. "That's all you have to say for yourself?" I ask.

She looks up, shocked. I rarely push back after she lays down the law. Now she blinks away tears, for real—except I'm unmoved. She's an actress. She can turn them on with a snap.

"You don't know how hard it is to be a working mom. Now that you're eighteen, I finally felt like I could breathe again. Like maybe the training wheels were off. And—"

"Spare me the bullshit, Mom. I'm not asking you to throw your career away. I just wanted an hour with you in Paris. To feel like I'm not the very last item on your to-do list. That's all."

"What the hell are you talking about? You're not a thing on my to-do list! I love you! But I'm not going to apologize for loving my career, too."

"When is it enough?" I demand. "You've already got an Emmy."

"Pfft. For a *limited* series," she replies.

"Mom, you're the highest-paid actress in Hollywood. You're a literal household name. What more do you want?" She belongs to the whole world, but she still wants more, she still wants it all. I'm clearly not enough to fill her up.

"I will not apologize for ambition!" For a moment I feel like we're on a movie set. She's slipped into her dramatic voice.

"I'm not asking you to," I say quietly. "But where do I factor in? Am I just a footnote in your obituary? World-famous actress, beautiful Hollywood icon—oh yeah, and there's her kid holding her back?"

She scans my face, looking genuinely hurt. "I had no idea you felt like this."

"Yeah, well, you'd need to pay attention to somebody other than yourself to figure it out."

I push my coffee away, standing up.

"Where are you going? Sit down."

I shake my head. "I'm done."

As I walk out of the café, I've never felt more alone. Like I'm stuck in place, while she's drifted out of reach, just beyond my grasp.

Maybe no matter how hard I try, I'll never measure up.

Maybe I need to stop trying.

CHAPTER THIRTY-FIVE

Piper
Paris, France

Today I have one of my rare free afternoons in Paris, so my dad and I plan to spend it together. I'm excited to put yesterday's humiliation with Sea Reilly's dad behind me. So maybe I don't understand the unspoken rules about how these people work. Is that a crime?

I tried and I failed. That's all science is, really: a series of hypotheses and experiments, each failure narrowing the possibilities, until, finally, observational success.

Onward. The experimentation continues.

Dad and I meet in the lobby. My dad's got a look of anticipation on his face and one of those glossy Paris guidebooks.

"They still make those things?"

"You expect me to wander around Paris with a TikTok video telling me where to go?" he jokes.

"Put the instruction manual away, Grandpa."

He pretends to look hurt. "I like these old travel guidebooks. They make it feel extra special." He flips through the book and opens a dog-eared page. "I went through it on the airplane. Found some great places."

"Oh God. We're gonna go to the Parisian Steampunk Firefighters Museum, aren't we?"

His face lights up. "Whoa. Is that a real place?"

"No."

"Damn."

We laugh, making our way toward the doors and stepping outside. It's a beautiful, sunny day. "Okay, do your worst. What's on the agenda?" I ask.

He looks sheepish, stepping out of the way of an ancient woman walking a dog that resembles a fluffy white hamster. "I have a few ideas. But now I'm thinking I'll save those for my non-Piper time. What are *you* thinking for today?" We continue down the street toward the Seine.

"Let's go to the Musée d'Orsay."

This stops him in his tracks. The Musée d'Orsay: one of the places Mom was always hoping to go. He closes the guidebook and puts it in his messenger bag, smiling. "That sounds perfect." I thread my arm through his and we're off.

The museum is a brisk walk just across the Seine from the hotel. Twenty minutes later, we're inside.

The d'Orsay feels completely different from the Louvre. It is a gigantic, light-filled space—exactly like the train station it apparently used to be.

Dad and I wander through the main hall together, examining various sculptures as we walk and talk.

"What's on the schedule for tomorrow morning?" he asks.

"You mean *other* than me forcing the waltzing instructor to question all his life choices?" I crack.

"He's teaching a bunch of teenagers to waltz. He brought this on himself."

I turn serious. "Tomorrow's the *Vanity Fair* photo shoot at Versailles!"

Dad whistles softly. "My daughter, the cover model."

"I don't think it's a cover."

"Their loss."

"We'll spend the morning at Versailles. We've got some downtime in the middle, and then our glam squad'll arrive to turn us into pumpkins for the ball."

"Mixing metaphors," he teases. He looks wistful. "I wish I could be there to see the photo shoot."

"Debs and cavs only. I think they're worried that sobbing parents will ruin the vibe."

We smile at each other. "Hey, your mom and I dealt with sleepless nights for two years straight. A few minutes of yelling, 'That's my girl!' as I snap photos of your magazine debut and moan how it all goes so fast are my God-given right."

We continue through the museum into the smaller galleries with famous Impressionist works.

"What's on the books for you tomorrow?" I ask him.

Dad shrugs. "I'm leaving it all up to Ethan—Dr. Hughes. My new buddy."

"Oh, we're on a first-name basis with the big celebrity now?" I'm trying not to laugh at how casually Dad is mentioning his new friend, seeing as Dr. Hughes is pretty much a household name.

"I am extremely charming. Is it any wonder all the celebrities want to hang out with me?"

"Humble, too," I tease.

"After he saved me from the moms, he's been showing me cool spots. We took in an exhibition at the Pompidou this morning. And yesterday we went to Shakespeare and Company. Tomorrow I think we're doing the Museum of Inventions. Did you know he started a corgi rescue charity?"

I smile at Dad's mention of Shakespeare and Company but let it pass. "Two peas in a nerd pod," I groan. "Typical."

"Hey, I still got some surprises up my sleeve for you," Dad says, grinning at me. "Don't think you can predict my every move."

"Sure, Dad."

Dad nods his chin toward the Van Gogh room. "You wanna?"

We examine the room of iconic paintings and self-portraits, full of Van Gogh's distinctive swirly brushstrokes and eye-popping colors.

The room is gorgeous and I can't believe I'm seeing these paintings in person. But everywhere I look, all I see is Mom.

Dad comes over and throws his arm around my shoulders, and we stare at one of Van Gogh's most famous paintings, a self-portrait that looks like he's challenging the viewer to a staring contest.

"I can't stop thinking about her," Dad says quietly.

"Me neither." I look across the gallery, where two women are walking arm in arm. They're clearly related, probably a mother and daughter, judging by how the younger one's face looks like the older one's DNA hit copy and paste. They chuckle, and the daughter leans her head on the mom's shoulder.

I told myself I wanted to stop living Paris for my mom and start enjoying it for myself, but it's hard when there are reminders of her loss everywhere.

"I wish she were here," I say.

We stand in silence, staring Van Gogh down, each of us missing Mom with every fiber of our being.

CHAPTER THIRTY-SIX

Chapin
Paris, France

I'm sitting on the couch in the suite's living room, mindlessly scrolling my phone, when Piper comes in.

"Hey," I say to her.

She takes one look at my tear-streaked face and moves to sit next to me on the couch. "You okay?" She's holding a plastic bag with the Musée d'Orsay's name emblazoned all over it.

I shrug. "Shitty day." I nod toward the bag. "It's a gorgeous museum, isn't it?"

She reaches inside and pulls out a few postcards depicting iconic paintings, including *Le Moulin de la Galette.* "My mom always wanted to visit. I thought I could frame these in her honor."

"That's sweet." For some reason, this makes me feel even

more depressed. Maybe because Piper had a mother who clearly adored her.

To her credit, Piper doesn't ask me to elaborate. Instead she leans over and plucks the room-service menu from the table. "Whenever Seb and I are depressed, we order takeout and watch movies." She picks up the room-service menu with one hand and grabs the TV remote with the other. "You wanna?"

After we each order a burger and fries, we settle in. Piper picks up the remote again and starts scrolling.

"No . . . no . . . no . . . ooh!" She turns to look at me. "*Notting Hill*? It's one of my favorites. What do you think?"

I smile, grateful for the pick-me-up. "One of my favorites too."

But as we watch the movie, I can't stop comparing Julia Roberts to Mom. In fact, I think she said once that she was up for this role. Our burgers arrive just as Julia Roberts is telling Hugh Grant's family how she's been on a diet since she was nineteen, which only makes me think more of Mom and all her bullshit.

Piper closes the door behind the room-service attendant, then sits back next to me. We dig into our burgers, but as I begin eating, she pauses. "You sure you're okay?"

I take a massive bite of the burger, relishing it. "That transparent, huh?"

"I probably should have suggested another movie. Maybe something that's not about a movie star and how hard her life is."

I snort. "Yeah, maybe. It's all good." I offer Piper the mini jar of ketchup and she accepts. "She deigned to hang out with me today. I thought we'd finally have some bonding time. Instead she spent the whole time on her phone frantically texting with her agent."

"That's gotta be hard," she says quietly.

"Nothing's ever good enough. It's not just me. It's her whole entire life. She doesn't see how lucky she is."

Piper dips a fry into the ketchup, not quite meeting my eyes. I flush as I realize how tone-deaf that might sound. Shouldn't *I* be realizing how lucky *I* am? At least I have a mom.

Piper doesn't say that, but judging by the look on her face, I bet she's thinking it.

And somehow it only makes me feel worse.

I know I'm lucky.

So why do I always feel so terrible?

CHAPTER THIRTY-SEVEN

Piper
Versailles, France

Today's going to be nonstop, with only twelve hours to go until the ball. But first, very important business: the annual *Vanity Fair* photo shoot.

Me. In *Vanity Fair*.

Even more *pinch me*: It's taking place in Marie Antoinette's private chambers at the Palace of Versailles.

Versailles was always at the top of Mom's to-do list. She didn't go to college, but she loved history and was always paging through magazines and books and encyclopedias, trying to better herself.

And of course there's that whole "if you don't learn history, you're doomed to repeat it" thing.

"*Bon!*" Amélie shouts. "Everybody, listen to me."

We huddle up, the din quieting. We're all gathered in one of the salons, which has been turned into a makeshift dressing room, lounge area, and staging area. The room is dotted with dressing chairs and standing partitions and lighted mirrors, seemingly every available inch of space taken over by makeup, clothing, or camera equipment.

"This is one of the most historic monuments in France. Versailles is of enormous cultural importance. I had to pledge my firstborn's firstborn for us to shoot here. You cannot possibly understand the sacrifices made and strings pulled to get us here today! It is the honor of a lifetime to be photographed for *Vanity Fair*, and it is the honor of a lifetime to be let behind the scenes at Versailles. You are all responsible for keeping your spaces pristine. If you muck this up, you will be on the first plane back home. Do I make myself clear!"

Like I said, dramatic.

"Yes, Amélie . . ." we reply dutifully, like schoolchildren.

Chapin and I exchange amused glances. She's across the room, next to Face. The two of them have been exchanging little glances nonstop today. I smile. Chapin was so depressed last night as we watched *Notting Hill*. She deserves a win.

Behind Amélie, Bardot holds a clipboard. She's wearing a walkie-talkie headset and looks like she's about to pass out.

The two of them survey all of us doubtfully. What could go wrong?

"We got this, Amélie," Chapin says authoritatively.

Within five minutes, it's chaos.

"I said *teal*, not *aqua*!" Peach pouts.

"No, no, that look is all wrong," Lottie says to a stylist, crossing her arms. "I refuse to be photographed in flats—even Bottega ones."

"This isn't on *loan*—it's *my* Boivin starfish," Zella says to her own hapless stylist, full of indignation. "We can't *swap* it for another piece."

I watch the debutantes as they throw one tantrum after another, equally horrified and fascinated.

"Piper, you go over here!" Bardot shouts above the chaos, directing us all with the precision of an air-traffic controller. I do as I'm told, walking to the far end of the ballroom and greeting a fashionable man and an edgy woman with a shaved head and blue eyeliner.

"Sit!" the man says in a French accent. "Now you're ours."

Over the next hour, one of them tugs and pulls on my hair—brushing it this way, curling it that way, spraying something all over the top—while the other begins spackling me with enough makeup to withstand a category 5 hurricane.

Chloe is at the station next to me, going through her own levels of beauty torture.

"Too high, do you think?" her hairstylist is saying to the makeup artist. He's got an English accent. Chloe's hair is piled on top of her head as if she's Medusa and her thick raven coils are snakes.

"Hmm." The makeup artist takes a step back, assessing Chloe. She's got one of those unplaceable accents. Dutch? South African? "Actually, I don't think it's high enough." Chloe and I exchange a look. *Help me*, she mouths.

Me first, I mouth back.

We both giggle.

Chloe looks down at her phone and then leans over to me, showing it.

"Did you see this?" she asks.

I shake my head.

"Sit up straight!" my stylist demands, yanking on my hair. I yelp from pain. He shoots me a dirty look, as if I've wounded him.

"What's this?" I call sidelong to Chloe, afraid to look down or turn my head.

"Deuxmoi posted about you!" she says, breathless with excitement.

"Do-who?"

Chloe laughs. "Okay, Piper, I know this isn't exactly your scene, but *really*? You don't know Deuxmoi?"

Again, I shake my head no without thinking, earning another rebuke from my stylist. "Head straight!"

"They're, like, the biggest gossip site," Chloe says. "Except they're not really a site. They're an Instagram account. But still."

"And they're notoriously unreliable," Chloe's makeup artist says grumpily. "Absolutely anybody can send in tips. They swore up and down that a client of mine got married, and I'm telling you, unless she did her makeup herself, I'd be the first to know!"

"Mmm, maybe she's lying to you, sweetie," my hairstylist says, giving her a pitying look. "We all know these clients have no loyalty."

"Please, she would never double-dip," Chloe's makeup artist shoots back.

"Sorry . . . um . . . but what did they say about me . . . ?" I ask tentatively.

"Oh right!" Chloe says. "They posted about you and Dalton!" My heart slides into my stomach like it's been liquified. "What . . . what did they say?"

Chloe looks at her phone again, her eyes scanning the screen. "Says he's your cavalier . . . you two have blazing chemistry but you're avoiding him like he's a bad disease. Speculates that either Amélie demanded you stay away from him or you just have awful taste. Sorry—just the messenger." Chloe puts the phone down, looking intrigued. "*Did* Amélie demand you stay away from him?"

I feel queasy. Across the room, Chapin is eyeing me suspiciously. I wonder if she's seen the gossip item too. We've been bonding the past couple of days. I want to stay on her good side.

I clear my throat. "Amélie didn't need to say anything. I have zero romantic interest in Dalton. I'm here for the dance, end of story." Even if Chapin can't hear me from the other side of the dressing room, I hope my declaration will get back to her.

"Wait, that was about you?" my hairstylist says. "*You're* the girl Dalton Buckingham is thirsting after? With *those* nails?"

What's wrong with my nails? I look down at them, embarrassed.

"I'm just saying a coat of nail polish and a cuticle trim wouldn't kill you." He turns toward my makeup artist. "You got any lacquer in there?"

"Yes, but she'll have to do it herself. I'm not a manicurist." I swivel my head toward the nail polish on the counter, causing my makeup artist to shriek. "I give up! We're gonna have to do a smokey eye!"

"Thirsting?" I ask, disbelieving, still stuck on what the hairstylist said about me and Dalton.

"Don't sound so shocked—you own a mirror." Chloe smiles.

Chloe's girlfriend, Margarita, strolls up. She's already done, her hair flowing down her back in goddess waves, her makeup bronzed and dramatic.

"Oh my God, you look insane," Chloe says, leaning over to give Margarita a sweet kiss.

Chloe's makeup artist sighs. "Thank God I already set your lips."

Chapin walks up. She's already done too, her hair piled on top of her head in a chic, throwback twist. She looks like a perfect, icy temptress from the 1950s.

"Wow, Chapin, you look incredible," I say, eager to stay on her good side.

The way she's looking at me, I'm certain she read that blind item. I don't want to go back to Chapin hating me. Everything in Paris has been a million times easier since she started actively liking me. But then she smiles.

"I cannot wait to wash this makeup off," Chapin says. She laughs. Oh, thank God. We're still cool.

"Sit up!" my hairstylist snaps. "I'm not done with you yet!"

Suddenly a loud voice booms from across the room. "Chapin, daaahling. I'm here!" It's Otis Buckingham.

CHAPTER THIRTY-EIGHT

Chapin
Versailles, France

Dad glides across the room and pulls me into a huge bear hug.

"Dad!" I yelp. "You're screwing up my hair!"

"Oh, who gives a toss about your hair?" he says impatiently, pulling me in harder.

He's right.

I melt into the hug, throwing my arms back around him. "You came," I murmur into his shoulder, slightly disbelieving. "Wait, what are you doing here? No parents allowed."

"Oh, hush." He finally pulls back, holding me at arm's length. "Let me see my gorgeous girl." I rifle my hand through my tight chignon, feeling like my head is about to explode from the pressure.

Behind Dad, I can see my hairstylist practically having a

panic attack. "I spent an hour on that," she whispers to another stylist in French.

"That's much better," Dad continues. "It's more you."

He turns, arm slung around my shoulder, so we're both facing the mirror. My hair is still in the chignon, but now, instead of giving Hitchcockian goddess with a stick up my bum (as Dad would say), I look like a much cooler seventies rock goddess. The hair is artfully undone, with messy tendrils around my face.

"It does look incredible," I admit. I look over at the hairstylist for confirmation. She reluctantly nods, displeased that all her work has been altered—but even she must admit it looks great.

"Now, as for that conformist makeup . . ." Dad says.

I squirm out from under his arm. "Thanks. I'll fix it later." Behind him, the makeup artist sighs in relief.

He shrugs. "Your funeral. None of this perfect-perfect, matchy-matchy business, though. Let's leave that to good ol' Mummy, shall we?" Dad sighs, stretching his arms exaggeratedly as he yawns. "I'm beat. Played a show in Berlin last night and didn't get to bed till five a.m." That's par for the course with Dad.

"Oh, yeah, that sounds—"

"Coffee!" he screams at nobody in particular.

This is what he does. He just yells orders and expects people to fulfill them.

"Um, Dad, I'm not sure if the assistants here—"

"COFFEE!" he bellows, this time even more insistent.

"I'll get that coffee for you, Mr. Buckingham," some poor assistant with a clipboard squeaks, scuttling away.

"Five sugars!" he demands.

I've long since learned there's no breaking him of that particular habit. Dad had already been a household name for thirty years before I drew my first breath.

Dad surveys the room. "So when are we shooting? It's *Vanity Fair*, no? Better be." He laughs. "Didn't fly all this way for some ghastly photo shoot in a tabloid rag."

I sigh. Part of me wonders if Dad would have flown halfway across Europe if it weren't *Vanity Fair* photographing us debs, but I squash that thought down. It doesn't matter why he's here.

The important part is that he actually showed up.

My parents so rarely show up.

"Yes, Dad. It's *Vanity Fair*. But they're not photographing you. Just me."

"Goody," he drawls, surveying the dressing room as if it belongs to him. He approaches a mirror and begins touching up his own hair and makeup. First he relines his eyes with black eyeliner—Dad pioneered the guyliner look—and then he uses a bit of hair gel to fluff up the hair around his crown. Even now, in his eighties, he's got more hair than most men in their forties.

Well, he's not a—*gross*—sex symbol for nothing, I guess.

"Once everybody's done with hair and makeup, we'll be doing individual shots and then a group portrait, I think?" I say. I don't know why I'm saying it tentatively, as if I'm unsure. That's exactly what's happening.

"Oh, hello, darling," Mom says, entering the dressing room. "I could hear your growls from the Petit Trianon." Dad grabs Mom and then pulls her into a deep kiss. Mom accepts it primly, surreptitiously wiping her lips after Dad turns his attention elsewhere.

I'm staring at her in disbelief, not because she and my dad are making out in front of everybody, but because I can't believe she had the balls to show up here today.

Mom just looks back at me, smiling. As if nothing happened. As if I'm just going to roll over like I've always done in the past.

"Um. Hi?" I say.

Mom's face falls into a frown as her eyes sweep over me. "What's this hair?"

"It looks better that way," Dad says.

"It looks too messy for *Vanity Fair*."

"It looks *perfect* for *Vanity Fair*."

"Otis, it's not a spread in *Rolling Stone*. This is a debutante ball."

"Which is exactly why she should look fucking rock 'n' roll, m'dear." He scoffs. "In all your years as a cover girl, you think you'd have learned a thing or two about the uncanny valley. Perfection is boring. You've gotta give 'em what they *don't* expect."

"Not when it's a full-page spread in *Vanity Fair*," she hisses.

"Enough!" I shriek. "What part of 'no parents allowed' did the two of you not get?"

Mom looks taken aback. But Dad's attention is already elsewhere. "Dalton!" Dad bellows. "M'boy!"

Dalton catches my eye for a split second—*yikes, here we go*—and then he approaches, giving Dad a handshake and a hug. Face trails behind him.

"Hi, Dad."

"Hi, Dad? 'Hi, Dad'? That's all I get? How about a 'How's the tour going? What's the latest with you? How's the record coming along?'"

"How's the tour going? What's the latest with you? How's the record coming along?" Dalton repeats dutifully, with just enough sass hidden that it doesn't trigger Dad's radar. Mom notices it, though. She looks at Dalton sympathetically.

"Bonkers, thanks for asking," Dad says.

Face steps forward and shakes my dad's hand. "Pleasure to see you, as always, Mr. Buckingham. I caught you on the Isle of Wight last summer, and it was *epic*. You are absolutely *incredible*. I cannot *wait* for your new album." He's effusive in the way that Dad loves, expects, and desperately needs.

Dad steps forward and throws an arm around Face jovially. "Always liked you, Miles! That's the spirit!" He wrestles Face as if about to choke him, turning him to face Dalton. "A little more of that effusiveness, eh, son?"

Dalton nods and smiles dutifully before making an excuse that he's needed in wardrobe.

Face laughs charmingly as Dalton retreats. "Duty calls, sir. I promised Dalton I'd help him choose something that doesn't scream *GQ* 2012. These stylists are *so* stuck in the past. Tragic."

Face gives my father a gracious little bow and then follows Dalton into the dressing area.

Mom watches him go admiringly. "Isn't he delightful?"

"Now that's class," Dad agrees. "Why don't you marry him, Chapey?"

My eyes bug out of my head. *"Marry?* Are you—I cannot even—"

He interrupts my spluttering, turning toward Mom. "What is he, twentieth in line?"

Mom shakes her head no. "He's rather far down the line of succession, I'm afraid. Two hundred and fifteenth, I think. Give or take."

"Not that you've checked," I mutter.

"Sadly, he's not even on the balcony," she sighs. "But he's still divine. So well raised." She turns to me. "You would be *amazing* together! The media loves a power couple, you know."

The irony of my parents plotting to marry me off while standing in the bedroom of an ill-fated teenage queen is not lost on me.

"I am not marrying Face! Or anybody. I'm freaking eighteen years old." Sometimes I cannot believe these two lunatics are my parents. How they get through the day in one piece is beyond me.

Of course, I know the answer: assistants. Lots of assistants.

"But God, imagine if he *were* higher up in line? Can you picture Chapin on the balcony?" Mom loses herself in a reverie, smiling. "Wedding at St. Paul's just like Diana. Horse-drawn carriage? We could get Sarah to do the dress. She did a marvel with Catherine's."

"Mom!" I shriek. "You're killing me!"

"Okay, jeez," she says, as if I'm the weirdo, not her. "Relax, Chapin. I would think you'd be ecstatic. I've seen the way he looks at you, you know."

My heart stops. "The way he looks at me?"

Her lips curl into a smile. "And judging by that reaction, the feeling is mutual."

I turn shy. "I mean, I have eyes."

"Yes, he's gorgeous, isn't he?" she sighs.

"Face like a Greek god," Dad agrees. "Body, too, by the looks of it."

I shudder. "Oh my God. You two are—I can't. Bye."

I scurry away from my parents, who have now switched gears and are comparing travel schedules next week. Mom'll be in Greece; Dad's onto Stockholm.

But as I walk into the wardrobe area, I find Face waiting for me.

"Your parents are a riot," he says, smiling at me.

My heart skips a beat. Did he hear them?

I lick my lips, trying to keep my voice even. "Yes, well, you try growing up with them."

Face laughs. "My father is the Earl of Debenham. I know a thing or two about kooky parents."

We share a smile.

"Face! You're up!" somebody calls from across the dressing room.

He turns back to me. "Gotta go." But then he takes a step forward. We're so close our bodies are only an inch apart. He smiles impishly. "For what it's worth, you'd make a beautiful bride, Chapin, eighteen or no." He leans over and gives me a sweet little kiss on the cheek, his lips lingering, before trotting over to the stylist waiting for him.

I'm dying. I'm dead. I just died.

CHAPTER THIRTY-NINE

Piper
Versailles, France

I take my place alongside the other debs, feeling a bit like a piece of furniture as the photographer, Cairo Mickelson, barks out orders to his assistant. (Seriously, what is with these entitled old men shouting orders to underlings?) I allow myself to be pliant, moving this way and that as Cairo tries to compose the perfect debutante group shot. I try to keep my hands out of the way. After being nail-shamed by the hairstylist, I took the time to slap a quick coat of OPI on, but it's barely dry.

In the other room, we can hear the cavaliers laughing and shrieking, sounding more like elated middle schoolers than like suave, sexy young men.

"OH, DO SHUT UP!" Cairo bellows at them in his weird accent. It's unplaceable, sort of vaguely mid-Atlantic, like in those old-timey Katharine Hepburn films my mom used to love.

The guys quiet for a few seconds into a low-level buzz before starting up again.

Cairo turns back to us. "You and you. Swap."

He's pointing at me. I step out of line, tentative. "Where do you want me?"

"There," he says languidly, pointing across the lineup at Zella.

She sighs, swanning across the room. Her skirt swishes as she glides.

I switch places with her, taking care not to ruin my dress again. It arrived via messenger only thirty minutes ago, and it took a team of four people to get me into it without destroying my hair and makeup. All the stylists and assistants seemed extra anxious, and I briefly wondered if the garment bag came with a note pinned to it that said CAUTION, THIS DEBUTANTE IS A TRAIN WRECK. I had to shut my eyes to pretend I wasn't basically naked in front of a group of people I'd only known for an hour, but strangely, adrenaline and the desire to just get in the freaking dress kicked in.

So maybe now I *do* understand how Christy, Linda, Naomi, and Cindy did it.

"I cannot believe he's moving me around like a vase on a shelf," Zella mutters as we cross paths. "In my country, I'm an icon."

"Ha-ha, yeah," I say weakly. I mean, how do you respond to that? *Me too—my Saturday afternoons working at the King of Prussia Mall are legendary.*

Zella was next to Chapin, and as I take my new place by my

suitemate, I understand why Cairo wanted us to switch. My gown and Chapin's look wildly different. The skirts are both made of tulle, but mine is whimsical and bursting with colors, while Chapin's is strikingly monochromatic. However, next to each other, Chapin and Zella's dresses are vaguely similar.

But as I come to stand next to Chapin, she grabs my hand. "Oh good," she says quietly. "Switch with me?"

"Huh?" I'm confused.

She does a little *psst* movement with her head, inclining it toward Imogen. "I would like *away* from her blood diamonds, thank you very much," she whispers.

Uh, I don't want to be standing next to blood diamonds either. But it's the least I can do for Chapin, since her helicopter stage parents care so much about this shoot.

"Sure," I whisper back, waiting until Cairo's attention is elsewhere and then quickly swapping places with Chapin.

The next time he looks up, the two of us are staring straight ahead as if nothing has happened. He peers at us, recognizing that something's different but not quite sure what. We beam back innocently.

"Nice one," Chapin whispers to me, giggling.

After twenty more minutes of minuscule tweaks and tinkering, the photo shoot finally begins.

When I envisioned a photo shoot in my head, it was a photographer standing in front of the model, yelling out things like "Love it!" and "Gorgeous! More!" and "Make love to the camera!" as the model twisted and turned her body every which way, from every conceivable angle.

And, in fact, that's exactly what happens.

He doesn't yell anything about making love, but he does shout encouraging words, telling us how BEAUTIFUL we all are and how much he LOVES it and how GREAT this photo shoot is going to turn out and YES, A LITTLE MORE and PERFECT, PERFECT, MORE OF THAT ATTITUDE.

However, I'm not giving any attitude, because I seem to be the only person up here who *didn't* attend modeling school. Everybody's channeling their inner Gisele, while I'm just sort of awkwardly angling my body this way and that, hoping I'm not the one ogre who ruins the princess photo.

"Angle your chin down," Chapin whispers.

"Huh?"

I look over at her.

"Eyes ahead, darling!" Cairo calls, his voice suddenly soft and caressing. "You look amazing!" Despite his abrasive personality before the shoot, it seems that he's a "catch more flies with honey than with vinegar" person when behind the camera.

I turn my face back to face Cairo, slapping a massive smile across my face that probably resembles something from a horror movie.

"Your chin," Chapin continues. "Push your neck out a tiny bit and then angle it down a few degrees."

I dutifully obey.

"Love it! Loooove it!" Cairo continues, snapping photos in a frenzy.

"Every few seconds, shift your weight a little bit," Chapin continues, muttering under her breath.

Roger that.

"Now shift your smile a bit. Wider . . . smaller . . . teeth . . . tight-lipped . . ."

I run the gamut of facial expressions, now pretty sure I look like an overcaffeinated serial killer.

"You're doing great," she whispers out of the corner of her mouth, even as she smiles brightly for Cairo's camera. She puts a hand on her waist and I tentatively follow suit.

"Attitude! Sassy! I love it!" Cairo continues. "Don't be afraid to be yourself, girls! You are the debutantes to end all debutantes! You are gorgeous! You are fierce! Own it!" I can't help it: I burst out laughing.

Cairo frantically continues snapping as Chapin follows suit. The laughter is contagious. First Margarita, then Peach, and then even Lottie starts laughing, high on the absurdity and delight of it all.

Chapin looks over at me and we laugh at each other, pure joy across our faces.

Cairo shoots us furiously, delighted. "YES! YES! You've got it! There it is! DON'T STOP!"

I look back at the photographer, still full of joy. Chapin and I are finally friends, I got a free trip to Paris, and I'm on track to get my scholarship and attend Columbia after all— hell, maybe Chapin will even get off the wait list. We could be roomies!

I feel blissful.

Click, click, click.

After nearly an hour of photographs, Cairo calls a break.

"Take thirty, everybody!" he calls. "We'll do the individual debutante and cavalier photos next. First up will be Chapin Buckingham."

Chapin's glam squad swarms in, pulling her away for a hair and makeup refresh.

All the debutantes wander this way and that, some sipping on Perrier out of straws, others burying themselves in their phones, AirPods nestled into their ears as they stare at their screens.

I stand aimlessly, taking it all in.

"Quite crazy, no?"

I turn to find Face. I smile at him. "You can say that again."

He leans in more closely to me, whispering in an overly silly voice, "Quite crazy, no?"

I laugh.

"So how's it all going for you, Piper?" Face asks. Cairo shoots us a dirty look—what are you still doing here?—and Face gives him a *mea culpa* gesture. Face gestures toward the hallway, indicating I should follow him to give Cairo and his team space as they set up the next shot.

I follow Face into the next room and find us surrounded by mirrors as far as the eye can see. "Wow," I say softly. "This is gorgeous."

"I know. Pretty wild."

"Have you been here before?"

"Oh God, yes. Too many times. In fact, I was here just last summer for a wedding. Four days of madness. Nearly turned into an international incident, in fact."

"A wedding at Versailles?"

"No crazier than a photo shoot at Versailles, right?" he says impishly. "Pomp is pomp."

I pause. "And money is money."

He laughs, surprised and delighted. "I know this can all seem quite overwhelming to most people, but you seem to be doing a bang-up job at it."

"Thank you," I say. "That means a lot."

"We can be a scary group to infiltrate—"

"You make yourselves sound like the CIA," I joke.

"And you just slotted yourself in like it was nothing."

"Well," I say gamely, "I wouldn't call it nothing. But I'd agree with you on the 'scary' part."

"Not *me*, surely," he says, smiling rakishly at me.

"Oh, you're the worst of the bunch," I say, going along with it. "Totally intimidating. Very unfriendly. Zero out of ten, would not recommend conversation."

"You wound me," he says, clutching his heart.

I smile, relaxing into our exchange.

He nods back toward the room where we just had our photo shoot. Cairo is bustling around, barking orders at his poor assistant. "Seems like you and Dalton are getting along well, no? If that gossip column is anything to believe . . ."

I stammer. "Oh—are we? Well, no—I mean, it's not . . ."

"Ah, so it's more than just a crush," he teases. "It's love. *L'amour.*" I furtively look around, praying Amélie isn't nearby to hear this.

"It is not love," I say firmly. "We're just friends."

"Really?"

"Really," I say firmly, in case anyone is eavesdropping.

Face leans in conspiratorially.

"That makes me happy to hear," he murmurs, his eyes fixed on mine.

My face and neck immediately turn hot. This is Not Good.

Face smiles, leaning down toward me. His lips make their way toward mine like heat-seeking missiles.

"What are you *doing*?" I shriek, pushing him away roughly.

Face looks confused. "Oh. Piper. I'm so sorry. I completely misread—yikes. Wow. I'm so sorry." To his credit, his own face is red now.

"I think we got our wires crossed."

"Yeah, no, totally. My bad. Argh." Face buries his head in his hands, and while it's semi-charming, I'm also horrified. Forget the Deuxmoi blind item—this situation is somehow worse. Consorting with not one but two cavaliers? Not to mention that if Chapin saw me with him, she'd jump to all the wrong conclusions, and then she would definitely never forgive me.

"Face?"

Oh, God. It's Chapin.

Face and I both turn to find Chapin standing there, a quizzical look on her face. "You ready?" she asks him, her voice tentative. "Cairo wants to get our deb-cav photos quickly, before he does my individual."

"Of course," Face says smoothly, hopping to attention. "Sorry, Piper, duty calls." He trots over to Chapin, a slightly guilty look on his face, and offers her his arm.

But as Chapin takes it, walking with him into the ballroom, she looks back at me, brow furrowed.

And as I anxiously look around the salon, I see Ella Somerset herself staring at me from across the room, furious.

CHAPTER FORTY

Chapin
Versailles, France

As Face and I go through our paces, posing this way and that for Cairo's portrait, my mind is racing.

Piper and Face?

It can't be.

Face puts his arms around me and smiles down at me tenderly. I smile back, desperate to make everything seem okay. I don't want him to see my confusion.

It must have been my imagination. It was kind of a weird angle. Sure, it looked like they were kissing—or about to kiss—but his back was to me. I couldn't see their faces. I couldn't see the space between their bodies. She knows I like him. Hell, *he* knows I like him.

They wouldn't.

She wouldn't.

Would she?

CHAPTER FORTY-ONE

Piper
Versailles, France

I feel numb as I make my way back to the ballroom for my photo session with Dalton.

My heart pounds as I wait in the corner, trying to avoid the TikToks that McCrae and Peach are filming together.

Dalton has a wide smile on his handsome face as he makes his way toward me.

"You look gorgeous," he says softly.

I blush so deeply, it's like my face caught fire.

"Okay, darlings," Cairo says. "Dalton, I want you to stand behind—what's your name again, dearie?"

"Piper."

"Mmm, of course, of course, Piper. Dalton, stand behind our *chère* Piper." Dalton obeys, but keeps a respectful distance between us.

"You're not playing 'follow the leader'! This isn't the school playground. Put your arms around her, for Christ's sake!" Cairo instructs.

Dalton leans over. I look back at him. "Is this okay?" he asks.

"Of course."

Consent-minded king.

He wraps his arms loosely around me, like in the old-school prom portrait of my mom and dad that's yellowing and gathering dust on a shelf somewhere in our living room. There's still an appropriate bit of room between our bodies, Dalton clearly hesitating to disrespect my personal space.

"Nestle in a bit closer, Dalton, boy. My God, she doesn't have cooties," Cairo says.

"It's all good," I whisper to him. "You're fine." Surely Amélie can't get mad at this. This isn't canoodling. This is PR.

Dalton nestles closer to me, gently tightening his arms just so. Now we're in a full-on embrace, my back pressed snugly to his chest. His arms feel strong and sturdy wrapped around me. He's so close I can smell him: all clean and fresh and soapy. Even his pheromones are delightful. But Ella's furious face is burned into my brain, ruining what should be an incredible moment.

"Oh, YES!" Cairo bellows. "Now *this* is *it*. Incredible." He picks up his camera hurriedly and begins snapping. "Now, Piper, lean back against Dalton . . . that's right . . . that's right . . . now Dalton, lean your chin against Piper's shoulder a bit . . . that's right, even more, drop it down . . . perfect, perfect . . ."

As Dalton and I obey Cairo's instructions, I feel a lump rising in my throat. I try to quash it. I already lost my shit during the group debutante session. I need to keep it together. I promised Amélie I'd be a professional.

Except Cairo isn't fooled. "Smiles, Piper! You are in a MAGAZINE, not at a FUNERAL!"

Dalton looks down at me, concerned. "Everything okay? Are you uncomfortable?" Why does he have to be so charming? And why does everything about this stupid ball have to be so complicated? I'm so close to the finish line—I refused to stumble now. I push down my anxiety and rearrange my face.

"Just nervous, I think. I'm good!" Dalton looks uncertain, but Cairo is calling for our attention.

"Eyes on me, please! You're at a photo shoot, not a therapy session!" I square my shoulders and lean into Dalton. I can do this. Literally ten minutes ago I would have died at the chance to cuddle up to Dalton. I channel Piper from this morning and pretend Amélie and her stupid rules don't exist. It seems to be working, based on Cairo's enthusiastic encouragement.

As the shoot continues, there's a moment where Dalton is looking down at me and I'm looking up at him, and everything fades away. It's like we're not in a fancy tux and a couture gown, not in a ballroom, not with a hopped-up photographer barking orders, but just the two of us in real life.

"Hi," he murmurs, his arms wrapped around me tightly. His pupils dilate as his eyes sweep searchingly across mine. He's so close I could stand up on my tiptoes and kiss him. I wish the two of us were in the real world, away from the cameras. Away from the stress of worrying what people like Amélie and Chapin will think. Away from the panicky memory of what just happened with Face.

In that other world, I'd reach up to Dalton, pull his lips down to mine, and kiss him. I don't think I'm imagining it. He seems to want me as badly as I want him.

But we're not in that world.

I take the tiniest step away from Dalton, widening the space between our bodies almost imperceptibly. A micro frown flickers across his face.

We turn back to look at Cairo, dutiful.

After our photo shoot is over, Cairo calls up the next two debutantes and cavaliers: Zella and Von Dodo (as I've never stopped calling Klaus). But when I return to the dressing room area, Zella and Von Dodo are still standing there.

Everybody else is too, staring at something in shock.

I glide up to Chloe. "What is it?" I whisper. "Is everybody okay?"

Chloe turns to face me, her mouth agape. She turns and points to something, and it's only then that I see my dressing area.

Which has been absolutely trashed to hell.

CHAPTER FORTY-TWO

Chapin
Versailles, France

"She trashed her dressing area? What a loser," Lottie sneers, barely above a whisper.

Piper's dressing table is covered in makeup, with powder spilled everywhere on the mirrored surface, as well as smudged across the floor. An open bottle of OPI nail polish drips onto the floor. It's a mess.

I turn toward Piper, scanning her face.

"Did you leave the bottle of nail polish open?" I whisper.

She looks genuinely stunned. But then her face goes from stunned to fearful as we all hear the *clack-clack-clack* of high-heeled footsteps.

Oh God, it's Amélie.

"*C'est quoi, ce bordel? Putain, mais non! Moi, je . . .*" Amélie swears furiously in French.

With every word flying out of Amélie's mouth, Piper's body language seems to visibly shrink. I swear, if she could, she'd crawl under the table.

Amélie switches to English. "What were you thinking, Piper? What insanity is this? I was explicitly clear—we are to be on our best behavior here! I had to pull ten thousand strings even to get this permit. You don't even want to know what I was forced to promise to Ludovine!"

But Amélie pulls herself together, switching from stressed to calm in front of our eyes.

Et voilà, fix-it mode.

"*Bon.*" She turns to Bardot. "We must clean this up. And *now.*"

Bardot nods, turning away. As she scurries into the distance, I see her bringing her phone to her mouth, dictating something. It sounds like she's explaining the situation to ChatGPT, asking how to get nail-polish stains off priceless ancient surfaces without permanently ruining them.

One of the official flunkies arrives, looking like he's about to have a heart attack. He immediately begins screaming in French.

Amélie puts her hand on his arm, and he shakes it off, spittle flying everywhere.

Amélie pulls him into the corner of the room, where the two of them begin shouting at each other as we debs and cavs watch breathlessly.

"Twenty quid on Amélie," Face whispers.

"I'll take that bet," Dalton agrees.

Every time Amélie seems like she's calmed him down, his temper flares up hotter than before. For her part, Amélie is a lion tamer, a matador, a crocodile wrestler. She zigs where he zags. She makes herself larger than him, then shrinks appropriately. She bats her eyelashes. She puts her finger in his face. She wails in agony. She shouts. I swear to Valentino, at one point it looks as if she pulls him into her arms and clutches him to her breast.

Whatever she does, after several mesmerizing minutes where the debs and cavaliers are in complete silence, the man stalks away. Amélie returns to us, emotionally bloodied but triumphant.

"*Bon*. That's settled. He wanted to call the police but through SOME MIRACLE"—her voice raises incongruously to a shout—"I have calmed him down and managed to avert disaster that would spell the end for La Danse." She peers at all of us, disdain etched across her gracefully aging face. "I know you are a bunch of messy teenagers, but trashing a national monument is a crime." She takes several menacing steps forward, as if she's about to throw hands. Margarita and Peach step back. Lottie holds firm, returning her gaze challengingly. Lottie has gone to war with the Sovereign Grant. She's not about to get bowed by some French lady—genuinely intimidating though Amélie may be.

"McRae, I would like to speak with you," Amélie says.

McRae's jaw drops.

"It wasn't me! I didn't do anything! This is—"

"I believe you," Amélie says smoothly. "I'd simply like to discuss keeping a lid on this. Making sure this doesn't make its way to the papers, no?" She affixes a hard gaze on McRae, who flinches underneath it. "If your father found out, I wouldn't want there to be any unintended blowback or unfortunate consequences." She doesn't need to finish the sentence: *unfortunate consequences . . . for you*. McRae nods, nerves visible.

"I won't say a word, I promise," McRae whispers.

Amélie looks satisfied, then turns and fixes her cold stare on the rest of the debutantes and cavaliers. "That goes for all of you. This story in the press would be our undoing. Do you understand?"

"Yes, Amélie," we all chant in unison.

"And as for *you*, we'll speak in private," Amélie says, turning toward Piper with quiet rage.

"But I didn't have anything to do with it! I swear!" Piper wails.

Amélie silences her with one furious, cutting look.

She stalks into another room. After several heavy beats, Piper reluctantly follows—a lamb to the slaughter.

"Jesus," I whisper to nobody in particular. "You don't think Piper really did that, do you?" She's thoughtful, not the type to leave behind a next-level mess like that.

"I saw her doing her nails," Peach says. "She was pretty bad at it too."

"And then she got called to her photo shoot," Lottie agrees.

Peach nods. "It feels obvious to me."

Not me.

But then I remember Piper going behind my back to *maybe* flirt with Face, and I feel like I no longer know anything.

CHAPTER FORTY-THREE

Piper
Versailles, France

I follow Amélie into the Salon de la Pais. She's several steps ahead of me, walking angrily. Her heels are making an ominous *clack-clack-clack* on the polished floor. From behind, even her shoulders look angry. I need to let her know this isn't my fault.

"Amélie, I didn't do it, I swear—" I start to say.

She stops so abruptly that I physically run into her. My face gets tangled in her bouclé jacket and her lion's mane, strands of artful balayage flying up my nose. I've gotten a mouthful of her perfume, too. I don't know my amber from my jasmine, but it's spicy-sweet with a hint of floral. Exactly the sort of expensive-smelling thing you'd expect Amélie to wear—but with a surprising edge, as if anybody who gets this close to her will find out a secret she's trying to keep. Very *not* House of Erijan.

She swivels around to find me spitting and gasping, trying to disentangle strands of her hair from my face. "Sorry," I say. "I just—"

"Do you think I'm an *imbécile*?" Amélie asks.

I'm stunned by the non sequitur. "I'm sorry?"

"Do. You. Think. I'm. An. *Imbécile*?"

"No. Of course not."

"Then why are you insulting my intelligence?"

I don't know how to respond to this. Is she just going to keep throwing out one aggressive rhetorical question after another, or are we going to get to the bottom of whoever's trying to sabotage me?

"First you skipped the yoga class. Then you *continued* to go behind my back with Dalton, making eyes at each other every chance you get. Next thing I know you are kissing Face Wellington. And now you are making a bloody mess of your dressing station with your sloppy ways." She grabs my hand. I instinctively pull it away, but not before she manages to sniff my nails. "Not fully dry. Just as I suspected."

"Amélie, I put the bottle away, I swear. I'm not stupid enough to leave my dressing room as a mess when you specifically said not to—"

"Oh, you're only stupid enough to break all the *other* rules?"

Well, she's got me there.

"Face kissed *me!*" I protest. Seriously, is this lady the NSA? How does she have eyes everywhere?

"I know you're a smart girl. Obviously. You placed first at the International Coding Fair —"

"International Science Fair" I mutter, unable to help myself. I regret the words as soon as they're out of my mouth.

"A National *n'importe quoi*. You are mentally gifted. *Très intelligente*. And despite your shoddy manicure work—especially your right hand—I don't believe that you would have assessed the situation and decided the momentary thoughtlessness of trashing the room was worth the lifetime of *disappointment and failure* you would experience after we had to boot you from La Danse immediately and you *couldn't go* to Columbia because you couldn't pay for it and your life was *ruined*." She says this last part ominously, as if it's a prediction, rather than a hypothetical.

"Exactly," I say, unsettled. "Good. Thank you. I appreciate i—"

"But what you frustratingly seem to fail to understand is: That's entirely beside the point. Perception is everything, and you are blowing your shot."

My face falls. "But—"

"You're completely out of the running for Deb of the Year. There is absolutely zero chance I can award it to you now." She looks weirdly furious. Did she *want* me to win? "Don't you remember? I had one rule: no bad press. So I really don't care who did what to whom—what I care about is protecting the reputation of this debutante ball and ensuring it remains immaculate."

Hypothesis: Amélie is mad at me for taking away her chance at more positive publicity. After all, what would garner more PR than me, the scholarship girl, winning the socialite crown?

"Yes, but—"

"I'm not going to kick you out of La Danse, Piper. That would be even worse press. Jettisoning our scholarship girl? On the heels of the Storey Ricci *scandale*? Can you imagine?" She shudders. "However! I *will* withhold the money if you don't perform to standards, as you promised you would. Forget Deb of the Year. Now you just have to survive tonight."

All the fight escapes from me. I believe her. She'd do it.

Amélie continues to scrutinize me.

"You know, if you have found yourself in somebody's crosshairs to the point that they're willing to sabotage *their* entire reputation in the hopes of getting *you* expelled, then something has gone quite amiss. I cannot concern myself with the emotional affairs of debutantes right now. But perhaps some deep soul-searching is required. Who have you betrayed? Who have you wronged? Find that person, and I don't care what you have to do, but *fix it*."

Okay, I'm going to set aside the fact that Amélie is literally victim blaming. The only person who might remotely have it out for me is Chapin. I'm unwilling to entertain the thought that Chapin might have trashed my dressing station as payment for Face trying to kiss me. I know she has a jealous streak, but she's not like that. Is she?

Suddenly my eyes widen. Unless it was . . . Chapin's *mother*?

Amélie nods, studying my face. "So you *do* know who the culprit is. Tell me."

I feel sweaty. I can't betray Chapin like that—even if she did betray me first. It would be crushing to her to know that her mother is interfering once again, and on such an offensive—not to mention illegal—level.

I lick my lips, my brain spinning. "Well, if I told you, you'd kick them out of La Danse, right? Or at least make such a huge spectacle that all the girls couldn't help but talk and it'd get back to McRae's father and then it would be front-page news. And then that would bring bad publicity to the ball, which would be terrible for *you* . . . which you'd blame on *me*, no? So maybe I'll just . . . say nothing. Try to be invisible." Amélie's mouth widens into a smile.

"*Bon*, Piper. You're finally beginning to understand how the game is actually played. *Bravo*." She wipes the smile away. "But I mean it. No bad press. Keep your head down. Don't make me talk with you again."

She turns on her heel and walks confidently back toward the debutantes. *Clack-clack-clack*. Her mane swishes.

I watch her go, distraught. This is my least-favorite recurring theme: rich people reneging on their promises when I've done absolutely nothing wrong.

I'm now alone in the hall. I take it all in. This gorgeous, ethereal palace, famous around the world and through the ages, synonymous with wealth and power and might and beauty. And yet darkness lurks here, simmering beneath the surface. This palace represents the aristocracy partying while the people toiled and starved. From here, Queen Marie Antoinette fled after a violent mob of women came for her, armed with pitchforks and a sense of righteous anger.

All that glitters is not gold.

But I know Amélie is at least partially right. On the face of it, this might just be a ball, but the stakes are high.

On the way back to Paris, we're all herded into Sprinter vans. I sit alone in the last row, feeling wounded. A few rows up from me, Face has his arm around Chapin, who has her unbothered poker face on. Neither of them so much as glances in my direction. I'm nothing to either of them.

I remember Face trying to kiss me and I feel my stomach twist in agony again.

Dalton comes to the back, bowing his head to avoid scraping it on the ceiling, and sits next to me.

"Hey," he says. "You okay?"

I nod.

"That was pretty intense. I'm sorry."

"Yeah. Thanks."

"I know you didn't do it."

I nod again, wanting to confide in him but forcing myself to stay silent. It doesn't matter that he gives me butterflies and makes me feel safe. It's not like Dalton Buckingham was ever going to date me, and butterflies can't pay for Columbia. In fact, now that Amélie is so pissed at me, Dalton can hurt my college chances. After this week, we'll go our separate ways and this whole thing will be a weird, distant memory.

Except for the fact that, if this actually works, you'll be at Columbia together, a little voice in my head reminds me.

Dalton gives me a little nod and small smile in return, then stands up and hunch-walks back to his seat.

As he walks away, emotion takes over me. This feels so deeply unfair. I can't remember the last guy who made me feel like Dalton does—and what's incredible is that he seems to like me, too. But I have to be sensible. I have to put my future first. And no matter how much Dalton makes my stomach flutter, no matter how much I lose myself in his eyes, he's standing in the way of my future.

It's for the best, I tell myself, blinking away the traitorous prickle in my eyes.

Conclusion: This week is turning out to be an unmitigated disaster.

CHAPTER FORTY-FOUR

Chapin
Paris, France

Even though it's been an exhausting morning, once we're back in the hotel lobby, everybody is buzzing, high on adrenaline and way too much coffee.

We've left our gowns in the care of representatives from the fashion houses, due to be delivered to our hotel rooms this afternoon. We only have a few hours before we have to regroup and get ready for tonight's ball. So obviously the smart thing to do would be to retire upstairs, take a quick nap. Maybe a face mask and a shower before our stylists and makeup artists and hairdressers attack us all over again.

But we don't do the smart thing. We do the deb thing.

The debutantes and cavaliers mill around, draping ourselves on lounges and chairs across the lobby.

These people might be weird, maddening, entitled, ridiculous, profane—but they're mine.

I plop down on a love seat, and Face quickly follows suit.

"I think we did rather all right back there, don't you?" he drawls.

"Yeah, it was a good shoot."

"You would know. Queen of the photo shoot. Not hard to look good together when I'm following your lead."

"Aww. Thanks." I'm touched. My eye falls on Dalton across the room. He's following a dejected-looking Piper, who sits down on a couch on the opposite side of the lobby.

"That Piper business at Versailles was weird, though." I frown, remembering how she drew Amélie's wrath. "It didn't seem like her at all."

Face knits his brow. "That's what everybody was saying. Something doesn't add up. She's not *my* cup of tea, but she doesn't seem like a bad person. Just a bit . . . clueless."

"She's actually incredibly smart."

"No, of course, obviously. I don't mean intellectually clueless. I mean . . ." He gestures lackadaisically to the lobby, where debs and cavs huddle in twos and threes. "All this. Socially." He pulls a face, groaning cutely. "Oh *God*, I sound like my father."

I laugh. "I think you're all right." I stretch, blood pooling in my arms, before standing. "I should head upstairs. Maybe catch a quick catnap before this afternoon."

"I'll come with you," Face says, standing up as well.

I think he means he's going to his room, but after he exits the elevator with me and then follows me to my door, I realize he means he's coming to *my* room. My heart pounds with excitement. Ohmigod. Is he . . . ? Are we . . . ?

My question is answered as soon as we reach the suite.

"May I?" he asks gallantly. He waits until I nod, and then holds the door open for me.

He's a real-life Prince Charming.

"Lock it, please," I request. "I don't want Piper—or housekeeping, or, God forbid my mother—waltzing in right now."

"Of course," he says.

The door closes behind us. I turn to find Face mere inches from me. We're so close, the proximity is dizzying.

"Is this okay?" he asks tentatively. He's looking at me with those big, gorgeous eyes, those mesmerizing lashes. I nod, entranced by his beauty, even as I'm not really sure what exactly I'm agreeing to.

He takes a tiny step closer to me, putting his hand on my face, and my heart begins jackhammering against my chest. *Ba-dum, ba-dum, ba-dum.* Holy shit, holy shit, holy shit.

"You're so beautiful it makes me nervous," he confesses.

"Oh, stop."

"No, really. I mean it." He blushes a little. "I feel very lucky to be here with you, Chapin." Face leans down and gently kisses me.

It's a perfect kiss, soft and tender, but as our lips touch and he lightly teases me with his tongue, it turns hungrier. He wraps his arms around me, and I lean into him, elated. I cannot believe this is finally happening again. I'm kissing Face. I'm kissing Face. DEFCON 1.

He's an even better kisser than last summer.

"You taste like peppermint," he says, smiling.

"Oh God. Sorry."

"No, no, it's good!"

Before I can say "royal wedding," we've migrated to the couch. He moves from my mouth to my neck, his hand roaming under my shirt. Every step of the way, Face continues to check in on me, solicitous. "Can I . . . ?" he whispers, tugging at my top.

I nod, breathless.

Face sits up, and I follow, and in one swift, sure motion, he whips my shirt off. Thank God I'm in a cute bra. His eyes light up like a kid on Christmas. "Good God, Chapin, you are impossibly gorgeous," he says.

I melt into a giggly puddle of goo, feeling my face and neck blush like a tomato.

"I mean it," he continues. "You are just compulsively kissable." He quickly unbuttons his own shirt and throws it carelessly onto the floor before pulling me down on top of him. We're a huddle of arms and limbs. My hands lightly run all over his chest and back, marveling at the feel of his smooth, muscular skin.

His hands migrate down to my bra, tugging at it impatiently. "Can I . . . ?" he asks again.

My heart pounds as I nod. "Yes, Face."

Yes, yes, so much yes.

CHAPTER FORTY-FIVE

Piper
Paris, France

After we get back to the hotel, I eventually make my way toward the elevators.

"Piper."

I turn and find Dalton, still with me.

"You sure you're okay?" he asks quietly. "You seemed kind of off in the van." I look down at the floor. I desperately want to confide in him.

"You can tell me," he continues.

I look over toward where Chapin was sitting with Face a few minutes ago.

Chapin.

Face.

The dressing room.

My face tightens again.

What is there to say? Dalton claims to be a good listener, and I know he's a good guy, but he's still Chapin's family. At the end of the day, if a disagreement happens between Chapin and me, she will always win. And I don't want to make a guy choose between me and his family.

Speaking of family, I promised Dad I'd text him when I got back from the photo shoot.

But when I reach for my phone, I realize I don't have it.

I paw through my bag, through my pockets, increasingly confused.

"Everything okay?"

"I can't find my phone."

"Oh shit. Maybe you left it at Versailles?"

"Maybe." I pause, trying to remember the last time I had it. I don't remember using it during the shoot. "Or maybe I left it upstairs? I promised my dad I'd let him know when we were back."

Dalton inclines his head toward the hotel's café. "I'm gonna grab a coffee. . . ." The message is clear. Do I want to meet him when I'm done finding my phone?

Well, yes. Obviously.

But I can't. Not if Amélie's around.

I keep a poker face. "Nice. Enjoy. See you later."

I turn and head for the elevators, but not before I see the disappointment on his face.

Outside my suite door, I think I hear laughs. I open quickly, not wanting to bother Chapin. I'll just pop into my room and then run back downstairs.

The first thing I see is a phone on the console table near the couch. There it is! But then I realize it's not *my* phone.

And then the next thing I see is Chapin half-naked on the couch, and a shirtless Face underneath her.

"Aaah!" I shriek. "Sorry! I didn't—"

"Piper!" Chapin shrieks back. "What the hell? Get out!"

I briefly make eye contact with Face. His reaction chills me to the core. He gives me a little smirk, making me feel like he's undressing me with his eyes, yanking me right back to the moment between us at Versailles. I quickly scurry out of the room, my heart racing as I get back in the elevator—still without my phone.

I don't know what to do. I don't know where to go. I find myself back in the lobby, as if in a daze. Dalton and I lock eyes from across the grand space. He's there, an empty chair next to him in the café. I could just go, plop down next to him, pour my heart out . . .

I turn away, overwhelmed.

Chapin has no idea Face tried to kiss me. He's a snake. But if I tell her, she'll hate me even more. If this week has made one thing abundantly clear, it's that my life is better when Chapin Buckingham is on my side . . . and is much, much worse when she's my enemy.

I'm completely screwed.

CHAPTER FORTY-SIX

Chapin
Paris, France

I bury my face in Face's chest after Piper leaves, totally mortified.

"That was so humiliating!" I groan. But then I look at him. "I thought you locked the door!"

He groans. "I'm such a dolt."

I throw a blanket over my body as I jump up and race over to the door, deadbolting it to ensure we won't be interrupted again.

"Okay, sorry. No more interruptions."

Face is smiling at me from across the room.

He opens his arms wide. "Come here."

I rejoin him on the couch. He immediately whips the blanket off me and begins kissing me again, his hands roaming over my breasts and underneath my hips. His lips are just as kissable as they were earlier, but now I feel unsettled.

Something feels off.

Face stops kissing me and leans back. His eyes sweep mine. "Is everything okay?"

I nod, pulling the blanket around myself. I try to ignore the strange feeling in the pit of my stomach. "Yeah. It's just—sorry. That was weird."

"What was weird?"

"Being walked in on."

Face shrugs. "She's your roommate, right? Nothing she hasn't seen before. Who knows . . . maybe she even enjoyed it." He laughs and then pulls me back into his arms, trying to undo the blanket from around my shoulders.

But I push him off again.

"What?" he asks, exasperated.

Okay, I don't love his tone.

"I have to ask you something," I say in a small voice.

"Okay . . ."

"Did you and Piper kiss?"

He looks shocked.

"What would make you think that?"

"At Versailles. I thought I saw something. . . ."

"Me and Piper? No. No way." He pauses. "She *has* been following me around, and there *was* a moment where she tried to kiss me but . . ." He shudders as if the thought is disgusting. "Pass. She's not even my type. Not like you."

"Okay," I say, feeling uncomfortable. "Sorry."

For me, the right response would be for him to apologize too. To tell me I have no reason to apologize in the first place. And then maybe to place the blanket back on my shoulders and say he's simply happy to be here with me, and why don't we just hang out and talk.

To make me feel comfortable and safe.

But he doesn't do that.

Instead he looks visibly annoyed. I swear, it seems as if he's trying to keep himself from rolling his eyes. "Do you want me to leave or something?" he asks in an aggrieved tone.

"No! That's not that I meant at all! Sorry!" I hate that I keep apologizing. But I'm so used to trying to keep the peace with Mom that he's triggering my conflict-avoidance button.

"I don't know," he says, now even more annoyed. "It certainly doesn't seem that way. It feels like you're blaming me for your rando roommate crushing on me. And that's not really fair."

I back up across the couch. "Wait, what? I'm confused." Why is he being so aggressive?

He comes closer to me on the couch, switching tones. Now he's being sweet and lovey-dovey again. "I'm sorry. I'm being such a numpty. Let's just put this behind us and try to start over." He reaches out to pull me into his arms a third time. He tugs the blanket off my shoulders again.

This time I push him away firmly, wrapping the blanket around me like a burrito. "I think you should leave."

He looks shocked. "So you *are* blaming me."

"You know what?" I say, gathering courage. "I'm done with this conversation."

"Wow." He stands up, his face cold. "I didn't expect this from you."

"Why are you being such a dick?" I ask him.

He looks haughty. "I'm not being a dick, darling. I'm just not willing to let a girl walk all over me."

"Calling you out for gaslighting me is not walking all over you. It's called meeting the consequences of your actions."

"And I certainly don't need to be lectured. Consequences are a two-way street."

"Good for you. I don't care."

His eyes bug out. He looks shocked that I'm standing up for myself. "What are you—"

"I'm serious. Leave. I don't give a shit who you are. You are cordially invited to get the fuck out."

Now he does actually roll his eyes. "Whatever. I'm outta here." He picks his phone up off the console.

"Good," I say, escorting him toward the door. "Bye."

"Crazy bitch," he mutters under his breath.

"You did not just call me crazy for standing up for myself!" I shriek.

But he's already hightailing it down the hallway. I think I hear him mutter "psycho" under his breath.

I slam the door behind him as loud as I possibly can, fuming.

I cannot believe I ever thought Face Wellington was dreamy.

What a dick.

Screw him, royalty or not. Onward.

CHAPTER FORTY-SEVEN

Piper
Paris, France

Our glam squad arrives: a SWAT team of hair stylists, makeup artists, Dior atelier staffers, and assistants.

Horrible nail-polish incident notwithstanding, I'd previously thought this morning was the height of glam. After all, how can you top getting ready at freaking Versailles for a *Vanity Fair* shoot?

Turns out, getting ready in your private suite at the Ritz comes pretty damn close.

The stylists have turned our living room into a beauty command center, with Chapin getting ready on one side of the suite and me getting ready on the other. The room is a swirl of energy, with hair dryers whirling, fluffy brushes flying, and an endless array of lotions and potions and creams. I've always thought of makeup as something that takes five minutes if you're *really* feeling inspired—but I'm more than an hour into my makeover and they're still not done. The front door of our suite is a revolving door as Ella flits in and out, nervously moving from space to space as if she's trying to burn off energy.

But things are beyond awkward between Chapin and me. There's a palpable tension in the room. Today has been a complete shit show.

"Stop," Chapin says coldly to her mother at one point, after Ella tries to tame Chapin's flyaway strands for the third time. I'm surprised; I don't think I've ever heard Chapin talk to her mother like that.

Seems like Ella hasn't either. She slinks off to the side of the room without saying anything, looking wounded. Instead of looking at Chapin, she turns to face me, icy.

I look away anxiously, not wanting to get into a stare-off with Ella Somerset. That's a game for stronger women than me.

How much did Ella see? Clearly, it was just enough to think that I was trying to make a move on Face, rather than the opposite. And then she retaliated by trashing my dressing room to send a message: *Don't screw with the Buckinghams.*

Which makes my walking in on Face and Chapin even more uncomfortable. I look over at Chapin in her chair, feeling like I'm standing on quicksand: no idea what to do, nowhere safe to turn. I was so naive to think everything in Paris was all sunshine and rainbows. I'm a mouse in the viper's nest.

But my attention is yanked back to the matter at hand—glamming—as my makeup artist begins, I swear to God, gluing eyelashes to my face. Is this how celebrities look so glamorous all the time? Foundation laid on with a trowel and eyelashes hot-glue-gunned to their skulls?

There's a knock on the door, and Bardot peeks her head in. "Knock-knock! Everybody decent?"

"Even if we weren't," Chapin drawls, "come on in. The more the merrier."

Bardot walks in, smiling brightly. "So. Big night ahead. How're we doing?"

"We're . . . doing," I say helplessly, as my makeup artist says, "Oops!" An eyelash falls onto my cheek. I catch a glimpse of myself in the mirror. The lash is hanging messily.

"Surviving, not thriving," Chapin deadpans. Her foundation is done but not the rest of her face—no lips, brows, or eye makeup—leaving her looking strangely ghostly.

Bardot looks down at her iPad, frowning. "So, are you feeling good about everything tonight? You know the schedule? You're confident about the dance?"

"I'm good," Chapin says firmly, dropping her jokey manner. "I got this, Bardot. Thank you. For real."

Bardot nods, looking overwhelmed. "Okay. Okay. Good."

"It's gonna be great. It's gonna be better than great," Chapin says.

I don't know where all this newfound confidence in our debutanting abilities is coming from, because from where I'm sitting, it's going to be a disaster.

Bardot catches the look on my face, and her anxiety flares up again. "And you, Piper? You sure? Everything better after this morning?"

I look over at Chapin, but she ignores me.

I nod, faking assuredness. "All good. Amélie knows that the dressing room thing wasn't me."

"I *told* her," Bardot says emphatically.

Now Chapin does meet my gaze. "But if it wasn't you, who was it?" There's a hard tone to her voice, as if she doesn't really believe me.

Chapin's clearly no longer presiding over the I Heart Piper fan club.

Ella jumps up and leaves for the bathroom, face buried in her phone.

"It doesn't really matter, does it?" I say hastily. "Emotions are high, shit happens, we put it behind us. And as far as tonight, we're good. Really. At the end of the day, it's just a dance."

Bardot's eyes widen. *Just a dance?* I suddenly wish I had some anti-anxiety medication to pass along to her. "Okay," she says doubtfully. "Well. Just text me if you have any problems?"

"I kind of lost my phone," I say, but rush to change the subject when Bardot looks concerned. "It's totally fine—I'm sure it's around here somewhere."

I can sense Bardot's anxiety growing by the second. "Do you want some chamomile tea?" I ask her. "Something nice and relaxing?"

"Get out of here!" Chapin laughingly says, shooing her away. "Forget the tea—go have a glass of wine!" As Bardot exits, glued to her iPad, Chapin calls after her, "Just not more coffee!"

I'm encouraged by Chapin's light laughter. But after Bardot leaves, her happiness drops and she goes back to ignoring me.

"God, Amélie works her to death, doesn't she?" I say tentatively.

Chapin looks over at me, face impassive. "Mmm," she finally agrees. "Nightmare."

CHAPTER FORTY-EIGHT

Chapin
Paris, France

Two hours into our glam-squad prep, and I'm still not fully ready for the ball.

I stretch my limbs, yawning, as the hairstylist yanks my head this way and that. She's giving me a deceptively simple hairstyle—long, loose waves coiled into an artfully messy bun, very similar to my look this morning at Versailles for *Vanity Fair*. However, I know from years spent observing Mom that sometimes the easiest-looking styles actually take up the most time.

First she needed to blow-dry my hair stick straight and empty a half bottle's worth of product into it for hold. Then she curled it into fat, barrel waves—never a mean feat, thanks to my lion's mane of hair. (Looks great, drives me insane.)

Then she began pinning up waves one by one, tongue pressed between her teeth as she concentrated. And now, even though my hair is fully up, she's seemingly still not done, slowly coaxing tendrils out at random intervals.

There's a knock at the door. Mom opens it, leading somebody in with a smile playing at her lips.

"Chapin," she says. "For you."

Three men enter in black suits, carrying briefcases.

"FBI? Are we under arrest?" I joke.

A woman enters from behind them. "Miss Buckingham, Miss Woo Collins, we are with Cartier," she intones dramatically. "We are here to—"

I gasp, jumping to my feet, nearly knocking the blow dryer out of my stylist's hand. "Jewelry!"

Cartier is sponsoring the ball tonight. In all the chaos and turmoil of today, I completely forgot that each of the debutantes will have the chance to pick out jewelry from Cartier on loan for La Danse.

After Piper and I each sign our lives away, the men open their boxes with a satisfying pop, revealing trays lined with the most gorgeous jewelry I've ever seen.

I stare at the gemstones, dazzled.

There are waterfall diamond earrings, ruby-studded bracelets that catch the light, and a glittering sapphire ring. Piper reaches her hand out wonderingly toward the diamond earrings. But my gaze strays toward the necklaces in the third briefcase: specifically a stunning showstopper with an ethereal alexandrite gemstone in its center.

"That's it," I say softly, pointing toward the alexandrite necklace. "That's the one."

The woman gently picks the necklace up from the velvet-lined tray and fastens it around my neck. The weight of it is incredible.

I turn and face the room. My mother gasps, tears coming to her eyes.

"Oh, Chapin. You are so beautiful."

She comes over and impulsively gives me a hug. I stiffly allow it. I'm aware I'm being a bit of a brat, but I've realized now that she'll always be like this. I have to stop making myself so vulnerable to her. It's the only way to keep from getting hurt.

She pulls away, hands still on my shoulders. "Do you remember the alexandrite necklace I wore to the Met Gala when you were little? It looked just like this. It's perfect."

Tears prickle at the corner of my eyes. My makeup artist will absolutely slaughter me if I undo her work. "I do." I nod, clearing my throat. I remember that moment so well.

"This is all I ever dreamed of," Mom says, gazing at me proudly. For the briefest of moments, I feel victorious. When Mom looks at me like that, like I can do no wrong, I finally feel like I'm enough. And then her gaze shifts down to my nails, frowning at the shade. "Maroon?" she says, wrinkling her nose. "Who chose that? You need Ballet Slippers. A tasteful, neutral pink."

"We're done here," I say icily. She'll never change.

She looks hurt. The Cartier team leaves as swiftly as they entered, and I sit back down to let my stylist finish my hair.

Suddenly my phone starts pinging. A push notification.

Both makeup artists' and one hairstylist's phones go off, too.

Whatever it is, it's something all four of us have subscribed to.

I turn my phone over, peeking at it.

Ah, it's just *TMZ*.

But as I peer at the news alert, my heart stops.

DEBUTANTE DEBAUCHERY!!! the headline screams.

I gasp.

"What?" Mom asks.

Piper looks over at me, now wearing the cascading earrings. "Is everything okay?"

Time slows to a halt.

I stare at the screen hard, as if blinking several times will wipe the headline away. Will change the fact of the photos staring back at me.

"Chapin, you're freaking me out," Piper says. "You look like you've seen a ghost." Slowly, I swivel my phone around, holding out the screen for Piper to see.

It's *TMZ*. With compromising photos of *me*.

In the hotel suite.

Today.

CHAPTER FORTY-NINE

Piper
Paris, France

As I stare at Chapin's phone, I'm trying to make sense of what I'm seeing.

Like, I understand that I'm looking at a photo of Chapin in our hotel room, on the couch, hooking up with Face, even though his face isn't visible. Objectively speaking, my brain is able to piece together these details.

Logically, I understand that this is what everything adds up to.

Chapin.

Today.

In the bedroom.

Half-naked.

But emotionally, I'm flattened. Why am I looking at half-naked photos of Chapin? Why is *TMZ* publishing them? And why are they now public, on Chapin's phone?

The makeup artist gasps. "*Putain, non.* Is this you?" she asks Chapin.

"What the hell *is* this?" Ella shrieks.

Chapin doesn't say anything. She turns and stares at the phone again, as if she's finding it similarly impossible to comprehend. We're both at a loss.

All I can think is: Who would *do* that to her? And *why*?

Somebody wants both of us to go down.

There's a sharp, insistent rapping on the door of the suite, rapid-fire: KNOCK-KNOCK-KNOCK-KNOCK-KNOCK.

I'm closest to the door so I move to open it. Dalton enters the suite, clearly distressed.

He doesn't even look at me, instead laser-focused on Chapin. "Are you okay? Have you seen it?" he asks.

Chapin nods, looking faint.

Only now does Dalton make eye contact with me. We share a distressed look. "What the fuck?" he asks.

"It's awful," I agree.

Ella has her head in her hands.

"What is this horseshit?" she demands. "Is this really you?"

I feel sick to my stomach as I realize that Ella is about to yell at her daughter. The only thing worse than bad press is bad *naked* press.

Chapin waits several beats before responding. I know her well enough by now. She's gathering her courage. "Yes." Chapin nods, her voice steely.

"Unbelievable," Ella seethes. "How *dare* they? This is despicable. I'm so sorry, honey." She pulls Chapin into her arms, hugging her fiercely.

Oh, thank God. I feel mildly less sick to my stomach realizing Ella isn't slut-shaming Chapin. Far from it. In fact, she's being protective. But then I'm confused: Isn't Ella the one who orchestrated my dressing-area disaster this morning at Versailles? Did she whip up this publicity for Chapin in some sort of sick bid to gain sympathy?

I know Ella Somerset isn't normal, but she's not *that* big of a monster, is she?

Dalton sinks onto the couch in the center of the suite as Ella begins stalking the exterior, pacing like a tiger in heat. "They messed with the wrong family," she mutters, scrolling through her phone.

Chapin's got a nervous look on her face. She must have been on the receiving end of this version of Ella before. "What are you going to do, Mom?"

"Don't you worry, lovebug," Ella says. "I'll fix it. We just need to—yes, hello? Yes, it's Ella. Ella Somerset, that's right." Ella first smiles through the phone, on the receiving end of some pleasantries, and then begins nodding in a frenzy. "Mm-hmm, mm-hmm, exactly. Well, you can imagine my surprise . . . mm-hmm, mmm-hmm . . . right? I mean! That's exactly what I said . . . mm-hmm . . . well, no, that's actually not true, not that kind of publicity, not at all, in fact—"

"Did somebody really just try to tell my mother that all publicity is good publicity, even when it comes to revenge porn of her eighteen-year-old daughter?" Dalton snarls. I've never seen him so angry.

Chapin looks across the suite at him, alarmed. "Revenge porn?"

"I don't know, what else would you call it?" he asks. "Sure feels to me like somebody has it out for you." He looks across the room at me, his gaze fixing on me intently. "You and Piper both, actually."

I watch Ella on the phone, feeling helpless. Part of me wants to scream: *It's her! The phone call is coming from inside the house!*

I mean, after all, Ella clearly already has *TMZ* on speed dial.

But then Ella gasps, horrified.

So, look, Ella Somerset is an award-winning actress. We've all seen that clip of her in *Double or Nothing*, where she bluffs in the final scene to save her sister's life. It's practically a master class in America's Sweetheart Wins Her Oscar.

But something in the tone of her voice feels like she's not acting. Her voice is strangled. Her face goes red. The pitch goes up an octave. And she says, "Wait? I need you to say that again. I must be certain I'm understanding you."

She grips her cell phone so tightly her fingers go white.

And she doesn't say anything else for the remainder of the phone call, simply nodding, speechless.

As she hangs up, Ella takes a deep breath, as if centering herself. She puts the phone calmly back into her purse. And then she turns to face the room, knowing that every eye is on her.

"Well?" Dalton asks.

Ella closes her eyes and looks up at the sky, as if summoning the heavens. (Okay, now it does feel a little like she's acting.) "The photos came from Piper's email," she says quietly.

My heart stops.

No, really. It stops. It skips a beat. It falls into my stomach and it leaps into my chest and every other cliché you've ever heard and it's all actually true because I cannot believe what she's saying and, for a split second, I feel like I'm genuinely going to die.

Ella opens her eyes and locks her gaze onto mine. It's so steely and penetrating that I feel like I'm Jon Snow being stalked by a White Walker.

"Ella," I say. "I didn't—I would never—"

"But you *did*, PWCScience@gmail.com," she says, full of quiet fury. "*You* sent those images to *TMZ*. You took compromising photos of Chapin—Chapin who trusted you. Chapin who opened her home to you—and you *sold* them to *TMZ*. You threw my sweet Chapin under the bus in your sick, disgusting attempt to win the debutante crown for yourself and secure your pathetic future. Appalling." Ella is practically spitting at me, her words are so clipped and angry.

"Ms. Somerset, I swear—"

"I don't want to hear it!" she shrieks. "I saw you leaping onto Face today, trying to kiss him! After all Chapin did for you!"

Chapin quickly swirls to catch my expression. Dalton frowns.

"Chapin," I say, the panic rising in my voice. "You have to believe me."

Chapin backs up, refusing to make eye contact with me. She clutches her necklace, looking pained, as if somebody has stabbed her.

I feel desperate. Why won't anybody believe me?

Dalton.

I swivel toward him, stepping closer. "Dalton, you *know* me. You know I would never do this. I would never, ever do anything to hurt Chapin like that. I wouldn't do that to my worst enemy. I'm not capable of it."

He takes a tiny step back from me.

"I don't even have my phone. Remember? I told you I lost it."

"I *can't* believe you would do something like this, Piper," he says quietly, agreeing with me. "It's not in your nature."

"Dalton!" Ella shrieks. "You're choosing her over your own flesh and blood!"

"Thank you, Dalton," I say, relieved even as I'm still sick to my stomach.

"But . . ." he says, and my heart sinks again. "It is . . . weird."

Oh. Shit.

"When you went back to the suite for your phone. Was Chapin there?"

"Yes, but—"

"With Face?"

I swallow. "Yeah, but—"

"Who you kissed?"

"It wasn't like that at all—"

"He rejected her, and Piper lashed out," Ella says with authority in her voice.

"It feels convenient that you came back upstairs, supposedly looking for your phone, and supposedly couldn't find it, and at that exact same time, a photograph was being emailed to *TMZ* from your phone of Chapin kissing the guy who rejected you? It doesn't look great," Dalton says.

"I trusted you," Chapin says, finally speaking.

"Chapin, I promise—"

"I thought we were friends."

"We are, I'm so grateful—"

"I didn't imagine it." Chapin sounds like she's foggy, underwater. "You did kiss Face."

Everybody's heads swivel toward me again.

I put my hands up, self-protective. "*He* kissed *me*."

"Wow," Ella says, voice hard. "So you admit it."

"I didn't let him! We didn't even kiss—"

"Get out," Chapin says, furious.

"But—"

"I mean it, Piper. Get out. I don't ever want to see you ever again. You're dead to me." She closes the door, kicking me out.

I back into the hallway, dizzy and confused.

Chapin's voice rings clear and strong through the door:

"Get me Amélie now. Piper's *done*."

CHAPTER FIFTY

Chapin
Paris, France

"I cannot believe the nerve of that girl," my hairstylist says, running her fingers soothingly through my hair. "Don't worry about her, love. We'll sort you out."

I stare at her, unable to focus. All I can think is, why does she have a British accent?

We're in Paris. Shouldn't she sound French?

"Where are you from?" I ask.

She blinks back surprise. "London."

"Why are you here?"

"Because I live here?"

"Oh. Okay." I nod, staring at myself in the mirror, feeling a million miles away.

"Poor love, she's cracking up," my hairstylist whispers to my makeup artist. "Talking gibberish."

I can hear you! I want to scream. But I'm used to being invisible to everybody. For the first time in my life, *I'm* the story. And, surprise surprise, I hate it.

I feel like I'm underwater. I fight back panic, trying to center myself. *Breathe in, breathe out. Breathe in, breathe out.* What's that meditation my mom always does?

Nam-myoho-renge-kyo. Nam-myo-ho-renge-kyo. I silently repeat it to myself over and over, as if the rhythmic chanting will somehow erase the betrayal ripping me in two.

I don't care about the dumb photos. I've shown plenty of skin on the beaches of Miami, practically naked. It's not about that.

It's the fact that I let my guard down. I trusted Piper.

Our Upper East Side world seems picture-perfect, but it can be so complicated. From the time I was eight years old, when Ava Cooper lied to everybody in second grade and told them she saw me kick my nanny because she was mad I took Kiara Stevens to Mom's movie premiere, I've known that you have to be careful. Choosing the right friends is everything: not so desperate they'll want what you have, not so indifferent they won't notice when you're hurting. I've cultivated my circle carefully. No, Lottie and McRae and Peach aren't perfect. But they understand the unique pressures of our world.

They know the rules.

I thought Piper was one of the good ones. It didn't matter where she came from, it didn't matter if she didn't know the rules: She was a friend. But it turns out she's just like Ava Cooper: She wanted what I had, and she hated me for having more, so she betrayed me.

She's not different at all.

CHAPTER FIFTY-ONE

Piper
Paris, France

Outside in the hallway, I sink to the floor. I'm barefoot in my debutante dress, and it's not lost on me that I suddenly feel a little bit like Julia Roberts in *My Best Friend's Wedding.*

Amélie rushes down the hallway toward me. I steel myself. Here we go.

"I know, I know," I say glumly.

"The photos," Amélie replies, equally downcast.

Look at us. Two peas in a glum pod.

"You put trust in me, and somehow I screwed it up, yet again. I let down my end of the bargain."

Goodbye, Columbia. Goodbye, Dalton. Goodbye, Chapin.

I failed.

But Amélie gently places a hand on my shoulder. She gingerly sits on the floor next to me, primly smoothing out her expensive suit. It's Chanel, by the looks of it. Well tailored. Well loved. Full of care. Even in this short week, my thinking has been transformed.

Amélie pats me on the shoulder sympathetically, if awkwardly.

"You tried," she says. "Going away quietly is for the best, for everybody. If you don't make a fuss, perhaps we can . . . work something out after."

It all comes back to publicity for her.

Of course, I'm not surprised she's ejecting me. But faced with the reality of getting booted from La Danse, my competitive juices stir.

"I'm sure it must feel unfair—" she begins.

I interrupt her. "You know it wasn't me. With my literal future on the line, you really think I would have stirred up *merde* twice in one day?"

"I think it's my fault for throwing you in over your head."

I stand up. This entire situation has been so wildly out of my control. Maybe I need to say screw it.

If I'm getting kicked out, I might as well go down with a fight.

"I think it's *my* fault for not properly showing you what I'm made of." I hold out a hand. Amélie looks intrigued, pausing before taking my hand and standing.

Amélie's eyes sweep over me, sizing me up. Pity mingles with something that almost resembles affection. I can practically see her wheels turning. Weirdly, I now feel like I can read the normally opaque Amélie's mind. I suddenly know *exactly* what she's thinking: Amélie is desperate for good publicity—and I'm good publicity—so she's forcing herself to summon her inner psychologist rather than lose her shit. She's weighing her options.

I still have a chance to salvage this thing.

"All publicity is good publicity, right?" I say.

She shakes her head. "*Non.* I hate that idiotic saying."

I can't believe I didn't see it earlier. For a supposedly smart girl, I can be ridiculously obtuse. But I guess that's human nature: We only see what we want to see.

"I will fix this," I say, a wave of determination washing over me. "I simply need to approach this scientifically." I begin ticking off things on my fingers. "First, I have to convince Chapin I didn't do it. *Because I didn't.*"

Amélie raises an eyebrow.

"Number two, I have to convince Chapin to take down the asshole who did—together."

"Right," Amélie says, still looking unconvinced. "And you know who that asshole is?"

"I do now," I say, continuing to stew in emotions. Relief mingles with disgust. "Most importantly . . ."

I pause for maximum effect. Amélie subtly leans in. She's curious as hell to hear what I'm going to say next.

"Tonight," I say, "I'm gonna dazzle the shit out of the press. Maybe you can't make me Deb of the Year, but I deserve to be here just as much as everybody else."

Amélie's desire for publicity seems to have won out. Her eyes sweep over me again, but this time—instead of resigned pity—they show something closer to admiration.

"I didn't backstab Chapin, I didn't trash Versailles—and I'm going to prove it."

"*Bon.*" She shrugs, equally jaunty and world-weary. "Well then, Piper. Show us what you've got."

I take the words to heart, strangely fired up, before reentering my hotel suite, ready.

CHAPTER FIFTY-TWO

Chapin
Paris, France

I tell the glam squad to leave so Piper and I can talk. Dalton and my mom scurry out after them.

My makeup artist and hairstylist both look at me dubiously. "But, like, fast, okay? We don't have that much time."

"My hair is literally done," I say.

"Your hair needs at least another twenty minutes!"

"Okay, okay!" I say, trying to summon patience as I shoo her out the door. "Just five minutes, please!"

"Why do we take these gigs?" I hear her muttering to the makeup artist. "They never appreciate it."

"Money, babe," the makeup artist replies.

I close the door behind her and then turn to Piper.

She looks apprehensive. "Chapin, it wasn't me."

I hold up a hand. "Oh, we're doing that? Save it. Let's just get through the night and then we never have to see each other again." I walk toward the door, ready to summon hair and makeup back inside. I'm not in the mood for anything other than Piper accepting full responsibility.

"I swear I didn't leak the photos," Piper says in a rush. "You might be kind of a diva at times—"

"Is this supposed to be an *apology*?"

"But you're also beyond cool and I really respect you. I . . . I value our friendship. I lost my phone at Versailles. So I'd bet my International Science Fair prize that whoever leaked those photos is the same person who took my phone, and probably the same person who trashed my makeup station this morning. And why would I do something stupid enough to put my scholarship in jeopardy? You know how much I need it. I swear it wasn't me. All I'm asking is for the chance to let me prove it to you."

I squint at her, taking it all in. It definitely doesn't look good for Piper. But at the same time, I truly can't believe she'd be reckless enough to throw away her chance at a scholarship. And she probably wouldn't be dumb enough to use her own email address.

Piper watches me, anxious, waiting for me to speak.

"I'm not saying I believe you," I begin. "But if it wasn't you, who was it?"

She looks guilty. "I . . . think I know."

Okay, this should be good.

She swallows, as if gathering courage. "I think it might be . . . your mother."

My jaw drops. "Piper, it's not my mom."

"I know it sounds crazy, but hear me out. Your mother is the only person who's had it out for me from the beginning. She thinks I'm stealing the crown from you, but you know I don't care about it. The only thing I care about is keeping my head down and keeping Amélie happy, so she'll fulfill her end of the bargain. There is no way I'm drawing attention to myself and rocking the boat."

"But my mother would never." I think about my mom. Even with all her craziness, it's not in her. "I know my mom seems like a nutjob at times, and she has a difficult personality, but she's not evil. She would never trash another girl's chances like that, and she'd never release photos of me. She wants me to succeed. She doesn't want other people to fail."

Piper huffs in frustration. "Okay, how about this. If we find my phone, we'll find whoever's behind this, right? If I can borrow your computer, I can access the Find my iPhone feature."

I let out a laugh of incredulity. This situation is so fucked. But there's a tiny part of me that really wants Piper to be telling the truth, and it's loud enough for me to give her this one chance. "All right," I say. "Go ahead."

We log into Piper's account on my laptop and trigger the Find My iPhone search. We both gasp.

The phone is somewhere in the hotel.

I grab my phone, logging into Piper's account there too. "Let's go."

We go from floor to floor, room to room, trying to get closer and closer to the source.

Finally, we're standing in front of the door.

It's Face's.

My chest feels hot as awareness crashes down on me. *Of course.* I'm not sure which is worse—believing it was Piper, or realizing it was Face. "Face was cut out of all the photos."

"And he tried to make out with me."

"And then he blamed you and was like, 'Gross, she's not even my type.'"

I'm mildly worried Piper will be insulted, but she bursts out laughing.

"Wow. That's textbook DARVO shit. What a douchebag."

"He really is." I feel rage bubbling up inside me, and I raise my fist to start banging down his door. But Piper grabs my hand before I make contact.

"Wait!" she whisper-yells. "Let's think about this for a minute. If we confront him, he'll just deny it. We need to figure out a way to fully prove it's him. What if he doesn't let us into his room and then he gets rid of my phone somehow?"

I pull my arm back, but I can't deny she's right. As great as it would feel to dress Face down, I want to make sure he suffers consequences.

"All right, fine. Let's regroup upstairs." We hustle to the elevator, and in minutes we're sitting back in our suite.

Piper looks energized. "Okay, let's put this together. He tried to kiss me. He tried to sleep with you. And when we each turned him down, his fragile baby ego couldn't handle it and he decided he'd take us both down a peg. This was after his little scheme to get Amélie to boot me at Versailles didn't work."

"Two birds, one phone," I agree. I feel sick. "He was being all sweet to me, but now I'm wondering if he was recording me for his private collection or something. God knows how many women he's recorded without them knowing."

I'm disgusted. Fucking Face.

Piper shakes her head. "I thought Paris was going to be about proving myself to Amélie, but I've realized: This whole situation was about proving everything to *myself*. Staying true no matter what circumstances are thrown my way. Realizing maybe I can't control everything—no matter how much I try—but that's okay. I can pivot. Life isn't a perfect science experiment."

I snort. "You are *such* a dork. This Hallmark moment brought to you by La Danse."

Piper flicks me off, but she's laughing as she does it.

We stare at each other as our laughter fades. Now is the moment of truth. "Are you thinking what I'm thinking?" I ask Piper.

She nods, grim. "You text Bardot. I'll call the front desk and ask for Raphael."

It's time for Face to get a taste of his own medicine.

CHAPTER FIFTY-THREE

Piper
Paris, France

Let the show begin.

The group of debutantes stands at the top of the steps on the second floor of the hotel, while Bardot waits next to us with a clipboard and a headpiece. Amélie is at the foot of the stairs, alongside the waiting cavaliers, and the parents and assembled guests wait beyond.

"Everybody ready?" Bardot asks anxiously. "Everybody know their marks?"

Chapin puts her hands on Bardot's shoulders. "Relax. Breathe. We got this."

Bardot nods, letting her anxiety dissipate. "I know you do. You're right."

"We won't let you down." Chapin grins at her. She then looks over at me and winks, and my stomach explodes into a nervous roller coaster.

Here we go. . . .

I wait between Valeria and Peach, at the top of the steps, watching a parade of debutantes glide down the grand stairs of the hotel, one after another. . . .

First up is Chloe in, well, Chloé. She's wearing a pink bohemian gown that is just frilly enough to be incredibly chic. After all, none of the debs wanted to wear "cupcake dresses." Halfway down the stairs, she does a little twirl, pivoting on her heel as the crowd below oohs and aahs.

Next up is Imogen in a striking yellow Lanvin gown. Naturally, she shows off her ancestral jewels to the photographers, ensuring they capture every piece.

Then it's Lottie in blue Giambattista Valli . . . and Zella in a Givenchy gown that looks so avant-garde it could go in a museum. Knowing La Danse, it will probably end up in the Costume Institute.

I'm toward the end of the line, just ahead of Chapin.

As I inch closer toward the top of the stairs, I can feel my anxiety starting to rise. What am I doing here? Am I crazy for feeling like I could pull this off?

This isn't what I do. I run experiments on bioplastics that might replace single-use packaging. I dig through journals researching bioengineered enzymes to break down toxic pollutants. I debate carbon-capture strategies.

What I *don't* do is stand at the top of grand staircases at the Ritz sandwiched between the most glamorous young heiresses on the planet, dressed to the nines in couture that could fund an entire year's worth of lab equipment.

Chapin is behind me, wearing her gorgeous Dior gown. True to form, she's decided against heels, and is instead wearing bespoke Celine platform sneakers. "They look perfect," I whisper.

She smiles back at me, radiant. "Thank you." She pauses. "My mom's gonna be furious."

I reach out, squeezing her hand. "You got this."

She nods, taking a deep breath to inhale courage as Margarita descends the stairs.

It's finally my turn. I step forward, the spotlight shining on me.

Smile, Piper. Breathe. My gaze homes in on Amélie, watching me apprehensively from the bottom of the stairs. We lock eyes and she nods at me, faintly encouraging. *You can do this.*

I can do this.

I breathe, I smile, and I steadily step down onto the staircase in my heels, all eyes on me.

My Dior confection is a total pastel dreamscape. With every step, as I descend, I feel like I'm moving further and further into a new life. Every step is taking me closer to my scholarship. Every step is taking me closer to smashing my illusions about the kind of person I am, about what kind of space I can take up.

Inspired by Chapin, I've added my own item of fashion defiance: I'm wearing the Claire's chain belt that Amélie demanded I take off on the boat. Irritated anger flashes across Amélie's face, but I finally have her number. Once people see that *the* Chapin Buckingham is wearing sneakers, my unique piece will all be chalked up to some high-low, mix-and-match trend.

I've had enough of playing by everyone else's rules. There's nothing wrong with not spending thousands of dollars on an accessory: Chapin would be the first to say style doesn't come from the price tag, and she's the most fashionable teenager in the world.

Besides, my dress is all about a nod to where I'm from—and nothing nods to where I'm from more than Claire's at the mall.

Another step, another step, one foot in front of the other.

For the briefest of moments, as I continue down the staircase, I close my eyes.

I remember right before I accepted the invitation, picturing my mother waiting for me there at the bottom of the stairs. Obviously, she's not here now, but she's in my heart.

I know she would be proud of me. I deserve to be here just as much as everybody else.

I smile, opening my eyes. I see Dad across the room, watching me with love and pride. We grin at each other.

Dalton is at the bottom of the stairs waiting, a strange look in his eyes. He looks delectable. Does he still blame me for what happened to Chapin? He saw us whispering earlier; he must realize something's up. I can't believe I wasted so much time trying not to rock the boat with Amélie when Dalton Buckingham was right there in front of me.

He looks at me quizzically.

I reach out my hand and smile.

In that moment, something flashes between us. It's like he can read my mind, and I get the sense that he understands that everything is not as it seems.

He smiles back as our hands clasp.

CHAPTER FIFTY-FOUR

Chapin
Paris, France

Here we go.

La procession des filles et cavaliers, as Amélie calls it.

I descend the steps as music plays in the background. Benoit, La Danse's master of ceremonies for thirty-five years and counting, announces my name with such gusto that I'm practically expecting confetti cannons to explode and trumpets to blare. "Chapin Pearl Fantasia Madeline Buckingham," he says, struggling to get through my obscene number of middle names. "Hailing from New York City, Mademoiselle Buckingham will attend Columbia University this fall, where she plans to study earth science. Her other interests include fashion, art history, and supporting numerous charitable endeavors. Tonight she was dressed by Dior and Cartier. The Most Honorable Miles

Wellington, Marquess of Debenham, will be her cavalier."

I brush off the pang that I feel when Benoit mentions Columbia. I don't have time to dwell on my wait-list status. Right now, I have to devote every ounce of energy to making a flawless debut. My mother catches my eye as I step slowly down each step, my sneakers visible. I'm waiting for her to clock the sneakers. For her to look at me with her thunderous *Chapin, WTF, are you* kidding *me?* face. But she doesn't. Instead she smiles and raises her eyebrows mischievously.

It's only when I descend another couple of steps that I see it.

Mom is wearing sneakers too.

I mean, they're high-fashion tweed sneakers costing more than two grand.

But still. The moment of solidarity brings a sharp feeling of tears pricking to my eyes.

I raise my head higher, throw my shoulders back, and continue descending, sending a dazzling megawatt smile her way. As soon as I smile, the photographers go into overdrive, the cameras click-clicking in a frenzy.

Face is waiting for me at the bottom of the stairs, a picture-perfect, dutiful little escort. He looks handsome: hair slicked back, suit perfectly pressed. He smiles at me as if nothing has happened between us, face relaxing, teeth gleaming, every inch the star-wattage royal. *He* wasn't in any of the photos, just me, so nobody knows his secret. But *I* know. His pretty outsides don't match his dark insides.

He reaches out his hand for mine, just like every escort has done with previous girls—but unlike the other girls, I ignore his hand, stepping past him with all of high society before me, watching, waiting.

Gasps erupt through the room as I ice Face and step onto the dance floor alone, escort-free, presenting myself.

Chapin Buckingham, high society rebel, I think to myself, silly, slightly giddy. But I don't let the smile appear on my face, instead keeping myself looking poised and professional.

I'm no longer another damsel in Dior.

Screw expectations.

And now it's dip time.

One of the highlights of the debutante ball is the curtsy performed by each deb after being presented. It's a deep curtsy crossed with a bow. I once looked it up, and apparently the origins come from the early 1900s and a ballerina whose dance resembled a dying swan.

I might have jettisoned Face for the dance, but I'm not about to miss my chance to execute a flawless swan dip.

I take my place in the center of the dance floor, all eyes on me, debutantes and cavaliers circling me, and begin the dip, lifting my arms to my shoulders and then extending them to the side, as if about to soar right out of the ballroom. Next, it's time for a deep swan curtsy—so deep, I'm pretty sure Queen Elizabeth would have awarded me a knighthood on the spot—with my knee touching the floor and my ear pressing to my lap. I swear, my mother is holding her breath, looking at if she's about to pass out from the sheer suspense of whether I'll wipe out. Finally, I look back up at the audience, still dipped at the waist in a bizarre pretzel shape, before unfurling myself and gracefully standing back up. Phew.

Debutante Mode activated.

My mother bursts into spontaneous applause, visibly moved. We grin at each other.

Since I'm the last debutante, traditionally, the waltz would now begin, with everybody coming together with their cavaliers for the first dance.

Instead I motion toward Bardot, who scurries over and hands me the microphone.

"Thank you all for coming tonight," I say grandly.

Amélie looks at Bardot like, *What the hell is this*? Bardot looks back innocently, shrugging.

"I know that I was in the news earlier today, so rather than hiding and feeling all ashamed and pretending like nothing happened, I would like to take this opportunity to set the record straight. First of all, yes, those photos were of me. They weren't doctored. They weren't faked. They weren't AI. It was me." The room begins to buzz.

"But secondly, and more importantly, is the reason *why* the photos were leaked—and by *whom*. Here are the facts. The photos were shared with the press out of revenge, to shame me," I continue, looking around the room before going in for the kill. Everybody stares back at me, rapt. "And the person behind the compromising photos is the same person who took them, unbeknownst to me, while we were together today, the same person who then emailed them to *TMZ* to shame me for changing my mind and kicking him out of my room. . . .

"*Face Wellington.*"

CHAPTER FIFTY-FIVE

Piper
Paris, France

I watch, giddy, as Chapin accuses Face of secretly recording her and leaking images to *TMZ* out of revenge.

"That's a lie!" Face yells.

"*Merde,*" Amélie mutters, rushing toward us.

But Bardot puts a hand out, gently restraining Amélie. She gives us a meaningful look: *You're on, girls—don't screw it up.*

Face swivels toward me, pointing his long pointer finger in my direction. "It wasn't me—are you *absurd*? It was *her*! It was Piper Woo Collins. She's jealous of Chapin. She's been trying to take her place. And this was all part of her plan to humiliate Chapin so she could win Deb of the Year tonight." He sneers in my direction, dismissive. But I see the embarrassment and anger behind his eyes and know the truth—I rejected him, and hell hath no fury like an entitled heir scorned. I rejected him, so he decided I needed to pay the price. "But are we surprised, really? She doesn't belong here."

"Yes, she does."

I hear the voice before I see the face, but my mind can't process it. I gape at her in shock.

Is *Ella Somerset* really standing up for me?

Ella lightly pushes through the crowd, coming up front to stand at the bottom of the steps behind Chapin. She rests her hands on her daughter's shoulders, squeezing supportively. My eyes stray toward her feet: She's wearing sneakers, just like Chapin. "If Chapin says it was Face, it was Face. And if Chapin believes Piper belongs here, so do I."

Chapin and I both look at Ella appreciatively. I move to take my place alongside Chapin, as if buffering her from Face. He sneers at the three of us. But I continue to analyze his face and can see in his eyes: His bravado is hiding fear. He knows he miscalculated. He didn't expect Chapin and me to team up.

"There's no use denying it," Ella says. "The hotel staff let us into your room to recover Piper's stolen phone. We have several witnesses who saw us discover it in your dresser."

Chapin looks toward Raphael and gives a small smile. Face turns beet red.

"Honestly, Face, I'm not really sure why you're doing this," Chapin declares loudly for all to hear. "Maybe powerful women turn you into a scaredy wittle baby man." She reaches out and squeezes my hand. "Or maybe you just want to punish Piper for turning you down too. But I don't give a damn. Your reason is not my problem."

The crowd gasps and starts buzzing at the revelation that I, too, rejected Face. I feel curious eyes probing me, but I keep my shoulders back, faking confidence. Internally, my heart is jackhammering like a construction crew. This is about eleven billion miles away from my comfort zone. *Goodbye forever, illusion of control.*

"But let's address the elephant in the room," Chapin continues. "As I already said, those photos were of me. But unlike what some people seem to think, *no,* I will *not* apologize for them. I'm not damaged goods, and I do not apologize for sex positivity. This does not define me," she says grandly. Commanding. Poised. Every inch Ella's daughter.

A couple of murmurs from the debutantes: "Hell, yes!" and "That's right!" and "Take out that trash!"

"By the way. Have you all heard of a little thing called the Digital Republic Act? Fun little French law. Does so much. Among other things, it protects those who have been victims of revenge porn, like what Face did to me."

"*Revenge porn?* That's utterly ridiculous—" Face begins spluttering.

"And since revenge porn is now a crime—as is the destruction of a national monument, which Face did when he trashed Piper's dressing area at Versailles and tried to blame it on her—"

"Absolutely not!" he continues.

"We have it on video, sweetie. You weren't smart enough

to realize you were in the background of McRae and Peach's TikTok drafts," Chapin says, shutting him up, before turning to the rest of the crowd and continuing. "So that's why the police are waiting outside. And you, Miles Wellington, are about to be under arrest. You should probably call the king. If he even picks up your call."

Over Face's angry protests, I look across the room to see Bardot and Raphael opening the ballroom doors. Several police officers enter and handcuff Face, arresting him.

"This is bullshit!" he bellows. "Get your hands off me! The king will be furious about this! This is an international incident! A witch hunt!"

The police frog-march Face out the doors, seeming to take a particular pleasure in strong-arming him.

"The French *really* don't like the British royals," one of the debutantes murmurs, while the rest explode into chuckles. Chapin hands the microphone over to Amélie before circling back to our little group. The crowd has broken out into groups, all whispering to one another. A few people have pulled out their phones to record Face's arrest.

I lean toward Bardot. "I still can't believe you found that footage."

She shrugs. "McRae and Peach are always filming. I figured there was a good chance they caught something without realizing it."

I turn to Chapin. "You are so amazing," I sigh, full of admiration.

She high-fives me. "Right back atcha."

I look at Ella apprehensively. "Thank you, Mrs. Buckingham."

"I'm sorry that horrid boy dragged you into anything," she sniffs back. "Just goes to show that royalty isn't everything." Chapin gazes at her mother, her face softening. "Amen to that." Ella reaches out and grabs Chapin by the hand, squeezing tightly. They lock eyes, so much love passing between them.

"I'm proud of you, darling," Ella says to Chapin. I can tell she means it.

"*Attention!* Ahem!" Amélie tries to get everybody to focus. She has to step onto the stairs in order to be seen above the crowd. "I have an announcement to make." Chapin and I look at each other expectantly.

She cocks an eyebrow. "Oh, this should be good."

CHAPTER FIFTY-SIX

Chapin
Paris, France

I'm expecting Amélie to go nuclear on Piper and me.

To my surprise, she instead reaches out her hands, beckoning us toward her.

I look at Piper, confused. "Is she gonna kill us?" she whispers.

"Stay behind me," I whisper back.

But we dutifully make our way to Amélie's sides, nervously flanking her on the step below.

The crowd is buzzing, but as we stand there next to Amélie, a hush falls over the room.

"First let me say this. It has always been important for La Danse to change with the times. We are an organization that continues to face battering from every angle, and yet we soldier on, secure in our mission." She looks around the ballroom, her eyes sweeping from person to person, her voice clear and commanding. "Tonight proves that our ball is keeping pace. Our debutantes have found themselves battling adversity, and rather than allowing themselves to bow and break, they have survived. Indeed, they have thrived!"

Amélie dramatically turns toward me, and then toward Piper, resting her arms lightly on our shoulders. "I could not be prouder of my debutantes for standing up for themselves. This is true courage. Fortitude. Grace. This epitomizes La Danse."

I catch Bardot's eye from across the room. She's watching the whole spectacle with a wry smile on her face. I don't have to chat with her to be able to read her mind: Amélie can't control us, but she can't buy this type of publicity either, so she's *working* it.

"That's my girl!" Ella calls loudly, beaming at me. Everybody's eyes—and camera lenses—swivel toward Ella, capturing her proud reaction as she radiates joy toward me.

Look. I know my mother is not above a publicity moment. God knows I can count on twenty-seven hands the number of times she made Dalton and me do pap walks with her over the years while she was trying to send a *message* to this person or that studio.

But I can also tell when my mom is full of shit. And my heart soars because I know she's being serious. She *is* proud of me. I'm so happy, I have to pinch my thumb to keep the tears from flowing.

Amélie continues speaking, savvily eyeing the ravenous press, who are practically orgasming as they photograph and video the entire spectacle. "*Bon, alors.* It is time for us to crown the Debutante of the Year. And this year, in the spirit of courage and grace, but also change, I am proud to award the honor to *two* young women who embody kindness, charity, and strength of character. I am delighted to present our first ever Co–Debutantes of the Year . . . Chapin Buckingham and Piper Woo Collins!"

A few gasps ring out as the crowd begins buzzing.

The room explodes into a standing ovation as Amélie reaches out and grabs me and Piper by our hands, lifting them aloft in victory.

I look over at Piper, dazed.

She looks at me back, equally stunned. Behind her, I catch Lottie and Peach looking supremely annoyed. Meanwhile, Valeria is mouthing WTF! to her mom across the room.

Piper starts to wipe away tears with her free hand, but I pull away from Amélie, instead grabbing Piper and hugging her. "We did it!"

In my hug, I feel Piper's shoulders shake as she starts to cry. She's overwhelmed.

"You okay?" I ask, pulling away to look at her. In that moment, the din fades: It feels as if there are no crowds, no paparazzi, no jealous debutantes, not even Amélie and my mom. It's just the two of us, sharing a private victory that we've battled to earn.

"Yes." She nods, taking a deep breath to center herself. "It's just . . . what a dream." She continues to swipe tears away, almost angrily, laughing even as she cries. "I don't know why I'm crying! God! This is so silly!"

"It's not silly," I tell her, putting my arms on her shoulders firmly. "They see you. We did this on *our terms*. To hell with their rules for us."

Her eyes well up with tears again, and then *my* eyes well up with tears, and now the two of us are crying like we're watching the end of *La La Land* for the first time.

Amélie is next to us, smiling at the crowds, waving for the cameras.

Out of the corner of her mouth, smile never leaving her face, she whispers to Piper, "I need to see you in private."

CHAPTER FIFTY-SEVEN

Piper
Paris, France

Amélie pulls me aside, still smiling at me.

I grin back. "I told you I'd put on a show."

"And that you did, Piper. *Bravo.*" Amélie claps her hands at me discreetly. "Very well played."

Boldness is coursing through me. "So what do you say to our deal?" I ask.

Amélie cocks an eyebrow. "Our deal is off."

My heart stops. "I thought—"

"Piper, I told you earlier today."

"Yes, but that was before I got you the most incredible press in the history of La Danse! Every news site is champing at the bit. The ball's gonna be the top story everywhere in about an hour."

"Let us review. You alienated a member of the British royal family. You invited police into my ball without permission. You made my assistant go behind my back and disobey me. You wore a revolting accessory I *expressly* forbade. And you forced me to name not one but *two* disgraced Debutantes of the Year. I would say you certainly did *not* hold up your end of the bargain."

Oh. "But I got you all that publicity . . ." I say weakly.

"What did I tell you, *ma chère*? All press is not good press. This damage will take twelve months to undo, maybe longer." Amélie looks around the ballroom, which is filled with gleeful debutantes, cavaliers, their parents, and the photographers who worship them all. A smile plays at her lips. She might claim she's displeased, but I see through her. "I'll take it, all the same. But . . ." She shrugs. "I *am* sorry. This could have gone much differently."

"You're just like the rest of them," I say, suddenly furious. "Just like the people who revoked my scholarship in the first place. I only had to do damage control because of Face trying to take us down. You're punishing me for things that weren't my fault."

"Piper," Amélie says, patting my shoulder. "You are very resourceful. I'm sure you'll think of something. I have faith in you." I shake off her cold hand, disgusted.

Suddenly I see somebody across the ballroom and gasp, my tears stopping. Emotions flood my body: first disbelief, followed by elation.

It's Seb. He's here.

I don't bother saying goodbye to Amélie. I race across the ballroom, where my best friend is waiting in a sharp suit, with a huge smile on his face.

"Surprise!" he says, pulling me into his arms for a gigantic hug. "What, you thought I'd let you be the only one riding off into the sunset with a rich kid? I gotta find me a cute cavalier, *tout de suite*."

"Is that your best French?" I tease, still marveling at the fact that Seb is actually in front of me, in the flesh, instead of just on the other end of an iPhone screen.

"Shh," he whispers, playfully placing his finger over my lips. "*Je suis très* totally gonna leave here in *l'amour* if it kills *moi*."

We laugh at Seb's exaggeratedly atrocious French accent.

"But seriously! What the hell are you *doing* here?"

"Well, first, I have a lot of money saved up from my back-to-back shifts at Mrs. Fields. A guy can only buy so many video games. And second, once Tom invited me to surprise you, it was like, *obviously*. No brainer."

I look across the ballroom at my dad, who is laughing and chatting with Dr. Hughes like they're old pals. He catches my eye and waves at me proudly.

"*That* famous game-show host," Seb says, pointing discreetly at Dr. Hughes, "is totally your dad's new bestie. They're adorbs."

My dad breaks away from Dr. Hughes and makes his way over to us. "Seems like you saw my big surprise," he says, looking exceptionally proud of himself. He claps an arm around Seb's shoulder. "I thought he wouldn't be interested, but—"

"Are you kidding me?" Seb interrupts. "The second you even *whispered* the idea, I was ready to sell a kidney to make it happen. I was fully packed before the conversation ended. I already have a scholarship for next year, so a last-minute trip to Paris to surprise my best friend and crash in her fancy hotel suite"— he turns toward me—"yeah, that's happening, sorry, babe—is exactly what the money's for."

Scholarship. Money. The words momentarily bring me back down to earth. I shake them off.

Dad laughs, before getting a little wistful. He turns back to me. "You looked so strong up there. I'm proud of you, honey," Dad says, now extremely teary-eyed.

"Oh God, please don't cry," I say. "I nearly lost it up there already."

Seb looks between the two of us knowingly. "Okay, it's daddy-daughter time. I'll just be over there in the corner bagging me an earl. BRB." He makes a beeline for Count Von Dodo.

The music starts up, signaling it's time for the waltz. I hold out my hands toward my dad.

"Shall we?"

I'm half expecting Dad to step all over my shoes, but as we make our way onto the dance floor and begin stepping gracefully to the music, he's a surprisingly good dancer. "Who knew you could waltz?"

"What do you think I've been doing all week?" he jokes.

"I don't know—strolling the Left Bank with the other dads and hiding from the thirsty moms determined to lock you down?"

He winces. "Too soon."

"The truth hurts, Pops." We giggle.

"Amélie made sure all the parents had dance lessons. However, I did have a lovely afternoon with Dr. Hughes walking around the Île Saint-Louis," Dad admits. "He took me to this famous ice cream shop—"

"Berthillon!" I finish.

Dad looks impressed that I'm on a first-name basis with Parisian ice cream shops.

"I saw a TikTok about it," I explain.

"What a week," Dad laughs. "If you'd told me a month ago that the two of us would be waltzing together in Paris in the most expensive hotel I'd ever seen, while you were the literal queen of the world's most prestigious debutante ball, I wouldn't have believed you."

"To be fair, a month ago I was knee-deep in science labs, Claire's shifts, and Netflix binges. I don't think anybody saw this plot twist coming."

But then Dad accidentally steps on my foot, wrecking our perfect third step. "Oof. Sorry, honey."

In response, I stand on my tippy toes and try to twirl him. I'm not tall enough, so the two of us just get tangled up like a pretzel, laughing.

"Let's try that again," Dad says, twirling me instead.

"So, what about *you*? I've barely seen you since our flight. Ice cream and game-show hosts aside, did you survive the week?" I ask. "Are you poised to become the prince of a tiny mountainous enclave in Eastern Europe?"

"Oh man," he groans, running a hand over his face. "If only I'd known."

"Your face would look really good on currency. We should make this happen."

"Let's leave the lothario status to Seb." We look across the room, where James, one of the cavaliers, is happily flirting with him.

"I'm telling you, Dad. Klaus's mom has had you in her sights all week. I think you're missing your shot. You could become Emperor Von Dodo." We collapse into a laughing fit.

Dad turns more serious. "This has been one of the best weeks of my life. Seeing you here in Paris . . . *thriving* . . ." Dad's voice sounds like it cracks, and he clears his throat.

"Aww. You old softy," I say. I'm joking with him, but the reality is that seeing Dad emotional makes me feel emotional too.

What's incredible is realizing that my dad was a parent at my age. I can't even imagine having a kid now; I'm barely mature enough to handle myself, let alone be responsible for a whole-ass other life.

"You know, they say that kids start pooping in the nest before they leave for college. To make it easier for parents to say goodbye—"

"Who is this *they*?" I demand.

"—but I'll just say you're making it real hard for me, kiddo." I'm not gonna cry. I'm not gonna cry.

There's so much I want to say, but it's overwhelming. "Thank you," I finally say, voice slightly shaky. "You've aced this whole parenthood thing." I make a funny face at him, to bring the emotion down a notch. "I mean, so far, anyway. There's still time for me to go completely off the rails and horribly shame you."

"Here's hoping," he jokes. He twirls me again, bringing me close. "I think you turned out okay." He clears his throat, and I realize he's about to say something emotional again. It takes him several heavy seconds to finally get the words out. "Mom would be so proud of you." Okay, game over. I'm crying after all.

I don't want to burst our fairy-tale moment with the news that I've lost my scholarship *again*. If this week has taught me anything, it's that life has a funny way of plopping opportunities in front of you, as long as you're open to them.

Amélie might have turned out to be a traitorous publicity hound, but she was right about one thing: I have faith I'll figure it out.

But that's for tomorrow.

Tonight is one last night for pure enjoyment.

Dad and I dance together in silence, enjoying the music, the setting, just soaking it all in.

I see Dalton watching us from across the room. He raises a hand at me in greeting: an opening. One of life's little opportunities.

After the song is over, I leave Dad's side and make my way over to Dalton.

"May I have this dance?" I ask.

He smiles. "I'd love that."

We come together, staring at each other.

"Hi," I say softly.

"I'm sorry," Dalton says, looking ashamed. "I was horrible."

"You were being loyal to your sister."

"I should have known you wouldn't have betrayed her like that."

I smile. "We're all just fumbling our way through."

"But you forgive me?" Dalton asks tentatively. "I'd understand if you can't."

"I forgive you, Dalton."

As we stare at each other, Dalton's pupils dilate. My heart begins to rush with the feeling of his hands on mine. I gently pull us closer together, until we're pressed against each other. He continues to stare down at me, his eyes straying down toward my lips. He fixes his eyes onto mine again, mouth sliding into a tiny smile.

"Still nothing more . . . ? Or have things changed now that you're Deb of the Year?" I'm brought right back to our moment on the boat, the first time we almost kissed. This time, I'm ready to follow my heart.

"No." My heart pounds with newfound courage. "I want more."

I pull his face down to mine. As our lips gently touch, my body feels fizzy. It might be my imagination, but I feel like the crowd goes silent, all eyes on us.

I pull away from Dalton, dazed, and realize it's just my imagination—everybody's too caught up in their own worlds to pay much attention to the two of us kissing on the dance floor. Everybody, that is, except for a photographer in the corner, who's snapping photos of us in a frenzy.

Dalton looks down at me, his eyes hungry. I step up on my tiptoes to kiss him again. It's a kiss full of longing and promise. We're lost in each other. This time I lean into it, putting my hand behind his neck and gently pulling him tighter.

Photograph *this*.

CHAPTER FIFTY-EIGHT

Chapin
Paris, France

I watch from across the room as Piper and Dalton kiss. They pull away, grinning at each other. The sheer joy is palpable on both of their faces. Aww. That's cute.

Suddenly I feel a presence next to me. I look, and there's Raphael.

Do it, Chapin. Get up the nerve. You can do it!

"Thanks so much for your help."

"No worries. Thrilled to do it. That guy was a real—how'd you say it?—wanker."

I laugh. "In America, we'd just call him an asshole." He grins back at me. God, he's adorable.

"He deserves everything he gets for trying to hurt you," he says.

"So, uh, do you maybe want to grab a coffee sometime?" I ask Raphael shyly. "If you're not too busy with work? I'm in Paris a lot."

He smiles, giving me confidence.

"Or, you know, a drink, even . . . ?" I add, my heart jackhammering with frenzied nerves as if I've never before spoken to a human male.

"I would love that. Yes. Both. All of the above."

We laugh, but as we lock eyes, underneath my smile I feel all warm and fuzzy. Cute, non-psychopathic Parisian guy for the win.

"Well," Raphael says philosophically, "now you have something good to write about for your university wait-list essay, *non*? The girl who brought the stuffy old La Danse kicking and screaming into the future?"

"Maybe so." I nod, contemplating. I guess it could make a good essay. Humblebragging, no. Truly finding meaning and self-reflection in what I've been through this week? Could work.

"I'm really happy you came to Paris," he says, his face turning serious.

I feel a twinge of lust. Ugh, I really want to kiss him.

One step at a time, Chape.

The ballroom has been filled with the sounds of a stirring waltz, but it fades to silence. Instead of another classical song from the orchestra kicking in, a DJ takes the stage.

"And now the real party begins!" the DJ bellows in heavily accented English. *"Allez-y!"*

Dreamy synth pop begins to shimmer over the loudspeakers

as I realize it's a club remix of Taylor Swift's "Paris."

Piper and I look at each other across the dance floor and break into smiles.

". . . like we were in Paris!" everybody sings out as the dance floor erupts.

The parents scurry out of the way, looking baffled—everybody, that is, except for my mother and father, who join the scrum and begin dancing with abandon.

"Taylor!" my dad bellows. "Hell, yeah!"

But instead of cringing and falling through the floor, I just laugh. There are worse things than your rock-star dad and movie-star mom actually having fun together for once. A throng of debutantes and cavaliers exit the ballroom, still dancing, following one another out onto the portico beyond. From there we can see the lights of the Eiffel Tower popping and shimmering. I grab Raphael's hand.

"I can't," he whispers. "I'm on the clock."

I nod, understanding. I don't want to get him in trouble.

But he continues holding my hand and then twirls me.

"Oh, screw it," he says, laughing.

Hand in hand, we exit the ballroom and begin dancing with everybody else under the stars.

We dance together, my mother and father kissing each other like gross teenagers, Dalton and Piper twirling and laughing on the other side of the porch, her friend Seb dancing next to them, a motley crew of friends old and new surrounding me, and I've never been happier. To hell with the rules. Nothing feels better than living for myself—opinions be damned.

CHAPTER FIFTY-NINE

Piper
Paris, France

The next morning, I wake up dreamily in my hotel room.

Was last night real?

I spring up in bed, looking around.

I catch a vision of myself in the mirror opposite my bed. My hair is still piled on top of my head. My eyeliner wasn't fully removed, so it's smudged around my eyes—I look like a cross between a raccoon and Billie Eilish. Next to my bed, my ball gown is hanging precariously on a clothing rack, front and center. It's next to my bags—thankfully already fully packed, other than my toiletries in the bathroom. And next to me, Seb's on the other side of the massive bed, face down on the pillow, lightly snoring and drooling everywhere.

I hug myself happily, sinking back in the cushions.

Yes. It was real.

We all partied and laughed until five in the morning, dancing so furiously that I kicked my shoes off sometime around midnight. At some point, snacks were procured and we all furiously tore into street hot dogs in our fancy gowns. With my klutziness, it's a miracle I didn't get ketchup all over my Dior. The fact I kept it clean is testament alone to how much this week has changed me.

I wrap myself in a fluffy hotel bathrobe and exit bleary-eyed into the sitting room. Chapin is already there, showered and dressed. She's sitting at the desk by the balcony, furiously typing on her laptop.

"All good?" I ask. "I could really use an espresso. Or three."

Chapin's clearly in the zone, wearing a pair of noise-canceling headphones. Her fingers continue flying across her keyboard. She doesn't even look up.

I walk closer, peeking over her shoulder to see what has her so rapt.

She's working on her Columbia wait-list essay.

Good job, Chapin.

We've finagled a late checkout but still have to be out of the hotel in two hours. I sneak a peek into her room: She's all packed too. So she's got the time to focus on her application.

I back off, wanting to give her space.

Chapin notices me and removes the headphones. "I only need another fifteen minutes. Wanna grab that coffee then? We can sneak one last espresso in before checkout. Your friend can come."

"Yes!" I can't wait to debrief on last night.

Chapin looks at me. Her smile is warm and genuine. "Last night was the best night of my life." I know she's remembering that after we all moved into the street, Ella joined us at a café for a post-midnight meal.

"Me too," I sigh. "Grab us when you're ready for that coffee."

I retreat to my bedroom and lie on top of the bedsheets. Seb groans.

"You're gonna make me wake up, aren't you?"

"We've got fifteen more minutes before coffee with Chapin."

"And you're going to use every second to do a last-minute pack?"

"And I'm going to use every second to sleep in," I sigh, sinking into the pillow.

He doesn't move. "Who are you, and what have you done with my best friend? Piper Woo Collins *never* sleeps in."

"It's a whole new me, babycakes," I laugh.

"Mmmph," Seb grunts, already falling back asleep. "Still cheesy as shit, though."

I peck at my phone—I've got an Instagram notification.

I bolt upright, my jaw dropping. It's from Claire's corporate account!

"Oh my God!" I yelp.

"What? Who died?" Seb sounds panicked.

"Claire's saw that I wore their chain to La Danse!" I exclaim.

"That's nice," Seb says, settling back into his pillow. "Can we talk about this in fifteen minutes?"

"The story went viral, and Claire's is now *blowing up*," I continue. "And they want to fund my college scholarship!"

"Are you serious?" Seb shrieks, wide awake again. "Holy shit! You're going to Columbia!"

"I'm going to Columbia!" I scream. "I'm really going to Columbia!"

Seb instantly clicks the golden RING FOR CHAMPAGNE button next to our bed. After all, this turn of events calls for a major celebration.

I wish you were here, Mom. I think you'd be proud.

I stare up at the ornate ceiling in a bittersweet daze, listening to the comforting, rhythmic tap-tap-tapping of Chapin's inspired fingers flying across her keyboard.

Oh my God. Chapin! I have to tell her the good news!

I sprint into the living room. With her noise-canceling headphones on, no wonder she didn't hear my insane shrieks. I'm pretty sure they were audible from a remote research station in Antarctica.

I wave my hands to get her attention.

"Claire's came through and is now funding my scholarship. I'm going to Columbia."

Chapin screams. "Hell, yes!" She stands up and envelops me in a massive bear hug. "You so deserve this. Hopefully, I'll be there with you, come September." She gestures down at her computer screen shyly.

Suddenly inspiration strikes.

"Hey, Chape? I just got a brilliant idea. . . ."

EPILOGUE

Piper
New York City

BANG! BANG! BANG!

Somebody knocks on the door with what sounds like their foot.

"This box is crazy heavy!" a guy's voice calls through the door. "Open up, quick!"

I swing the door open to find Dalton carrying one of Chapin's boxes. It's massive and is simply labeled BEAUTY. He's staggering under its weight.

"Sorry!" I say, swinging the door open wide to let him in. As he passes, lumbering through the door and setting the box down with a plop on Chapin's bed, I try to jam the door open with one of Chapin's oversized suitcases. They are now taking over *way* more than half of the room. I only have one large suitcase and one medium one, while Chapin has four suitcases, several duffel bags, a Rimowa carry-on, and enough boxes that I'm pretty sure she's going to set up a boutique here on campus.

"I feel bad for you, rooming with Chapin," Dalton says. "Sure you don't want to flee? I bet you could find a nice single in John Jay. Get the closet all to yourself. Ensure that you won't accidentally suffocate in the middle of the night under an avalanche of J.Crew dresses."

I laugh, settling down on my bed. I've already started unpacking, organizing my clothes into piles. Chapin and I have to share a closet, and I know that my stuff's gonna be out in the cold. But hey, that's what you get when you sign up for a roomie, right?

"Oh, ye of little faith," Chapin says, rolling a clothing rack into the room from the hallway. "Piper and I are going to split the closet *and* split this clothing rack. You're both acting like I'm a monster. And joke's on you—I don't wear J.Crew." She strains as she rolls the rack farther into the room, settling it against the far wall by the window.

I giggle, but Dalton just looks at her, aghast. "How on earth did you get that thing up here by yourself? I told you I'd help."

"What, like it was hard?" she says innocently. "Don't underestimate how strong and cool and awesome and amazing your little sister is, Dalton." She turns toward me, lowering her voice. "A bunch of varsity crew boys helped me carry it up," she whispers, smiling.

"I don't know why you're fine with living in Carman," Ella says, entering. She's carrying a Bottega tote bag stuffed to the brim with God only knows what as if it's a throwaway burlap sack she found in the utility closet. "You could just live at home and save the money."

Chapin shoots her mother a dry look. "Because now you're penny pinching? Quick, how much did that Van Cleef necklace cost?"

Ella looks wounded. "My pilot got picked up, darling—you know I always treat myself after a green light. Self-care is nonnegotiable."

"There is absolutely no way I'm living at home for my first year of college."

"For your second year of college?" Ella asks hopefully.

"Wait till senior year; then we'll talk," Chapin says breezily. But I know her enough by now to read the pleased expression she's trying to hide. It makes her happy to know her mother genuinely enjoys spending time with her. And, as much of a diva as Ella Somerset is, Chapin's gonna miss her, too.

"Knock, knock!" My dad is at the door, looking inside expectantly. "May I come in?"

"Dad! Welcome!"

He enters, scoping everything out. "Wow, honey. This is incredible. What a cozy room."

I burst out laughing. "'Cozy' being a euphemism for 'size of a shoebox'?"

My dad holds up his hands innocently. "You're a college freshman. Tiny, shared bedrooms are a rite of passage. You're not supposed to be living at the Ritz."

"Or on Seventy-Fifth and Park," Chapin says pointedly, looking at her mom.

Ella brightens up when she sees Tom. Seems even the great Ella Somerset isn't immune to his charms. "Tom! What a delight to see you."

He hugs her awkwardly, and I can tell that he's still mentally freaking out that the star of one of the most popular sitcoms of all time knows his name. "Ms.... Ella ... hi ... hello!" Dad clears his throat, trying to hide his embarrassment.

I sit on the bed and Dalton plops next to me. Ella, Chapin, and my dad start a conversation about locks on the door—everybody agrees it's extremely important to have a deadbolt, but for different reasons—and even though we're in public, for a split second it feels like Dalton and I are alone, just the two of us.

"Hi," he says, looking at me with that adorable smile.

"Hi," I say back, feeling my heart swell.

He leans over and gives me a tiny, parent-approved kiss that activates the swarm of butterflies in my stomach waiting just for him.

"Okay, you two, get a room," Chapin groans.

We flush and pull apart. Dad politely pretends to suddenly be extremely interested in the activity outside our window down on Broadway.

My watch buzzes, reminding me: It's time for orientation.

"We have to go!" I gasp. "New Student Orientation in fifteen minutes."

"We can be fashionably late," Chapin says, slicing into her box of beauty products with a pair of scissors and pulling out a hand cream. She offers me a dollop and I gratefully accept. "Let's stop by Hungarian Pastry first."

"Mmm," Dalton agrees. "My favorite."

"Late to the first party, yes," Dad says. "But on the first day? To orientation? Maybe not."

I look up at my dad and suddenly feel such an overwhelming wave of love for him. I can't believe how transformational the past six months of my life have been. Here I am, living in New York City, a first-year at Columbia University, just like I always dreamed, rooming with Chapin Buckingham of all people, dating Dalton Buckingham (*Dalton Buckingham!*), and an alum of the most prestigious debutante ball in the world.

What a whirlwind. And it was all possible because Dad believed in me.

He looks across the room at me, and I swear, it's like a mind meld. I don't have to say anything—somehow he just *knows*. He mouths at me, *Love you, Pipes.*

Love you, Dad, I mouth back, wiping away a tiny tear.

I'm truly adulting for the first time.

"Oh!" Ella says, reaching into her designer Mary Poppins tote. "Before you race off, take a look at this. It was just published."

Ella produces the new *Vanity Fair*: the highly anticipated September issue.

"Ooh!" Chapin squeals.

Ella flips through the pages until she finds the article, turning it around so we all can see it. Cairo's group photo of the debutantes splashes across two pages:

BELLES OF THE BALL

Meet the Debutantes Changing the World

And in the group photo, front and center, it's Chapin and me.

"We should get them to cover your jewelry capsule collection for Claire's," Ella says authoritatively. "I'm good friends with *Vanity Fair's* style director. They'll love the angle." Ella begins painting a picture, using her actress voice. "Two young entrepreneurial college students, science mavens, teaming up on an affordable, eco-friendly jewelry line—combining their knowledge of sustainable fashion and a passion for gemstones—with a portion of the proceeds going to the Environmental Defense Fund." Ella finishes weaving her vision, looking extremely moved. "The article writes itself."

What's incredible is that the conclusion of La Danse wasn't a goodbye after all. Instead, it was an enthusiastic *bonjour*. To college. To friendship. To the next chapter. And to our joint collection with Claire's. I'd been burned enough by rescinded scholarship offers to realize the best way to guarantee my future was to invest in myself. So I countered Claire's offer, and they were all too happy to accept.

"Hey," I say to Chapin casually. "Have you heard from Raphael recently?"

She laughs. "He's always texting at the weirdest times. Time zones and all. But he's hoping to come to New York for my birthday."

I nod, hiding my smile. What Chapin doesn't realize is that Raphael and I are already working with Dalton to plan a surprise party when Raphael's here for Chapin's birthday. Raphael had the brilliant idea of a "Rocks and Rockstuds" theme, which she's guaranteed to love.

I pause, looking around the room and taking it all in.

It's almost perfect, but something's still missing.

I stand up, walk across the room, and rifle through a box of framed photos. I pull out the one I'm looking for: my favorite picture of me with my parents. We're all together at a state fair, me holding the world's biggest stick of cotton candy, my parents on each side of me. My mom and I are grinning at each other, and my dad's got his arm around both of us, looking on proudly.

Maybe this photo should make me sad—after all, my mom died less than a year later—but instead, when I look at it, all I feel is pride. I may not have had her forever, but in the short time I did, I know I was loved.

I put the framed photo in my place of honor, right next to my bed, on top of an Introduction to Environmental Law textbook, and beside the framed postcards from the Musée d'Orsay I bought in honor of Mom. I look across the room at my dad, but he's now wiping his eyes. I smile at him. "Damn allergies," he says.

Chapin claps her hands. "Okay! College! We got this!" She looks at me expectantly. "You ready?"

Am I ready?

I feel calm. After the La Danse scandals, infighting, falling in love, and more public attention than I've ever received before, I know I can handle anything.

I pop to my feet as our families look on proudly. "Yep. Let's do it." After all, compared to La Danse, college should be a piece of cake. . . .

Right?

ACKNOWLEDGMENTS

Much like a debutante ball, this novel took countless people behind the scenes to bring it to life. First and foremost, *By Invitation Only* would never have been possible without Serena Lese, my debutante ball fairy godmother extraordinaire. Serena, your generosity, genius, humor, and wit know no bounds.

An immense thank-you to Linda Medvene and Chloe Sommer, without whom so many elements of *By Invitation Only* would not exist. Both of you taught me everything I know about embracing originality through fashion, which plays a major role in this book. You have brought endless whimsy, vibrancy, and joy—not only to this story but to my life. I feel profoundly lucky to have you both in my corner.

Thank you to everyone at Simon & Schuster, whose brilliant contributions and hard work helped make this novel a reality. To my incredible editor, Kate Prosswimmer: I am beyond thrilled that this project ended up in your hands. Working together has been a dream come true! Your notes and insights were invaluable. I deeply appreciate your passion and enthusiasm for this book. Thank you as well to Andrenae Jones, Alex Kelleher-Nagowski, Lindsey Ferris, Karen Sherman, Sonia Chaghatzbanian, and Elena Masci.

I am also endlessly grateful to everyone at CAA. Thank you to Michelle Weiner for responding to my cold query email and introducing me to Mollie Glick, the best agent I could have ever asked for. Mollie, thank you for taking a chance on me and championing this story from the very beginning. Thank you as well to Berni Vann, Sarah Mitchell, Via Romano, Emily Calomino, and Alex Rice.

Thank you to the incomparable Nadine Jolie Courtney for your guidance, contributions, and mentorship. I am so grateful for your expertise, and I am in awe of your talents.

Thank you to my dear friends who graciously read the earliest drafts of this novel: Karen McCullah, Vandy Boudreau, Leslie Woods, Natalia Safran, Christine Varon, Grant Gordon, Lux Frisina, Katharine Leede, Izzy Simanowitz, Paloma Sommer, Saskia Sommer, and Andrea Greenburg. I am also deeply grateful to Heather Hach Hearne, Gabi Medvene-Cirigliano, Kelly-Marie Smith, Lore V. Olivera, Kira Kirby, Alex Varon, Emma Kami, Kiara Boboff, and Kiley Roache for their many years of friendship and support.

Thank you to Jim Hornstein for your wise counsel and thoughtful advice.

A special thank-you to my writing professors at Stanford, whose teachings continue to inspire me: Adam Tobin, Cheo

Hodari Coker, and R. B. Brenner. Thank you as well to Liz Magill, for your support, always.

Most importantly, I would like to thank my family, whose love and encouragement mean everything to me. Annabelle, Audrey, and Ames: Thank you for being my best friends and most dedicated readers. Many of the characters' most lovable traits are inspired by you. I will never forget receiving the news that my manuscript had sold while we were together. There is no one else I'd rather celebrate with, ever.

Of course, the greatest thank-you of all goes to my parents, Amanda and Justin. No words can ever adequately convey my love, appreciation, and admiration for you. Thank you for nurturing my love of reading and storytelling from the time I was young—that is the best gift in the world. None of this would have been possible without you both. Thank you for always believing in me. Thank you for everything.